The Social Exorcist

A pastor's supernatural journey to the Catholic faith.

by A.V. Vega

The Social Exorcist by A.V. Vega

Published by LuluBoss LLC

http://AVVega.com

Cover by Lesia germancreative.

ISBN: 979-8-9871116-0-4 (paperback)

Printed in The United States of America

First Edition: October 2022

10 9 8 7 6 5 4 3 2 1

This book is dedicated to all the Protestants who made the difficult journey into the Catholic Church and are now evangelizing their fellow Protestants.

A.V. Vega

"After Jesus rose from the dead early on Sunday morning, the first person who saw him was Mary Magdalene, the woman from whom he had cast out seven demons."

Mark 16:9

Chapter 1

Like the demonic horrors set in motion by events unbeknownst to him, Pastor Ed emerged from his office at Community Baptist Church and gazed at the northern summer blue sky, oblivious to the dark ominous clouds inching closer from the south. The church stood at the edge of an intersection, wrapped in red brick with a high white spire, commanding attention like an angry Bible-thumping Baptist shouting on a street corner. Only a block away was Pastor Ed's favorite coffee shop, Colorado's Best Coffee Co. With the next day's church service running through his mind, and the July heat taking a toll on his thirst, he realized how much he needed caffeine to get him through the rest of the day and walked to the coffeehouse.

Stepping inside, the aroma of brewing coffee made his nose twitch, and the live chatter made his ears perk up. He was such a regular customer, the cashier already had his order rung up by the time he reached the register. He paid, then drifted to the side to await his order. Seconds later, the front door swung open, and an appealing young lady in her early thirties stepped inside — dark hair and brown eyes, with an olive undertone skin color. She approached the front counter gracefully, her red dress accentuating her curves, her hoop earrings reflecting her grace, and her crucifix expressing her faith. After placing her order, she made her way to the waiting area.

His stomach fluttered and his shoulders tensed. *Okay, you've done this before. Remember, the key is confidence. No matter what happens, just be confident.* He took a deep breath and approached her. She turned her face toward him — quizzically, or fearful, or just pleasure — and it flooded him with adrenaline, compelling him and somehow giving him purpose.

"Catholic?" Pastor Ed asked.

"Excuse me?" she replied.

"I noticed your crucifix. I thought perhaps you're Catholic."

Colorado Catholic residents make up less than fifteen percent of the population, so whenever he came across one, he never missed the opportunity to evangelize. But it was sneaky of him to do so in a coffee shop, since people are reluctant to leave without their drinks. The trick was to evangelize before the barista called out their name.

"Oh that? Yes, it belonged to my mother."

"I see. It's lovely."

Not really. In Pastor Ed's eyes, keeping Jesus on the cross was heresy, but he knew compliments went a long way.

"Thanks, and yes, I'm Catholic."

"I'm Pastor Ed, and I'm the preacher over at Community Baptist Church. We get a lot of ex-Catholics over at my church and—"

She raised her hand and brought him to a complete halt. "I'm going to stop you right there. I attend St. Michael's Catholic Church and I'm quite happy there, but thank you."

He was used to pushback, but years of evangelizing taught him to never give up on the first sign of resistance. "I think that's great that you go to church. Do you mind if I ask who the priest is?"

"Father Garcia," she replied.

Pastor Ed drew his eyebrows together and tilted his head. "Father? You call your priest 'father'?"

She gave him a mildly quizzical glance. "Yes, that's what you're supposed to call a priest… Isn't it?"

"Well, Jesus says otherwise. According to the gospel of Matthew, chapter 23 verse 9, Jesus said, **'Call no man your father on earth, for you have one father, who is in heaven.'**"

"Tall, skinny latte," the barista called out.

"I'm guessing there's an exception for priests. Look, I'm sure your church is lovely, but like I said, I'm really happy with St. Michael's."

"I didn't catch your name, by the way," he said dismissively.

She crossed her arms. "Norma"

"Norma, it's great that you enjoy going to church, but over at Community Baptist Church, we simply preach the gospel. Bible only. That's it. We put nothing between you and Jesus. None of them…" He paused for a moment, then quickly snapped his fingers. "Sacraments! All we do is preach the gospel. In fact, I've got to tell you, I've read the Bible plenty of times and I've never come across a single verse that talks about the Pope. Have you?"

The espresso machines whirred, and the patrons turned their attention toward their conversation.

She glanced to the side. "Well," she said, uncrossing her arms, "now that you mention it, no."

"And I believe that the Catholic Church tells you to call the Pope 'Holy Father.' Is that correct?"

"Yes, I suppose you're right. But like I said, I'm sure there's an exception for the clergy."

"I'm afraid there isn't."

"Caramel iced latte and a ham panini for Pastor Ed," the barista called.

Norma gave a slow smile. "I think they just called out your name."

He raised his index finger, "One second," then scurried to the pickup counter. Grabbing his coffee and wrapped panini, he quickly returned to find Norma wide-eyed.

"Norma," he said, "in your church, do they have statues and images of the Virgin Mary and saints?"

Tapping her foot, she replied, "Yes, we do."

Struggling to hold his coffee cup and panini with one hand, he pulled out his phone and navigated to his favorite Bible app.

"Let me read to you what God said to Moses on Mt. Sinai in the book of Exodus, chapter 20 verse 4."

"Is this guy for reals?" one customer commented.

Ignoring the comment, Pastor Ed continued. "'**Thou shalt not make unto thee any graven image, or any likeness of anything that is in heaven above, or that is in the earth beneath, or that is in the water under the earth: thou shalt not bow down thyself to them, nor serve them: for I the LORD thy God am a jealous God.'**

"Norma, do people in your church bow down before statues and ima—"

"Ahem," the new store manager interjected, arms crossed with a stern look on his face. "Pastor Ed, no soliciting."

"I'm not soliciting, I'm evangelizing." Turning his attention back to Norma, he continued. "I'm going to be preaching tomorrow over at Community Baptist Church. It's the long brick building around the corner—"

"Alright, that's it." The store managed stepped between him and Norma, arm stretched out, pointing toward the exit. "Out! Let's go, outside," he said as he escorted Pastor Ed out the door to the sounds of the customers clapping.

Once outside, the store manager gave him a stern, uncompromising look. "The old store manager might have put up with you because he attended your church, but I sure as hell won't. Next time I catch you bothering my customers, I'm going to call the police and have you banned from the store. Understood?"

With a slight heaviness, Pastor Ed made his way to the street corner where a homeless man was panhandling. "Hey, George," he said, as he handed the man his panini.

"Oh, Pastor Ed! God bless you. You're too kind," the man said with affectionate eyes.

"You're very welcome, George. Don't forget tomorrow's church service," he said, and began tracing his steps back to the church.

Unwrapping the panini, George took a big bite, and with his mouth full said, "I'll be there along with all of God's angels to hear you preach, Pastor Ed."

* * *

The cool evening light poured through Pastor Ed's office window and overflowed onto the antique wooden panels. The stale smell of coffee was a telltale sign it was time to call it a day, but Pastor Ed sat behind his executive cherrywood desk, refreshing his YouTube channel's analytics page. Just ten new subscribers in the past month for a sad total of just over 3,000 subscribers. He navigated to Joel Osteen's channel.

2.5 million subscribers.

His assistant, Nancy, a blue-eyed blonde in her mid-50s with a gentle smile, peered into his office. "Staring at the sermon won't make it better," she said.

He smiled and closed his laptop. "Yeah, you're right."

She stood by his door with one arm holding the other at the elbow. "Before you leave, I'd like to remind you that the venue wants payment by Monday."

He stood up and shrugged his shoulders. "Okay, so pay it."

"Well, the thing is, we're way under budget for this year's evangelical mission, so I thought perhaps we should hold off on paying it."

Placing his cell phone and keys in his pocket, he said, "No way. Someone might snatch up that time slot. We can't risk it."

She scratched her elbow. "But what if we fall short on fundraising and we end up having to cancel?"

He shook his head. "That won't happen."

She shifted her balance. "Well, the thing is, this year's recession could force us to cancel. Perhaps we should find another venue. A less expensive one that is willing to hold off on taking payment until we're sure we have enough."

He took a deep breath. "That's the best deal in the area. Plus, going somewhere else is going to mess up logistics."

"But if we cancel, we won't get our money back. Perhaps we should just hold off on this year's mission until—"

"No. Absolutely not. This church has prided itself on its evangelical missions. I will not be the first pastor to cancel."

"But—"

"No buts. Just pay for the venue, okay? We'll figure it out. And don't stay too late. I need you bright and early for tomorrow's church service."

"Okay," she said, taking a few reluctant steps back to her chair.

Pastor Ed rubbed his chin and stared out the window for a short while before securing his laptop in his computer bag and pacing past Nancy toward the exit.

"Oh, Pastor Ed, before I forget," she said.

He halted within arm's reach of the door. "Yeah?"

"You know how the girls said they went out to the movies last night?"

He gripped the doorknob so hard that his knuckles turned white. "Yeah, what about it?"

"Well, they didn't really go to the movies."

He released the doorknob and turned to face her. "Where did they go?"

She frowned and played with her ring.

"Nancy, where did they go?"

"Rebecca confessed to me that they actually went to go see a medium."

"A what?!"

CHAPTER II

When Pastor Ed walked through the front door, Patricia was lying on the couch, her feet resting on the couch's arm. Her body faced the ceiling, and her arms were outstretched, holding her phone. She tapped her fingers rapidly at the screen, texting and ignoring the television playing in the background, a bad habit that drove Pastor Ed nuts.

"Patricia," Pastor Ed said. "What's this I hear you went to go see a medium?"

Patricia turned her head toward him, wide-eyed. "Who told you?"

Pastor Ed placed his keys on one of the end tables next to the couch. "That's irrelevant. What matters is that you lied to me about going to the movies last night."

She put her phone down and took a proper sitting position. "I didn't tell you because I knew you'd get mad."

"Of course I'd get mad." Pastor Ed's hard stare bore into Patricia's Spanish-green eyes. She looked much like her mother, brunette with a faun skin undertone. "What will the congregation say if they find out you went to go see a medium?" Taking a seat next to his daughter, Pastor Ed continued, "What on earth were you thinking? You're not supposed to be messing around with that stuff. You know that."

Patricia shook her head and flinched back. "Mediums aren't bad, Dad. They just want to help people reconnect with their loved ones."

Pastor Ed narrowed his eyes. "They're charlatans. They can't actually talk to the dead. Once someone dies, we can't communicate with them." He tilted his head to the side. "The Bible makes it very clear."

"That's not true. She knew things that only Mom would know. As a matter of fact, I saw a documentary that talked about how the police are now using psychics to help them solve cases." She grabbed the remote and pointed it at the TV. "Look, I'll show you."

Stopping her, Pastor Ed placed his hand over the remote. "That lady was only pretending to communicate with Mom. They're good at convincing people. She probably got her information from your friends or social media."

"No way, Dad." She set the remote down. "She knew really personal stuff that only Mom and I would know. She's able to tap into the spiritual realm."

"Spiritual realm?" He smirked. "What the heck is that?"

"You can mock me all you want, but I know what I experienced was real." Leaning toward him as if revealing a secret, in a soft voice she said, "Dad, it was like talking to Mom."

Pastor Ed released a deep breath. "Look, I miss Mom too, but I can't have you running around seeing psychics, mediums, or whatever. Not while I'm pastor. Understand? It's extremely dangerous to see these people. The Bible says that God will turn his face from you." *Not to mention the fact that I'd lose all credibility as a pastor.*

She sat back and stared at the television. "The Bible was written by old men thousands of years ago. I have the right to my own beliefs. You have to respect that."

Pastor Ed got up. "Your own beliefs don't pay the bills, nor place food on the table." Heading toward his bedroom, he began pacing across the living room. "So long as you live under my roof, you will be Christian."

"I'm off to college soon, so that's fine by me," she muttered.

Halfway across the living room, he checked his flight. "I'm serious, Patricia." He made an about-face. "If I find out that you continue to go to see one of these charlatans, I won't let you go to university." He pointed directly at her. "I'll send you to community college."

Patricia shot up. "You wouldn't dare."

"Oh yes I would, and I'd be saving a pretty penny too. So don't tempt me. And don't think that just because you're away at college, I won't know what you're up to." He pivoted and once again headed toward his bedroom. "I'll have eyes and ears on you there too."

"It was Rebecca, wasn't it?"

"Maybe it was. Maybe it wasn't."

"She must have told her mom. I knew we shouldn't have taken her with us," Patricia said in a low voice, but not low enough for Pastor Ed to miss.

"Us? How many of you went?" Pastor Ed shot back from his bedroom.

"Just two other girls from school," she replied. "But don't worry," she shouted. "They don't belong to our church."

* * *

The sun, deciding it had had enough, pulled the clouds over its face like a blanket, and as a result, no sunlight pierced through the long windows that ran across the sides of Pastor Ed's church. There were no icons or statues to be found. No images of Christ, Mary, or any saints. Just a picture of Pastor Ed with a small plaque underneath it, an American flag, and Bibles. Lots of Bibles. The congregation never missed church, and that morning's gloomy weather wasn't about to stop them from putting on their best garments and dowsing themselves with cologne and perfume.

"Thank you for coming," Pastor Ed said to one member. "Hope to see you next Sunday," he said to another. Having the feeling that someone was approaching him from behind, he pivoted to find Norma making her way through the small crowd. "Norma, you came," he said, with a smile fit for a dentist's ad.

"Yes, and I have to say, I'm impressed." A sweet smile slid across her face.

Pastor Ed shook her soft hand with a firm grip. "I'm glad to hear that. Did you like the sermon?"

"Yes. You're a talented preacher." She took in the room. "Does everyone bring their own Bibles?"

He nodded. "Yup, that's what being Bible-only is all about."

"I've never seen that before."

"Seen what?"

"People bringing their own Bibles to church."

A couple feet behind Norma, Albert and Frank chatted. Both men were in their mid-30s, but they couldn't be any more different from each other. With tilted eyebrows that gave him a look of being in constant fear, Albert Muller, sporting a buzz cut with a trimmed-down beard, stood at five feet six inches. He was Pastor Ed's wingman when it came to converting not just Catholics, but Anglicans and Lutherans too. To Albert, the Anglicans and Lutherans were basically on the other side of the Tiber River and, therefore, practically Catholic. Frank Truman, on the other hand, was tall, pushing six feet, sported a charming smile, and had almond-shaped eyes. To him, they were all brothers in Christ.

Pastor Ed waved at them. "Norma, I want you to meet Albert and Frank. Albert's a lifelong member of the church, and Frank joined us two years ago."

"Hello, Norma. What brings you to our wonderful little church today?" asked Frank.

"I met Pastor Ed at the coffee shop around the corner yesterday and he insisted I come."

"Norma is a parishioner at St. Michael's Catholic Church," Pastor Ed said.

Albert raised his chin. "Hey, did you guys know that the Roman Emperor Constantine started the Catholic Church?"

"I always thought it was started during the Middle Ages," said Pastor Ed.

"Nope. That's when the Catholic Church's persecution of the Christians was at its zenith," said Albert. "But two hundred years before the Middle Ages, Constantine wanted to unify the Roman Empire, which was splitting apart, so he combined Christianity with Paganism and created the Catholic Church during the Edict of Milan in 313 AD. He then created the papacy with Miltiades as its first pope."

Frank tilted his head. "Are you sure?"

"Oh, I'm sure," said Albert. "It's a mixture of both religions. That's why they have relics, statues, and sacrifices."

"Sacrifices?" said Norma.

"Oh yes. At the mass, the bread is believed to become the body of Christ through transubstantiation."

Norma turned to Pastor Ed. "That's true. They taught us that at catechism school."

"Right," continued Albert. "And the priest offers Christ's body as a sacrifice to the Father. Basically, Christ's sacrifice on the cross wasn't enough and—"

"Whoa, wait a minute. That's not true," said Frank. "The mass is a participation in Christ's death at the cross. The Catholics believe that, at the mass, they are mystically transported to the foot of the cross."

"What? That's crazy," said Albert. "And even if they do believe that, what they are doing is plain wrong. It's works-based salvation."

Norma stared at them both.

Frank rolled his eyes. "Oh, come on, Albert. No Christian Church teaches works-based salvation. The Catholic Church and the Lutheran Church both signed the Joint Declaration on the Doctrine of Justification, where they basically agree on salvation by grace alone."

"The Lutherans?" Albert jolted. "They're basically Catholic Light."

Norma looked at Pastor Ed. "We never talk about other religions at my church."

Realizing that he'd better get a hold of the situation before Norma went running back to St. Michael's, Pastor Ed grabbed the rest of the congregation's attention. "Hey, everyone. I want you all to meet Norma. She's new to our church."

The congregation swarmed on Norma like paparazzi. "Welcome, Norma. We're glad to have you," one member said. "Have you picked a

Bible study group yet? You should join our group," said another member. "Norma, come to tonight's family event with us," said another.

"Oh wow. It's nothing like this at my church." She turned to face Pastor Ed. "After mass, it's like a race to the parking lot to see who can get home first," she said, half jokingly.

While Norma tried to decide which Bible study group she'd join, a voice from behind caught Pastor Ed by surprise. "Pastor Ed?"

Pastor Ed swung around. "Oh hi, Mr. and Mrs. Chapman! How are you?"

"Not well, Pastor Ed, we'd like to have a moment with you in private," Mr. Chapman said.

Mrs. Chapman stepped forward. "It's about our son. He's in danger and—"

Mr. Chapman placed his arm in front of his wife. "It's best if we speak in private with the pastor, dear."

Chapter iii

The church's choir was practicing for that evening's family event, and their synchrony of beats flowed through the wall behind Pastor Ed's desk. On it hung a framed Billy Graham quote which read "Once you've been to the cross, you will never be the same."

Mr. and Mrs. Chapman sat directly across from Pastor Ed. Mr. Chapman, a clean-shaven man in his mid-40s, at least six feet tall with a full head of hair and thick eyebrows, wore an untailored gray suit which gave him a boxed look. Mrs. Chapman, a petite brunette ten years her husband's junior, with bangs parted in the middle, wore a navy-blue dress.

Pastor Ed leaned forward. "So, you said you wanted to speak to me in private about your son?"

Mr. and Mrs. Chapman stared at each other for a moment. "There's no easy way to say this," Mrs. Chapman said, "so I'm just going to come out and say it."

Mr. Chapman nodded. "Go ahead, dear. Tell him."

She bit her lip, then turned toward Pastor Ed. "Our son is possessed by some kind of demon, and we'd like for you to expel it."

The choir's angelic singing pierced through the thin wall.

Pastor Ed leaned back in his black leather chair. He had counseled plenty of families before. The entire congregation knew about his loss, and thus he could always relate to grieving families on all kinds of issues, but nothing like this.

He placed his fingers on his chin. "What leads you to believe that your son's possessed?"

"Our son was a good kid until we moved into the house," Mrs. Chapman said. "That's when we noticed a change in his behavior."

Mr. Chapman shifted his weight to the side. "It all started with that heavy metal music that his friend got him listening to. I told her that kid was bad news." He placed his hand over his chest. "I didn't want that kid anywhere near my son or my house, but she would let him in the house when I was away at work."

"I didn't think there was anything wrong with that," Mrs. Chapman said. "I mean, we listened to music that our parents forbade us from listening to, and we turned out just fine."

"That's different. The music we listened to didn't have any satanic lyrics in it. And we sure didn't dress like these kids do." Mr. Chapman leaned toward Pastor Ed. "You wouldn't even believe the shirts these kids are wearing. One of them's got an upside down pentagram. I get the chills just thinking about it."

Pastor Ed glanced at them both. "What else has your son done that is out of the ordinary?"

Mr. Chapman leaned back. "Well, for one thing, he's gone for several days at a time."

"I worry so much about him," Mrs. Chapman said. "We've filed so many missing persons' reports that the police stopped taking us serious any time we call to report him missing. I'm afraid that one day he will go missing and the police won't go looking for him."

Mr. Chapman extended his arms. "He started yelling profanities at us. You should hear the things he says. They're horrifying. And if that doesn't scare you, how he says them will. I mean, it's like he's a completely different person. His facial features change and his voice does too. My God, his voice." Mr. Chapman shook his head.

"Pastor Ed, sometimes he says things to us that we just can't understand," Mrs. Chapman said. "I found his notebook where he wrote some poetry. Here, take a look at this." She handed him the notebook.

Pastor Ed took a moment to read it, after which he placed it face-down on the desk. "That's very disturbing."

"I tried to get a hold of the situation," Mr. Chapman said. "I told him last week that I was going to place him in a boarding school. He got so angry at me, he started punching me. My wife called the police, and when they finally showed up, they handcuffed me instead. They said that I had to stay away from the house until they finished their investigation on account of him being a minor. I spent that night behind bars, worried he might do something to my wife and daughter."

"Luckily, nothing else happened that night," Mrs. Chapman added.

Pastor Ed leaned forward. "It sounds like he's got anger management issues. Have you tried getting him counseling?"

Mr. Chapman nodded. "Oh, we've tried. Believe me. We've tried. We've taken him to several, including anger management, but he's only gotten worse."

The choir ceased playing their melodies, and the room fell silent.

"I don't think that your son is possessed, Mr. Chapman, and I don't think possessions happen anymore." Pastor Ed leaned forward once more. "I understand that your son's behavior is frightening, but what I suggest for you to do is continue to seek professional help."

Mrs. Chapman pulled out a tissue from her purse. "We are at our wits' end, Pastor Ed. You're our last hope." She wiped her eyes. "With him disappearing for periods of time, I don't think we have much time left."

Mr. Chapman held his wife's hand. "All that we are asking is that you come and talk to him. See for yourself. If, after speaking with him, you still believe that it's not demonic, then that's all the proof we need."

Mrs. Chapman put her head down. "It would make us feel better to get your expertise on the matter." She lifted her head. "And while you're there, could you say some prayers over him?"

Pastor Ed tilted his head. *Great, first mediums and now demons.* He cleared his throat. "That I can do. It would be my pleasure to help in any way I can."

* * *

After his church's family event, the GPS system led Pastor Ed to a one-story house wrapped in orange bricks and divided in half by a staircase leading up to the front entrance, with its most prominent feature being two black garage doors resting on the right wing. Having parked his car and marched his way up the long driveway, he pivoted to the left and approached the front door. Reaching it, Pastor Ed was surprised to find Mrs. Chapman waiting for him.

After a quick greeting, Mr. and Mrs. Chapman guided Pastor Ed into the hallway. At the end of the hallway, there was an open door to a room with pink walls. A cute little girl of about eleven years stuck her head out the doorway and let out a big smile.

"Hi, Pastor Ed," she said.

Pastor Ed smiled back. "Hi, Julie."

Mrs. Chapman walked over to her. "Can you stay in your room until Pastor Ed finishes talking with your brother?"

Julie nodded. "Okay." She took one last look at Pastor Ed before closing the door.

To the left of the hallway was another door, and to the right was Randy's room. Mr. and Mrs. Chapman stood by Randy's door.

Mrs. Chapman knocked on her son's door. "Randy? Pastor Ed is here. He'd like to have a word with you."

Mr. Chapman gestured with his hand. "Go ahead. We'll be by the door just in case."

"I don't think that's necessary. I'll just have a talk with him."

Mrs. Chapman opened Randy's door. "It would make us feel better."

Pastor Ed nodded and slid into Randy's room, the air a mixture of stale cigarettes, old carpet, and dirty laundry. It was bright, too bright for a room its size, and except for two heavy metal posters and a bed that ran across the back wall, the room was barren. Sitting on his bed with headphones on that jammed heavy metal music, Randy stared at Pastor Ed, a tall skinny teenager sporting long hair that touched his shoulders, blemishes across his cheeks, and, except for a white outline of the grim reaper on his shirt, his outfit was entirely black; he was the definition of a 1980s metalhead.

Pastor Ed smiled and raised his right hand. "Hey, Randy. Can you take your headphones off? I'd like to talk to you."

Speaking gibberish in an almost catatonic state, he stood up and drifted toward him. The hairs on the back of Pastor Ed's neck stood up. "What's that? I don't understand what you're saying."

Ach, Randy cocked his head back. *Ptui*!

Pastor Ed flinched. *What the hell?*

With one eye closed, he stepped out of the room. "Where's your restroom?"

"Straight ahead," Mrs. Chapman said.

Pastor Ed rinsed his face over the sink.

"What happened?" Mr. Chapman asked.

Mrs. Chapman handed Pastor Ed a towel. "Did he spit on you?"

Mr. Chapman's face turned crimson red. He swung Randy's door open. "Damn it, boy!"

"It's okay. I'm fine, Mr. Chapman." Pastor Ed walked back into the room. "Really, it's fine. Give us a minute."

Mr. Chapman stood looking at Randy, square-jawed. "Okay, we'll be by the door. Just yell if he tries anything else."

"Will do, thanks." Pastor Ed closed the door behind him.

Randy was sitting on his bed, staring to his right. He turned and raised an eyebrow. "Oh, hey, Pastor Ed. What are you doing here?"

"Randy, why did you spit on me?"

"What? I can't hear you." He pointed to his headphones. "You're going to have to speak louder."

Pastor Ed signaled with his hands to take the headphones off.

"No can do." Randy shook his head. "You're going to have to speak up."

"I just want to have a word with you! It'll be quick. I promise!"

Randy leaned back. "No way!"

"Why not?"

"The voice. I don't want to hear the voice."

"Whose voice?"

"What?!"

Pastor Ed sighed. *Really, kid?* "Whose voice!"

Randy pointed to the corner.

Pastor Ed turned around. *Nothing.* "There's nothing there," Pastor Ed said.

"You can't see him, but he's there, and he looks mad. I don't think he likes you being here."

"Who's *he*?"

"The demon."

Pastor Ed took a long breath. "I'm a pastor! I'm a man of God! He can't touch me because God is more powerful than any demon!"

"He says there's no such thing as God."

"If there are demons, then there's a God!"

Randy stared at him for a second. "Okay, but you better make it quick."

While he took his headphones off, Pastor Ed sat next to him. "Randy, when did you start hearing voices?"

"Voice, not voices. It's just one," he said. "And it started when we moved into this house. I told my mom the house was evil, but she didn't believe me. They thought I was scared or something."

"Your parents told me you started acting up when you started listening to heavy metal music. They said your friend got you listening to it."

"Pfff. Yeah, they would say that." Randy stared at the ground. "No, my friend only recommended me heavy metal music because the other music doesn't work. I can still hear the voice. But with heavy metal music, the voice gets mixed in with the artist's lyrics." He looked up at Pastor Ed. "My friend was only trying to help."

"Oh, I see," said Pastor Ed. "Is that why you also run away?"

"Yeah, at first the voice follows me, but then it gets weaker the longer I stay away, until I can't hear it anymore."

"Um, so why come back?" Pastor Ed asked.

"Because that's when the thoughts of suicide come in." Randy wiped his nose. "The longer I stay away, the worse it gets. It gets to the point where all I can think about is ways to off myself."

Pastor Ed's eyes grew warm. "I won't let that happen, Randy. I know what that's like."

Randy flinched. "You? What do you know about it? All you pastors ever care about is your 10%."

"That's not true, and I do know what it's like. I've been there. I lost my wife and thought about ending it, but someone helped me out."

"Oh yeah? Who? A stupid pastor?"

Pastor Ed looked him in the eyes. "Yes. It was a pastor. And he's not stupid."

Music continued to flow from Randy's headphones.

"Randy, what does this voice tell you?"

"It wants me to do all kinds of evil."

"Murder?"

"Yeah."

"Rape?"

There was a pause.

"Sometimes."

"Is that why you attacked your father the other night?"

"I don't remember any of that."

"You don't remember? Your mom said the cops showed up and took your dad to jail."

"Last time I left, I was gone for a really long time and it got furious at me. And ever since then, I have blackouts where I don't remember anything."

"What does your counselor say about that?"

"Nothing. She just gave me pills."

"And are you taking them?"

Randy turned away. "Yeah… I'm taking them."

"There's nothing to be embarrassed about," Pastor Ed said. "Your parents think it would be a good idea that I come and see you. I think I can help you out, Randy. Is that alright with you?"

"Do I have a choice?"

"Of course you do. I also think it would be a good idea for you to attend church services with your parents."

Randy lifted his headphones. "You should leave. He's getting angry."

Pastor Ed stood up. "Okay, but before I leave, I'd like to pray over you."

He closed his eyes and placed his hands over Randy. "Dear Lord, we ask that you—"

Randy made a groaning sound. "Stop."

Pastor Ed peeked through his right eye. "What?"

"I said stop." Randy's nostrils flared. "Stop praying."

Pastor Ed flinched. "Why?"

"Because."

"Because why?"

"Because I hate it," Randy said in a deep voice.

"Randy, I just want to—"

Randy shoved Pastor Ed toward the door. He regained his balance just in time to catch Randy rushing him. Locking arms with Randy, Pastor Ed yelled out for help.

Mr. and Mrs. Chapman stormed in and restrained Randy.

Pastor Ed took a couple steps back, stunned and not really knowing what to make of what just happened. "It's okay, Randy. I'm going to help you. I promise."

"Get out." Randy's voice grew deeper. "Get out of my house."

"It's alright, Pastor Ed. We've got this," Mr. and Mrs. Chapman said.

"Are you sure?"

Randy bared his teeth. "I said get out. Now"

"Yes, Pastor Ed. Go on. We'll talk later," said Mr. Chapman.

Pastor Ed lifted his hands up. "Okay. I'm leaving." He saw himself out, but not before taking one last look at Randy.

CHAPTER IV

The dishwasher seemed extra loud that night at John Barrett's home. John, whose wife was out with friends, walked into the living room carrying two cups of tea. He placed one cup on the coffee table in front of Pastor Ed and then sat on his recliner. Pastor Ed took a good look at John, a retired ex-pastor with a bald head and deep wrinkles running across his forehead and around his mouth, wearing a mahogany flannel that made his skin look extra red. He was a man with a fragile look, who at one time ran an illegal Bible smuggling operation into an Islamic controlled region.

"I took one last look at him, and chills ran down my spine." Pastor Ed lifted his cup. "The odd thing is that it wasn't until I started praying over him that he began to change. His voice sounded like that of an older man, but deeper and raspier. Evil."

"How old's the boy?" John asked.

"I'd say he's fifteen." Pastor Ed sipped his tea. "Then his face changed too. It contorted, and you could just see the hate in his eyes. We've worked with drug addicts and ex-convicts in our outreach program, but this was on a whole other level."

John's eyes widened. "Really?"

"Oh yes," Pastor Ed said, "and that stuff that he said about not being able to leave the house for too long. Did you ever run across something like that back when you were pastoring the church?"

John shook his head. "Not exactly."

Pastor Ed put his cup on the table. "I told him I was going to help him, but I just don't know how."

John looked up to his right. "I'm guessing the family has him seeing a specialist?"

"Yes, but it doesn't seem to be working. He's getting worse."

John got up and headed toward the stairs. "Come with me. I want to show you something."

The two headed upstairs. "Back when I was pastoring," John said, "a family came to me with a similar situation, only it was a woman." John came to a full stop. "Funny thing was, she lived in the same house that the boy lives in now."

Pastor Ed had never been to the second floor of John's house before, let alone his home office, but it was just as he'd expected. A cherrywood desk sat facing out three long windows with beautiful white plantation shutters, and to the sides ran cherrywood bookshelves filled with books.

John fired up his laptop. "The gospels tell us that our Lord cast out demons." He looked out the window. "One can't believe in the gospels and deny the existence of demons. To deny demonic possession is to deny the gospels." He punched in his password. "I ended up performing an exorcism on the woman." John clicked on some folders. "My assistant recorded the event on his camcorder." He double clicked on a video file and skipped ahead several minutes. "It's dated, so the resolution isn't the best."

On the screen was the Chapmans' living room, only the furniture was different. A woman sat pinned downed to a chair by three men. She had the same evil look as Randy.

A young Pastor Barrett stood before her with his Bible. "I cast you out in the name of Jesus Christ."

The woman's eyes bulged out of their sockets. "Never!"

Pastor Barrett placed his Bible on her head. She shook violently and screamed. He recited verses from the Bible, which exacerbated the woman's reaction.

Pastor Ed leaned toward the computer screen. *Is this for real?*

John paused the video. "The exorcism took about an hour, but ultimately she was delivered."

"I can't believe what I just saw," Pastor Ed said. "Do you believe Randy is really possessed?"

"A Christian can't be possessed," John said. "If he's accepted Jesus Christ as his personal Lord and Savior, then possession is impossible." John pulled out a thumbdrive from his desk and inserted it into the laptop. "The woman in the video recited the sinner's prayer, but wasn't a true believer." John dragged the file onto the thumbdrive icon. "Do you know if the boy is truly saved?"

Pastor Ed shook his head. "Based on our conversation earlier, I'd say no."

John pulled the thumbdrive out. "He's never publicly accepted Jesus?"

"Not at the church, no."

"Then he's probably possessed." John handed the thumbdrive to Pastor Ed. "Here, take this. Get him to accept Jesus and the demon will have no choice but to leave. It won't be easy. The demon will fight you all the way."

Pastor Ed looked at the thumbdrive. "Is that how you were able to liberate her?"

John nodded.

"Why haven't you shown this to the congregation or posted it on social media?"

"I couldn't show it to the congregation for privacy reasons, and social media wasn't a thing back then, plus the resolution is poor for today's standards. People would just dismiss it as fake."

"I don't know about that. I think that video could make a difference. Something like this is sure to garner a lot of views."

"Well, either way, I'd need permission from the woman, and she's long gone now."

"I understand."

* * *

Pastor Ed took a seat in the Chapmans' olive-green loveseat. The air conditioner hummed, warm afternoon light pierced through the window, and an electrifying lime scent filled the room.

Mr. and Mrs. Chapman sat on the sofa across from him. "What made you change your mind?" they asked.

"After looking into the matter, I am convinced that demonic possession is possible," Pastor Ed said. "In fact, I've spent the last couple days researching how to confront the demon. Unfortunately, most of what I found is Catholic superstition, the kind you're likely to find in a Hollywood movie."

Mrs. Chapman placed her hands on her lap. "We also did our research on the matter. The Internet is filled with contradicting theories. It's hard to tell what's true."

"That's why I'd like to record the exorcism."

The Chapmans' jaws dropped in open disbelief. "Record the exorcism?"

Pastor Ed bit his lip. "Yes, I'd like to upload the video onto YouTube to help raise awareness."

Mr. and Mrs. Chapman glanced at each other.

"With your permission, of course."

Mrs. Chapman sat up straight with her arms crossed like a Civil War general. "I don't know how I feel about that. I mean, he's already a bit of an outcast amongst his friends."

"I understand your concern, Mrs. Chapman. However, I'm also thinking about the families that are struggling with the same situation but don't know that the problem is demonic. They'll never receive the help they need."

Mr. Chapman rubbed his chin. "I can see how it could help, but I'm not too sure we'd want a video of our son's possession on the Internet."

"The gospels tell us that our Lord commanded us to go forth and make disciples of all nations. It is our duty to convert nonbelievers."

Mrs. Chapman crossed her legs. "We do our best to bring the gospel to others. Isn't that right, hun?"

Mr. Chapman nodded. "That's right."

"The reason I bring it up is that my research shows that Christians can't be possessed. A demon can't possess someone that's saved."

Mrs. Chapman blinked several times. "Are you saying that Randy isn't saved?"

Pastor Ed shrugged. "You mentioned he likes to listen to music with satanic lyrics, and that he enjoys wearing shirts that depict satanic iconography like an upside down pentagram."

Mr. and Mrs. Chapman both looked at each other.

"Perhaps your son recited the sinner's prayer. However, if he was truly saved, he would never listen to that type of music, let alone wear those shirts. I bring this up because this video would not only help those who are currently afflicted by evil, but also to bring people to Christ."

Mrs. Chapman turned to her husband. He looked at her and shrugged.

"Pastor Ed," Mrs. Chapman said, "I understand that what you're trying to do is very important, but I'm really concerned about what this video could do to his future. I'm worried about the repercussions. How the rest of the kids will treat him. How it will affect his job prospects. I mean, what if the college admissions office sees the video?"

"Well," Pastor Ed said, "what if we ask Randy? See what he says?"

A grin appeared on the side of Mrs. Chapman's lips. "He's way too young to make that kind of decision on his own." She gripped her husband's hand. "Isn't that right, hun?"

Mr. Chapman stared at the floor. His lips narrowed until they disappeared.

Mrs. Chapman's grin quickly vanished. "Hun?"

He looked up and rubbed the front of his neck. "I think we should let the boy decide."

Mrs. Chapman drew her hand back. "What?"

"Hey, Randy!" Mr. Chapman cried out.

Mrs. Chapman's nostrils flared. She glared at Pastor Ed with so much dislike that he had to avert his eyes.

No response.

"He must have his headphones on. I'll go get him." Mr. Chapman got up and headed toward the boy's room.

The air conditioner stopped humming. Pastor Ed and Mrs. Chapman sat in awkward silence. Gripping his Bible, he did his best to avoid eye contact.

Minutes later, Mr. Chapman returned with a long face.

Pastor Ed's chest tightened. "What did he say?"

Mr. Chapman drew his eyes together. "He's gone."

Chapter V

Meanwhile, in Mexico.

Doña Gloria conducted business from her small house in the border city of Juarez. A witch's clientele is comprised mostly of women whose husbands had left them, whose sons had fallen victims to drug abuse, or who simply wanted the handsome man just outside their reach. Men came too, blue-collar men who sought promotions or better job prospects, businessmen wanting more clientele, and local politicians and drug cartel members seeking "blessings" in an upcoming election or border crossing.

In the past, seeing a witch, or *bruja*, was enough to make you the black sheep of the family, but things are changing in Mexico. Ever since social media penetrated the four corners of the country, the witch business has boomed. The church no longer seems attractive to the younger generations, who no longer concern themselves with the afterlife, but with the here and now — status, money, power.

Sella and two other women waited patiently in foldable chairs in Doña Gloria´s living room, which served as a waiting room. One of them, no older than twenty, simultaneously pressed her lips together in a pout and sucked in her cheeks, held up a peace sign, and snapped selfies with her phone. The other woman, who had to be in her late twenties, with tawny brown skin and thick eyebrows, smiled, holding a boy on her lap who watched cartoons on a phone he managed to yank from his mother's hands.

"First time?" the woman asked.

"Yes," Sella said. "You?"

"No, I've been coming for a while."

"Does it work?"

She shrugged. "It's worked for me."

At that moment, another woman stepped out of a room. "Gracias, Doña Gloria," she said, before heading for the exit.

Doña Gloria stepped forth. "Who's next?"

The two women nodded toward Sella. "She's next, Doña Gloria."

Doña Gloria signaled with her hand. "Come."

An intoxicating smell of herbs, wax, incense, and smoke hit Sella as she crept into the room cautiously, shoulders hunched, fear skittering around her skin, lashes flipped fully open, taking inventory of the room. It was dark, lit only by brightly colored candles running along the walls: one depicted a gagged man with the words "shut up" written above; another featured a man on his knees gazing up into a domineering woman's hypnotic eyes, with "do as I say" inscribed on it; still another had the words "Baron of the Cemetery" and pictured a bearded man raising a flaming sword above his head, stomping on a dead man's corpse.

The candles led up to an idol at the back of the room, a skeleton figure standing on an altar, wearing a bone-white hood with fool's gold trim, raising a balance with its left hand and clenching a black scythe with the other. *La Santa Muerte,* or "Holy Death" as it's known in the U.S.

A round table stood in the center of the room with two chairs on either side. Doña Gloria sat at one end of the table facing the door, and overlooking her from behind like a dark shadow was *La Santa Muerte*.

"Sit," she said.

Sella took one step back and turned toward the exit.

"Don't be afraid, child," Doña Gloria said. "Come. Sit. Tell me what's troubling you."

What's troubling me? Within arms reach of the door, scared, knees unwilling to bend and feet rooted into the floor, Sella thought about what brought her there. Forcing her heavy legs to turn around, she tore her feet from the floor and took a seat facing Doña Gloria, who was around forty years old with dark hair, hazel eyes, and terracotta-brown skin, high Mayan cheek bones, and a beauty mark right below her left eye.

"Tell me your name and what brings you here today."

"My name is Sella," she said, cotton-mouthed, "and my friend recommended you to me."

Doña Gloria raised an eyebrow.

Sella cleared her throat. "My boyfriend and I had a good relationship. We dated for a year, and shortly after we moved in together into a small house we purchased under my name. He took up the role of stepfather to my two little children, and they've come to see him as their biological father. Everything was great, but then, suddenly, out of nowhere, he changed. He began to be distant and often came home late, complaining about the kids, the bills, the way I dress. He even complained about the pictures I uploaded on social media, saying I was seeking male validation."

Doña Gloria reached for her tarot cards. "Go on."

"Shortly afterward, he accused me of cheating and left. I stayed up all night crying and got little sleep. The following morning, I arrived late to work and was written up for it. That same day, I became distracted and caused a mistake at the factory. My boss fired me shortly after. I've spent the last months looking for a job, but no one's called me back, and now my friends refuse to lend me any more money. I've fallen so far behind with all my bills that creditors are calling non-stop, and the bank is threatening to foreclose on the house. My friend suggested I come and see you as a last-ditch effort. She said you've been able to help people in my situation."

"I can help you." Doña Gloria shuffled her cards. "But first we must see what we are dealing with." She placed the deck on the table.

"Cut it."

Sella cut the deck and handed it back.

Doña Gloria whispered a prayer, then blew on the deck three times. She took several cards from the top of the stack and placed them on the table face up, studying them intently. "I see that there's another woman, a past lover — angry, jealous, seeking revenge. She has him wrapped around her finger. And—"

Lifting her head, she stared into Sella's eyes. "She's placed a curse on you."

Sella's stomach pitted into tight coils.

Doña Gloria gathered her cards. "I can remove the curse. It won't be difficult."

"So my boyfriend will return?"

"No," she answered sharply. "Removing the curse will simply put a stop to the downward spiral that has become your life."

Sella's heart sank.

"I can help you get your boyfriend back if that's what you want."

"You can?" Sella perked up.

"Sure. I can also help you with your financial troubles too."

"Really? How?"

Doña Gloria got up and retrieved a cigar, a lighter, some incense, and herbs. "First, we must do a *limpia*. The cleansing will remove the curse." She moved the table out of the way. "Put the chairs over there in the corner." Doña Gloria lit the incense and placed it in front of *La Santa Muerte*. Kneeling before it, she said a brief prayer before rising and lighting her cigar. Taking three puffs from it, she crossed to the center of the room. "Stand here in the middle."

Sella took two hesitant steps forward.

"Don't be afraid. Come." Doña Gloria grabbed Sella by the shoulder and drew her to the center. "Stand here and don't move." She took another puff of her cigar and started rubbing the herbs on Sella. She began by rubbing it on her head and worked her way down, then up again, all the while saying some prayers in a low voice and exhaling smoke. The temperature dropped, causing her breaths to become visible. Sella looked past Doña Gloria and found *La Santa Muerte* staring at her.

Doña Gloria finished her ritual. "There. That should do it."

Sella felt a little light-headed, but was relieved it was over. "How do I get my boyfriend and job back?"

Doña Gloria turned and walked to the altar of *La Santa Muerte*. On it sat three stacks of cards. She took one card from each stack and handed them to her. "Here. Say these three prayers every night before going to bed, and she will bring your boyfriend back."

"She? Who's *she*?" Sella asked.

"*La Santa Muerte.*"

Sella observed the bloodless, off-white skeleton.

"*La Santa Muerte* has performed many miracles for many of my clients. She'll do the same for you."

"I'm not sure if I want to pray to her. She looks scary." Sella looked down at the three cards in her hand. "Is there another way?"

Doña Gloria thought for a moment. "I can remove the spell that woman placed on your boyfriend, but he has to see me in person. Do you think you can convince him to come?"

"No, he would never come. He'd think I'm crazy."

Doña Gloria shook her head. "In any case, removing the spell won't guarantee that he'll come back to you, nor improve your financial situation."

Sella's legs weakened.

Doña Gloria grabbed the table and placed it back in the center. "Pray to her or don't pray to her. It's up to you." She grabbed the chairs and placed them in their original spots. "But it seems to me like you don't have much of a choice." She walked to the door and opened it.

Sella's mouth went dry. "Okay."

"Good, and if you need anything else, don't hesitate to call."

* * *

Exactly three days later, Sella woke up to find herself, unsurprisingly, still jobless and still single. Thinking she was a fool for wasting her time, not to mention what precious little money she had left, on a witch, she threw the three prayer cards into the trash bin and thought nothing more of it.

That afternoon, Sella was in the kitchen preparing *caldo de pollo* when her mother rushed through the door. "*Mija*, I've got good news."

Sella chopped unions, tomatoes, and *chile de arbol*. "What's the big news, Mama?"

"*Mija*, you're not going to believe it," her mother said, "but my *comadre* called to tell me that her daughter, Alicia, says she can get you a job at her office."

"An office job?" Sella said. "You're right. I don't believe it."

"*Mija*, she put in a good word for you."

Sella placed the chopped pieces into the blender. "But, Mama, I've never worked in an office before. I don't know the first thing about office work. They'll fire me right away, and it's going to reflect poorly on your *comadre's* daughter."

"You'll do great. You pick things up right away."

"I don't know, Mama." Sella added water and salt to the blender. "Those jobs require you to know how to use a computer. They'll know right away that I've never used a computer before. It'll be too embarrassing."

She ran the blender for a couple seconds.

"What are you talking about? I see you using that phone all the time."

"The phone isn't a computer, Mama. They're two completely different things. And I'm sure they require a high school diploma. They're not going to hire me."

"*Mija*, they will hire you."

Sella poured the salsa into the bowl. "Why? Why would they hire a person who couldn't finish school, has never used a computer, and has never worked in an office before? Huh? Tell me? Why?"

"You don't understand. I've been going to church and praying before Jesus every day since you lost your job."

Sella rinsed the blender in the sink. "Oh my God." Sella eyes widened. "It worked!"

"Yes, *mija*. God is finally answering our prayers."

Sella dried her hands. "What's her phone number? I'm going to call her right away."

Sella's mother gave her Alicia's number and prayed the entire time she was on the phone.

"What did she say?" her mother asked.

"I don't believe it." Sella stared at her phone. "She said I can start tomorrow."

Chapter VI

Although she adapted quickly to her new work environment, making new friends and even surprising herself with how quickly she mastered the computer system, Sella still struggled to make ends meet. Sure, her new position paid significantly more than her previous factory job, but three weeks after accepting her new position, she still found herself dodging bill collectors.

After work, contemplating whether she should take up a part-time job, Sella helped her two kids with their homework — Javier, an almond-skinned seven-year-old boy, sporting his cappuccino-colored hair in a faux hawk cut, and Little Maria, a six-year-old with porcelain skin and hard-angled eyebrows, who always wore a small bow in her chestnut hair; today it was pink. The phone rang once again. She glanced at the unknown number and quickly decline the call.

A few moments later, a text came in: *It's me answer your phone.*

Sella felt a heaviness in her stomach. Although the text didn't say who it was from, she knew exactly who sent it. *Did La Santa Muerte get the wrong ex?* Pedro was the ex-boyfriend she most definitely did not want back.

The phone rang.

She pinched the bridge of her nose and answered. "What do you want?"

"What do I want?" he said. "I want my money back. What do you think I want?"

She jerked her head back. "What money?"

"Don't act stupid. I want the money you took from me."

"I didn't take any money from you, jerk."

"Give me back the money you took from me or else."

"Don't threaten me. I didn't take your money." She gnashed her teeth. "I don't even know what the hell you're talking about."

"I'm talking about the money child support took from my bank account."

Silence.

"Are you listening to me? Hey, I'm talking to you."

"That's between you and child support services. You need to talk to them, not me. I haven't received a single peso from you."

"I'm not playing, Sella. If you know what's good for you and the kids, you'll give me back my money and retract the child support claim you have on me."

"Don't you dare touch my kids, or I swear I will go to the police. Are you loco or what?"

"Don't say I didn't warn you."

—Click.

"Pedro! Pedro!"

"Daddy!" The kids leaped up and, reaching over with both hands, they tried to wrestle the phone from their mother, yanking it as hard as they could.

Sella jerked the phone away, causing them to lose their balance. "Work on your homework."

"But I want to talk to my daddy," Little Maria said, jumping up and down.

"Me too," Javier said.

"He hung up already."

Javier let out a cry, followed by Little Maria.

"We never get to talk to Daddy," he said.

"Next time he calls, you can talk to him. Go finish your homework in your room." Sella got up and headed toward the door. "Stay here," she said, "and don't go anywhere. I'm going to the mailbox."

Little Maria looked confused. "Do we stay here or go to our room?"

"Go to your room and stay there," Sella said, locking the door behind her.

She speedwalked to the mailbox. When she got there, she found it stuffed full of letters. "Ugh. I've got to remember to get the mail more often."

She pulled the stack of letters from the small mailbox hole. Some fell to the ground. She gathered them all up as quickly as she could and, on her way back to her house, she flipped through the envelopes. *Water bill. Electric bill. Final notice. Bank notice.*

"Hey, señora! You dropped some mail," a boy on a bike yelled out.

Sella glanced at the piece of paper on the ground. *Brochure.* Turned around and continued walking. *Come on. Where is it?* She flipped through the envelopes.

She came to a fast halt. *Pension Alimenticia*!

Sella opened the envelope. A check fell out. She picked it up and flipped it around. *Payable to Sella* Castañon *for $204,454.46 pesos.*

He's going to kill me.

* * *

The following day after work, Sella sat in Doña Gloria's waiting room clutching a plastic bag. The other two women weren't there this time. She was alone. She'd been waiting for 45 minutes and worried that perhaps she might not have time to be seen.

A man stepped out of Doña Gloria's room. Sella recognized him as Marco, a local petty drug dealer that sold drugs across the street from her house. "Gracias, Doña Gloria," he said.

"Don't mention it, young man."

Marco, looking at Sella for a split-second, blushed and quickly left.

Doña Gloria flipped the WE'RE OPEN sign and locked the entrance. "Come in, Sella. You'll be my last client for today."

Sella took her seat facing Doña Gloria.

Doña Gloria looked at the bag. "Did you bring what I asked?"

Sella nodded and handed the bag to her. "It's all there."

Doña Gloria opened the bag and pulled out a picture, a long sleeve shirt, and a comb: items that belonged to Pedro. She held the picture in her hand. "Hmmm. He's no good." She looked up at Sella. "You sure know how to pick em, eh?"

Sella adjusted herself in her seat. "I'm scared that he might hurt the children."

"I see," Doña Gloria said. Rubbing his shirt with her fingers, turning her head to the side and leaning her ear to the shirt as if she were trying to hear something, her eyes bulged and she turned with a snap of the neck. "He's evil," she said. "He'll kill you and the children."

Impaled by fear, Sella couldn't move. The thought of him killing her babies tore at her insides.

She placed the shirt on the table. "But don't worry, dear. We can bind him with a powerful hex so that he doesn't hurt you or the children."

Air filled Sella's lungs once more. "Yes, please."

"Don't worry, child, I will. But first, did you bring the other item?" Doña Gloria asked.

Sella's mouth dried up. "Yes, I did."

"Well? Where is it?"

Sella rubbed her hands together. "It's in my pocket. I put it in a small case so that it doesn't break."

"Good. Now give it to me."

Sella looked around. She locked eyes with La Santa Muerte standing behind Doña Gloria.

Doña Gloria extended her palm. "Go on. Give it here."

Sella snapped out of her gaze and cleared her throat once more. "Growing up, the priest said it was the most holy."

"It is. That's why it's so powerful."

Sella's body felt heavy. Heavier than it had ever felt.

"The hex won't work without it," Doña Gloria said. "So if you want me to protect your children, you're going to have to give it to me."

Sella looked around. Her body trembled. In a flash, she put her hand in her pocket and gave it to her, hoping that if she did it fast enough, God wouldn't notice.

Doña Gloria smiled. Holding the container with both hands, she popped it open, revealing the white wafer celebrated in holy communion. The candle lights flickered, and Sella averted her eyes until she heard the container snap shut.

"Good," Doña Gloria said.

She got up and opened a small drawer. Placing the container in it, she retrieved three small human fetus skulls and a mortar and pestle. Doña Gloria laid the mortar on the table with the three skulls on it. Raising the pestle, she ground the skulls into fine white powder, then reached for the comb, extracted the hair follicles, and let them fall into the mortar. She took Pedro's picture and carefully placed it in the center of the mortar. Clasping her hands together, she closed her eyes and prayed in a low breath. The temperature dropped and her breaths became visible. Sella jolted from her chair as she watched in disbelief as Pedro's picture caught fire and slowly burned into ashes. Doña Gloria lifted the mortar and dropped its contents into the small hex bag and shut it tight with a knot.

Doña Gloria pulled out a piece of paper and wrote on it. "Is his father still alive?"

"His father? No, he passed away."

She slid the hex bag and paper over. "Go to the cemetery with your two children at midnight. Bury the hex bag three centimeters deep on his father's grave and recite this spell."

Sella rested her eyes on the hex bag.

"Go on. Take it," Doña Gloria said.

Sella took the hex bag. "And the other item? You said you needed it to make the spell work."

Doña Gloria smiled. "Let me know if you need anything else."

* * *

Shortly before midnight, Sella woke the kids up and put them in the back of her car.

"Where are we going?" Little Maria asked.

"We're going to the park."

"Right now?" Javier asked.

"Yes, right now. We have to run an errand."

She drove across town until she reached the gravel road that ran around the cemetery. She adjusted her rearview mirror; Javier and Little Maria were slumped over, fast asleep. She kept driving along the gravel road until she saw it — the big bright red Coca-Cola sign. The same one she remembered seeing when they buried Pedro's father several years ago.

Four-foot-tall plastered cement blocks divided the gravel road from the cemetery. Behind them was a desert of makeshift wooden crosses, gravestones, and raised tombs mixed in no ordered fashion. In the center was a mound. She canvassed the tombs resting at the base of the mound.

She opened the rear door. "Javier. Maria. Wake up."

"I don't want to go to school," Javier said, half asleep.

"Wake up!"

Little Maria looked out the window. Her eyes bulged in mounting terror. "It's a cemetery."

"What?" Javier hoisted himself up.

"Come on, kids, let's go."

"In there?" Little Maria pointed out the window.

"Yes, in there."

The kids backpedaled away from her side of the car.

"Get out of the car. Now!"

The kids shook their heads.

"I'm not going to ask you again."

"Why do we have to go?" Little Maria asked.

"Because we have to drop off a present with Grandpa."

Javier gripped his seat. "I don't want to go. I'm too scared."

"If you don't get out of the car right now, I swear to God!"

Javier cried heavily, followed by his little sister, large tears flowing down their cheeks.

"Okay, that's it." She took her belt off.

The kids trembled. "No. No. No."

"You see this?" Sella held her belt up. "The belt or the cemetery. Which is it?"

They held their little palms up. "Okay, okay, we'll go."

Sella popped her trunk open and pulled out a flashlight and shovel. They made their way to the base of the mound. Running her flashlight across the makeshift wooden crosses, she read the names of the deceased until she came across the one that read *Juan Carlos Lopez de Garcia*.

Sella handed the flashlight to her son. "Javier, take the flashlight and point at the ground here." Hands shaking, sobbing uncontrollably, Javier pointed the flashlight at the ground. Sella raised the shovel and struck the ground. With little Maria grasping onto her left leg and burying her head into her mother's jeans, Sella raised her right leg and stomped on the shovel, lifting it up and tossing the dirt to the side, then repeating until she dug a hole about a foot deep. She took out the hex bag and laid it in the hole, before covering it up with dirt.

"I don't want to be here," Little Maria said repeatedly, clasping onto her mother's leg.

Sella threw the shovel to the side and pulled out the piece of paper. "I'm almost done. I need you two to be quiet while I read this."

The kids nodded. "Hurry."

"Oh, holy death, all powerful. You who will claim our life at the moment of our death. Protect me and my two children from Pedro López de García and, in return, I offer you the lives of these three innocents. Accept this exchange on behalf of myself and my two children, and I promise you, my lord, my loyalty forever."

She paused, expecting something to happen.

Nothing happened.

Three days later, Sella's ex-boyfriend came crawling back.

Chapter vii

Back in the USA.

Pastor Ed recruited two men from his church for Randy's exorcism. Having recorded many of his wedding ceremonies, Mike, a local photographer of African descent with a high fade and a trimmed-down beard, volunteered to record the ritual. Joe, a bodybuilder sporting a pompadour hairstyle and a mechanic's t-shirt that gave him a rockabilly look, volunteered to help restrain Randy during the exorcism.

After they moved the Chapmans' furniture out of the way, Pastor Ed called everyone to gather around Randy who, having returned home the night before, stood in the middle of the living room. His headphones were blazing full strength, his hair was unkempt and greasy, and dark bags hung under his eyes. His right hand held his left arm above the elbow, and he wore his customary all-black heavy metal outfit, looking so depressed that he resembled death.

Mrs. Chapman removed his headphones. "You sure you want to do this, hun? It's not too late to say no."

Turning off his music and glancing to the side, he muttered, "I just want it to go away."

Pastor Ed leaned toward Randy, placing his hands on his shoulders and looking him in the eyes. "You're doing the right thing. People will find hope in this video."

"Yeah, Randy," Joe chimed in.

Pastor Ed turned his attention to the crew. "Is everyone ready?"

Everyone nodded except for Mrs. Chapman, who made her way to the corner — arms crossed, head tilted, eyes glaring at him.

Ignoring her ire, he picked up the microphone, and not knowing whether the red light meant that it was recording or that it was off, he tapped on it repeatedly, asking, "Is this on, Mike?"

"Yes, sir," Mike said.

Pastor Ed turned to the group. "Okay, everyone. I know the camera can be a little intimidating, but try to ignore it. Before you know it, you won't even notice it." He picked up his Bible with his right hand. "Joe and Mr. Chapman, the both of you stand on either side of Randy. Make sure he doesn't hurt himself or anyone else."

"You got it," Joe said, taking up position. Then, tapping three times on Randy's chest, he let out a big smile. "You got this, kid."

Randy turned his head to the side, paused for a split second, and let out a faint smile.

Mike pointed his camera at Pastor Ed.

Turning his attention to the camera lens, he adjusted his collar and then lifted the mic. "My name is Pastor Ed," he said, "and the young man standing next to me goes by the name of Randy. Randy is possessed by a demon that resides in this house. Today we're going to exorcise that demon, and in the process we're not only going to save his life, but also his soul."

Turning his face away from the camera and toward Randy, he asked, "Randy, is the demon here with us today?" and placed his microphone to Randy's face.

Speaking into the mic with his eyes facing the camera, he responded, "Yes, he's here."

Pulling the mic back to himself, Pastor Ed asked, "Can you show us where he's at?"

Drifting his gaze from the camera, Randy rested his eyes on

Pastor Ed for a brief moment before shifting them slightly to the side. Lifting his finger, pointing directly behind him, he said, "He's right there."

With the hairs on the back of his neck standing at full attention, Pastor Ed slowly turned and looked. *Nothing.*

He cleared his throat. "Randy, can you tell me what this demon has been doing to you?"

"He's been tormenting me. He tells me to do evil things." Randy lowered his head. "Things I don't ever want to do."

"I see," Pastor Ed said. "Randy, the last time we spoke, the demon talked through you. Do you remember that?"

"I remember talking to you, but then everything went dark."

"Right. Do you think I could talk to the demon now?"

Turning his head away, Randy shut his eyes tight. "He's standing right behind you and he's furious."

Pastor Ed leaned forward. "Look at me, Randy."

Randy shook his head.

"I need you to look at me."

Opening his eyes, he turned his head toward Pastor Ed, then began alternating his gaze between him and whatever it was that was standing behind him.

"I'm going to drive out that demon, but in order to do that, I need him to manifest himself through you."

"I don't know how."

"You leave that to me." Pastor Ed turned to the camera. "I'm going to use what's called religious provocation to get the demon to manifest itself by praying over Randy." Turning toward Randy and hovering his Bible over his head, he said a prayer.

Halfway through his prayer, squeezing his eyes shut, Randy groaned. "Stop."

Pastor Ed placed the mic up to Randy. "What's that, Randy?"

Grinding his teeth, he snarled. "I said stop."

"Why is that, Randy? Why do you want me to stop?"

His eyes shot open, pupils dilated. "I'm not Randy."

Pastor Ed nodded at Joe and Mr. Chapman, who, placing their

hands on Randy's shoulders, dug in their heels.

Muscles tensed, snarling, veins bulging from his neck, pressing up against their hands, he said, "I told you to leave."

"Why are you tormenting Randy?"

"Because he's mine."

"He belongs to God, not you, demon."

Randy's voice deepened. "No, he belongs to me. He gave himself to me."

Mrs. Chapman gasped.

"When? When did he do that?"

Randy stared deep into Pastor Ed's eyes. His hostile glare was hard as daggers.

"In the name of Jesus Christ, I command you to tell me."

Randy pressed forward, his momentum carrying the two men with him, extending his arms, hands inches away from Pastor Ed, trying to grasp a hold of him.

"Don't say that name," he said.

"You don't get to make demands here, demon. Now tell me. When did he give himself to you?"

Taking two steps forward, he dragged the two men behind him, leering with a wide feral grin, straining his hands to reach him. He grabbed ahold of Pastor Ed's shirt, pulling him closer, inches away from his face, gnashing his teeth with a foul breath, hissing and growling like a dog.

"In the name of Jesus—"

Thump. The camera fell to the floor, tumbling, coming to a full stop a foot away from where Mike was standing, blood drained from his face, mouth dropped open, rendered speechless. Seconds later, Mike was out the door.

"Where did he go?" Joe asked, pulling on Randy, who was trying to grab Pastor Ed's face.

"I think he got scared," Mr. Chapman groaned, struggling with his son.

Eyeing the camera and doing his best to keep Randy's hands off his face, Pastor Ed said, "Mrs. Chapman, get the camera."

Mrs. Chapman shook her head.

"Pick up the camera, dear," Mr. Chapman said, struggling.

"Mrs. Chapman, please," Pastor Ed said.

Mrs. Chapman shook her head again.

"I've got the boy," Joe said. "You get the camera, Mr. Chapman."

"Are you kidding me? He'll slip away," Mr. Chapman said.

"I've got it." Julie came running forth from the hallway, arms extended, pig tails bouncing.

"Julie, baby, no. Go back to your room," Mrs. Chapman said.

Swinging behind Joe and Mr. Chapman, she picked up the camera and pointed it in her brother's direction. "It's okay, Mom."

"Alright, Julie!" Joe cheered.

Turning his attention back on Randy and gripping his Bible tight, Pastor Ed placed it on Randy's head. "I command you in the name of Jesus Christ to tell me. When did he give himself to you?"

Shaking his head violently, screaming, Randy released Pastor Ed from his grip.

Looking disheveled, with half of his shirt untucked and wrinkled, Pastor Ed removed his bible from Randy's head. "Tell me!"

"When he muttered the lyrics," Randy fumed.

"The heavy metal lyrics?"

Randy growled.

"Randy said you started tormenting him before he started listening to heavy metal," Pastor Ed challenged.

"We are everywhere," Randy said.

"So you were here, but you got permission to enter Randy when he muttered the heavy metal lyrics. Is that it?" Pastor Ed placed the mic up to Randy.

Randy laughed.

Pastor Ed turned to the camera. "This is why I always tell parents not to let their kids listen to that music. It's got satanic lyrics." Turning back to Randy, "I command you, in the name of Jesus Christ, to go back to the pit of hell from which you came."

Eyes growing with hate, swinging his arms, attempting to free himself from Joe and Mr. Chapmans' grip, he spat, "Never."

Pastor Ed held his bible up like a knight's sword and swung it into Randy's chest. "I slay you with the Word of God."

Randy leaned forward, eyes bulging, hands clenching his abdomen, as if the air had been knocked out of him.

"Randy. Accept Jesus Christ as your personal Lord and Savior." Pastor Ed pressed his bible deeper into Randy's chest.

Randy shook his head and opened his mouth wide, gasping for air.

"Randy." Pastor Ed swung his Bible around Randy and pressed it up against his back, pulling him toward himself. He stood face to face with Randy. "Accept Jesus as your personal Lord and Savior and you will be saved."

Randy looked up at the ceiling and let out a cry.

"Do it, Randy," Joe said. "Accept Jesus."

Hand over her mouth and wide-eyed, Mrs. Chapman implored, "Do it, baby. Accept Jesus."

"Do it, son," Mr. Chapman added.

With tears rolling down his cheeks, Randy opened his mouth, but the words would not come out.

Pressing his Bible deeper into his back, Pastor Ed said, "Randy, I know you can hear me. Accept Jesus and this will all be over."

"Yes." He let out a long breath. "I accept you, Jesus."

Pastor Ed released Randy and turned toward the camera, holding up his Bible. "You see that? The devil is no match for the Word of God."

The two men lowered Randy's now limp body to the floor. Mrs. Chapman ran to him and embraced her son.

"Randy," Pastor Ed said. "Randy, is the demon still here?"

Pastor Ed placed his mic to Randy's face. "No. He's gone."

"Alleluia," Pastor Ed shouted. "You have been saved by the blood of Christ!"

* * *

For about an hour that night, Pastor Ed sat on his sofa, laptop open, index finger on the mouse pad, carefully placing the cursor on just the right frame, cutting and splicing his video.

The front door swung open.

"Hey, Dad." Patricia walked in. Making her way to the living room, she snatched an apple off the countertop. "Whatcha doing?"

Pastor Ed looked over his shoulder with a big grin on his face. "You'll never guess what I did today."

Apple in hand, she took a seat next to him, and noticing the irritating sticker, she began picking away at it. "What you do?"

"I exorcised a demon."

She cocked her head. "You what?"

"I exorcised a demon," he repeated.

Drawing her brows closer, she leaned forward. "Like an exorcism *exorcism*?"

"Yes, like an exorcism *exorcism*," he said mockingly.

"On who?"

"You know that Randy kid?"

"Randy Chapman?"

"His parents asked me to perform one on him."

Patricia perked up. "Randy's not possessed by no demon, Dad."

"Well, he's not anymore because I got rid of it."

"No, you didn't. He was never possessed. Randy's schizophrenic. He thinks there are demons in his house and runs away because of that."

"First of all, it's a demon, not demon*s*. Second, he would run away because it would tell him to do evil things, and when he's away from the house he doesn't hear the demon's voice anymore, but then—"

"But then he thinks about killing himself. Yeah, everyone at school knows the entire story." She took a bite out of her apple. "I'm telling you, he's schizophrenic. There's no such thing as demons."

"There's no such thing as demons? Wait. Wasn't it you who said something about tapping into the spiritual realm, and now you're telling me that there is no such thing as demons? How does that even make any sense?"

"It's simple." She took another bite out of her apple. "There is no such thing as hell, and if there is no such thing as hell, then there is no such thing as demons."

Pastor Ed let out a breath. "I'm not even going to go there with you right now." He plopped his computer on her lap and got up, heading toward the refrigerator. "I need you to work your special effects magic on that."

"What's this?" she said, staring at the screen.

Pastor Ed opened the refrigerator door and grabbed a Coke. "Randy's exorcism."

Her eyes widened. "You recorded it?"

"Yup." He opened the can and took a drink. "I'm going to upload it onto my YouTube channel."

"No way!" She hit the play button. "Does Mrs. Chapman know?"

"Yeah, I got her permission." He sat down again. "As a matter of fact, I just got off the phone with her. She wanted to thank me for helping them out. She says she's never seen her son so happy." Pastor Ed fast-forwarded the video to right before Randy accepted Jesus. "See that? Tell me he wasn't possessed."

Patricia hit the pause button. "Okay, hear me out. Randy is schizophrenic, so in his mind, he really believed that he was possessed by a demon. So if he believed that, then he must have also believed that the only cure was an exorcism."

"What? No way," Pastor Ed said.

"Dad, it's true. I saw it in a documentary they did on a psychiatrist that would send patients like Randy to be exorcised. He said that his patients got cured because they believed that they really had a demon inside, and once they went through the religious ritual, they truly believed it cured them, and *poof*, no more demons."

"You watch too many documentaries," Pastor Ed said dismissively.

"Well, you should too, because it would have helped you with your video."

"What do you mean?"

"Well, we get no backstory on Randy. You didn't even interview Mr. and Mrs. Chapman. You should have given them screen time. That way, people watching the video could relate to, or at the least garner sympathy for, what they were going through. No offense, Dad." She took the last bite of her apple. "But this video looks like an amateur film crew filmed it trying to start another ghost hunters YouTube channel."

Pastor Ed rubbed his chin and, after thinking about it for a brief moment, said, "Congratulations, you're now my assistant. Next time you're coming with us."

"What? No way."

"Why not?"

"Because I don't believe in demons, remember?"

Pastor Ed took a long look at his daughter. "Look, you'll be leaving for university once the summer is over. After which, I'll be here by myself."

Patricia let her head drop. "I know."

"This could be like a summer project we get to work on together."

"Can't we do something else? I mean, casting out demons isn't really what I would consider to be a father and daughter pasttime."

"No, but helping people like Randy is," Pastor Ed said. "You can't tell me Randy and his family aren't better off."

"Yeah, but… I had other plans for the summer."

"Think about it. If what that documentary said is true, then wouldn't we be helping people by performing exorcisms on them?"

Patricia lifted her head. "Yeah, I guess you're right."

"What could be better than to spend the summer together helping people like Randy?"

She let out a reluctant smile. "Okay, fine."

"Great. You're not going to regret this. I promise."

Patricia replayed the video. "So, this is a thing you're doing now?"

He nodded. "I think it can get us a lot of followers."

Chapter viii

A week after Randy's exorcism video was released, Pastor Ed received a plea for help from a couple living in Colorado who claimed that a demon was ruining their marriage. He rounded up his crew — Mike, Joe, and Patricia — into the church van and made the 45-minute drive to their home, a pastel-colored house with a white picket fence. Parking the van on the sidewalk, they exited the vehicle and made their way up the driveway. Knocking on the door three times, Pastor Ed could hear muffled sounds coming from inside the house. The door opened to reveal an odd couple in their mid-thirties. Valerie, a woman with way too much makeup on, who looked like she spent her best years partying it up, stood behind her husband, Daniel Torres, an overweight IT guy, who looked like he'd spend his twenties playing Dungeons and Dragons.

After making their acquaintance, Pastor Ed had Mike plant his tripod in the middle of the living room facing a large couch. Patricia sat on a stool next to the tripod holding the mic, while Daniel and Valerie sat on the couch facing the camera.

"Mr. and Mrs. Torres, how long have the two of you been married?" Patricia asked.

"April 15th was our two-year anniversary," Daniel answered.

"My girlfriend set us up," Valerie said. "I had commented to her how there were no more good men left, so she suggested I try meeting someone at church."

"She introduced us during our Sunday church service," Daniel said.

"Daniel really isn't the type of guy that I would normally go for," Valerie said.

Daniel smiled. "But I won her over, and after dating for several months, we got married."

Patricia smiled. "Do the two of you have any children?"

Daniel and Valerie looked at each other. "We don't have children together," she said, "but I do have two sons from previous relationships."

"I understand," Patricia said. "And what do the two of you do for a living?"

"I'm a software engineer, and she stays home and looks after the kids."

"And the kids' fathers? Are they involved in their lives?"

"No, they're deadbeats," she said. "I really don't want to get into that right now."

"I totally understand." Patricia glanced at her father. "So I'm guessing everything was fine until the demon showed up?"

"Not exactly," Valerie said. "I've been dealing with what's called a Jezebel spirit for most of my adult life."

"Jezebel spirit? Can you explain what a Jezebel spirit is?" Patricia asked.

"A Jezebel spirit is a demon that causes rifts in marriages through promiscuity," she said.

"I caught her cheating on me with her ex. I came home early one day and saw his car drive off. At first, she tried to convince me I was imagining things. She accused me of gaslighting her. She had me believing it, but I checked the dash cam and was able to confirm his license plate number."

"That's when I felt compelled to tell him about having the Jezebel spirit. I told him I was under demonic influence. He didn't believe me, but I showed him the video of the exorcism your father did on that boy."

"I was ready to file for divorce. I felt bad for the kids, because I've developed such a bond with them. The thought of not seeing them again really hurt, but I felt like I couldn't trust her anymore."

"That's when we reached out to your father," she said.

"What would you like to see happen today, Valerie?" Patricia asked.

"I would like for this demon to leave me alone so that I can be the wife he deserves," she said.

"And you, Daniel?"

"I want us to be the perfect family that I know we were meant to be."

Patricia turned to Mike. "And that's a cut."

"Now what?" Valerie asked.

Pastor Ed approached Valerie and guided her to the center of the room. "Now they're going to push the furniture out of the way and you are going to stand right here next to me."

Not forgetting Mike's sudden disappearance during Randy's exorcism, Pastor Ed asked, "Are you good, Mike?"

Mike blushed and gave him a thumbs up.

Pastor Ed placed his hands on Valerie's shoulders. "Okay, look at me and don't be afraid. God is in control, and no matter what happens, don't panic. Got it?"

Valerie nodded. "Got it."

"Are we all set, Patricia?" Pastor Ed asked.

Patricia gave the countdown, hand raised, five fingers extended. "Ready in 5. 4. 3. 2. —"

Placing his Bible over Valerie's head, Pastor Ed prayed, and after a minute or two, a small curl of a smile crept around her mouth. Her eyes closed, face muscles tensed, she began to grind her teeth, and when she opened her eyes again, Pastor Ed had the distinct feeling that it wasn't Valerie standing before him.

Handing his Bible off to Patricia, he grabbed her head with both hands, thumbs on her temples, and looked deep into her eyes. "Jezebel spirit, how long have you been tormenting Valerie?"

Valerie screeched, eyes bulging, mouth stretched open. "Eeeee. Eeeeeee!"

He planted his feet, giving two quick jerks to her head. "How many years, Jezebel? Tell me."

Her lips perking together in a twisted fashion, she shook her head.

Pastor Ed released his grip and turned to the camera. "The demon's not letting her speak." He wrapped his arm around Valerie's waist and pulled her toward him. "How many years?"

She raised her hands, palms facing up, as if in some kind of trance, and blurted out, "Blaaah. Blaaah."

Pastor Ed let out a sharp inquiry: "How many years?"

Locked jaw, eyes fully open, mouth stretched back, shrieking, "Eeeee. Eeeee," struggling to speak, she finally released a single word. "Eighteen."

Pastor Ed released his grip and took a step back. "Eighteen, huh?"

Shifting her weight from side to side, left palm faced up, right hand shaking, eyes closed, she shook her head in what appeared to be some sort of ritual. Daniel and Joe got within inches of her, placing a firm grasp on her shoulders.

Extending his hand out to his daughter, Patricia handed him his Bible, and holding it close to his chest, Pastor Ed stepped side to side in lock step with Valerie. The two looked like boxers in the ring, sizing each other up. "How did you get to possess her?"

She opened her eyes. "Teeees…in…saaaaaap."

"Tes in sap? Eh?"

Bible in hand, he jabbed her on the side of the neck, causing her to fall back, but Joe and Daniel broke her fall.

"Whatever that means, I rebuke it in Jesus' name."

Regaining her balance, she stood still with mad eyes and a devilish smile, bobbling her head from side to side, pupils locked on Pastor Ed.

Seeing that he was about to place his Bible on her forehead, Valerie made a dash for it, but crashed into Joe, who held her back, knees bent, hands on her shoulders, back arched. The two men pushed her back toward Pastor Ed. She shouted, "Tasho tasho," as Pastor Ed brought his Bible down on the back of her head, causing her to shake and raise her voice, screaming, "Taaaaasho, taaaaasho."

Pastor Ed handed his Bible back to Patricia and turned to the camera lens. "Must be some kind of evil ancient language," he said. "We rebuke it in the name of Christ."

"Amen!" the crew shouted.

Turning his attention back to Valerie, whom by now the two men had managed to turn around, he said, "I command you to repeat after me in the name of Jesus Christ." He placed his microphone up to her mouth. "I, Jezebel."

Valerie leaned back. "I, Jezebel."

"Break the curse."

Valerie twirled her hair in a childish manner, repeatedly saying, "Ta… ta… ta."

"Break the curse," Pastor Ed insisted.

She pointed at him, giggling.

Pastor Ed extended his hand. "Give me my Bible."

As soon as Patricia handed him his Bible, Valerie leaned her head forward, like a schoolgirl letting out a swear word. "I've had her too long," she spat.

"You've had her too long?"

She swayed from side to side in the confines of the men's grasps. "I've had her too long. She's mine."

Mimicking her movements, Pastor Ed pressed on. "Really?"

"Reeeaaaally," she said with a grin.

Pastor Ed leaned forward within inches of her face. "Is that so?"

She leaned her head to the side. "O-lowte— aaaah!"

Pastor Ed swung his arm around her waist, placing his Bible on her upper back. "Let her go."

Jerking her body, attempting to escape his grasp, "No," she said in a thick voice. "I've worked too hard."

Pastor Ed pressed his Bible deeper into her back. "Let her go."

Valerie convulsed, and the men struggled to hold her in place.

Pressing deeper, he commanded her, "Let her go now."

Valerie swung her upper torso around, pushing up against Joe and Daniel for a little over a minute. She fought to escape the men's grasps to the point of exhaustion. Pastor Ed retracted his Bible. "You're no match for the Word of God, demon."

Valerie's body went limb. Raising her head, she let out a low groan.

"It's been weakened," Joe commented.

Pastor Ed handed his Bible to Patricia. "Hold her up, men."

The two men lifted her limp body up and held her tight.

Pastor Ed placed his hand on her limp head and lifted it.

She had a demented look. Lifting her hand to Pastor Ed's face, she swung her index finger from side to side. "No. No. No."

Pastor Ed looked into her eyes. "Do you have a legal right to be there?"

She drooled and mumbled.

"Yes or no?"

Her muttering set Pastor Ed's nerves on edge. "A legal right, yes or no?"

She shifted her pupils toward him. "Hhhaaaaaaa."

"If you did, you would tell me, Jezebel."

A psychotic laugh escaped her lips.

He pushed down on her head. "I command you in the name of Christ."

She became stiff like a board.

"Repeat after me," Pastor Ed commanded. "I, Jezebel, break the curse."

"Mee-mee mee."

The crew laughed.

Pastor Ed held his hand out. Patricia handed him his Bible. "Oh, that was not nice."

Shaking her head wide, she dodged his attempts at placing the Bible on her head, but showed signs of exhaustion.

"Hold her tight, men."

Muscles flexed, veins bulging, knees bent, and feet grounded, they held her in place until she could resist no more. Strands of hair obscured her face, her arms dangled, and her head barely held up.

"I command you in the name of Jesus Christ to repeat after me."

"No." Her voice was faint.

Taking note of her physical exhaustion, Pastor Ed rested his Bible on her forehead. "I, Jezebel."

"I, Jezebel," she repeated.

"Break the curse."

She hummed a lullaby.

He pressed on her with his Bible. "Break the curse."

Her body gave off short trembles. "Break the curse," she said.

"Let's go." Pastor Ed jabbed his Bible in her abdomen. "Come on. Let's go. Now. Get out."

Valerie began to hyperventilate.

"The curse is broken. Leave now," he commanded.

She raised her head.

"Get out in the name of Christ."

She stood up and, lifting her arms up high, she let out a long cry, then let her arms fall on Pastor Ed's shoulders and sobbed.

Embracing her, he said, "It's all over."

She wept for a brief moment. Mike removed his camera from the tripod and panned it across the scene, capturing the moment.

Valerie stood up and cleared her hair away from her face.

Pastor Ed placed his mic next to her face. "Valerie, do you accept Jesus Christ as your personal Lord and Savior?"

Valerie grabbed the mic away from Pastor Ed's hand and looked into the camera. "Yes."

"You need you to say it so that everyone watching can bear witness."

"Yes. I do. I accept Jesus as my personal Lord and Savior," she said with a smile.

* * *

The following day after work, Pastor Ed drove home with two

steaming lattes in the cup compartment, windows down, the wind blowing through his hair. His aviator glasses reflected the sunset, and a grin crossed his face. His left hand was on the steering wheel while the other gripped his phone, his thumb swiping down repeatedly, refreshing his YouTube's analytics page: 30 thousand subscribers and counting.

"Hey, I'm home." Pastor Ed walked through the front door. "How's the video coming along?"

Patricia was on her laptop, editing Valerie's exorcism. She had the television on some documentary and, as always, she wasn't paying attention to it. "Ooh, latte." She extended her arm out, opening and closing her hand. "Gimme. Gimme."

Pastor Ed handed her the drink. "Is it ready?"

"Just about." She placed the playhead at the beginning of the film. "Here, check it out."

Patricia enjoyed her drink while Pastor Ed analyzed the footage.

"That was a good idea to include their wedding photos," he said.

Patricia clasped her drink with both hands. "Yeah, it was nice of them to let us use them in the video. I think it'll show the viewers what was at stake."

"I would've never thought about including the photos in the video." He pointed at the monitor screen. "Hey, check me out. I look like a boxer facing off against the demon."

Patricia laughed. "Calm down, Dad. Let's not get carried away."

Pastor Ed pointed at the screen. "Look at her eyes. She looks like a maniac."

Patricia took a sip of her coffee and placed it on the coffee table. "I'm just glad Mike didn't run away this time."

Pastor Ed laughed. "Thanks for helping me out, kiddo."

Patricia smiled. "You're welcome, Dad." She looked at the screen. "I think the viewers are going to love that scene. The way she fell on your arms and you had her accept Jesus."

Pastor Ed studied the video. "It's such a powerful moment when someone accepts Jesus into their heart." Leaning forward, he said, "How many subscribers do you think this video will get us?"

"Who knows, a couple thousand at least," Patricia replied.

"I'd say so. Randy's exorcism alone got me 27 thousand."

"Wow! Congrats, Dad," she cheered, raising her arm up, hand clasped, eyes shut.

Pastor Ed smiled and took a sip of his drink.

"Oh, before I forget…" Leaning over, she moved the playhead forward. "There's a minor problem."

"Oh yeah? What's that?"

"After the exorcism, I interviewed the husband to get his perspective, and this is what he had to say."

The video showed the couple sitting in the living room. Patricia was interviewing them. "Daniel, what ran through your mind at the last moment when your wife accepted Jesus as her personal Lord and Savior?"

"In all honesty, I was a bit confused."

"Oh, and why is that?" Patricia asked.

"Well, my wife had already accepted Jesus as her personal Lord and Savior at our church."

Valerie leaned forward. "Does it really matter?" She gripped his hand. "What matters is that the demon is gone and we can be a happy family again."

Patricia paused the video.

"That's not a problem at all." Pastor Ed got up and headed to the refrigerator.

Patricia took the laptop and placed it on her lap. "It isn't?"

"Nope. Not at all," he said.

"But isn't it going to confuse the viewers?"

Pastor Ed pulled some Tupperware out of the fridge and placed it in the microwave. "I'll just explain to them how she wasn't really saved."

"But you've always said that if we accept Jesus, we are guaranteed salvation. Isn't that what you alway preach?"

"Yes, it's true." He punched in the time and hit the start button. "But it's obvious that she wasn't truly saved. Committing adultery proves that a person isn't really saved."

"So if you commit a grave sin, then it shows that you weren't truly saved?"

"Exactly, the Bible says that we will know them by their fruits. Matthew 7:15."

"But you can't see into the future, right?"

Pastor Ed pulled his food from the microwave. "Right."

"So then you don't know if in five years you'll commit adultery."

Pastor Ed placed his food on the dining table. "Correct."

"So then, how do you know that you're truly saved if you can't see into the future? I mean, if you could see from here to the moment of your death, then I could see how you would know if you're truly saved today, but since you can't, then you really don't know."

Pastor Ed grabbed a fork. "Because the Bible says that Jesus will not fail to save his sheep from the clutches of the devil. John 10:28."

"Yeah, but it says nothing about a sheep wondering off on its own free will."

"Well, then they were never a part of his herd to begin with."

"But then we're right back where we started. Only this time we are asking how does one know if one is truly a part of the herd?"

Pastor Ed chewed his food. "You just have to have faith, kiddo." He lifted his fork up. "Hey, did we get any additional requests for exorcism?"

"Actually, we got a couple, but there's one in particular..." She turned toward him moon-eyed. "Dad. We've got to help these people out."

Chapter IX

Sella sat across from Doña Gloria. The candle lights flickered, and *La Santa Muerte* leered at them both.

"I didn't expect to see you so soon," Doña Gloria grinned.

Sella Cleared her throat. "It's my boyfriend."

"Oh?" Doña Gloria said.

Sella sighed. "Things haven't been as I expected." She placed her hands on the table. "I feel like now that I'm making enough money to cover the bills, he would…" She pinched her lips together. "He would try to get a better job."

"You want me to help him get a better job? I can do that."

"That's the thing. He doesn't want a better job. I told him he deserves a better job than the one he has at the body shop."

"I see," said Doña Gloria.

"I told him he should go back to school and get a degree."

"That's a great idea, and a wonderful opportunity for him."

"It is." Sella leaned forward. "But he said that he doesn't like school." She shook her head. "I told him we need to take advantage of our new situation. I even tried convincing him to tackle a part-time job.

He could save up to open his own body shop."

"What did he say?"

"He said that he's not interested in opening a body shop. He doesn't like the idea of managing people and he doesn't want to deal with all the other administrative duties that go with running a business." Sella threw her hands up. "It's just so frustrating. I'm trying to motivate him to become a better person, but he takes it the wrong way and starts arguing with me." She took a breath. "I want to see him succeed. The men at my office are always well-dressed. They drive nice cars and are always working on ways to drum up business."

"Perhaps I can help him be a little more motivated. Tell him to come see me."

"Yeah right." Sella rolled her eyes. "He'd laugh at me and probably think I'm crazy for even suggesting it."

"Sounds like he's contempt."

The candles flickered.

"I'm curious, Sella. If you already knew that he wouldn't be open to seeing me, why are you here then?"

Sella sat back in her chair and twirled her hair. "There's this young engineer at work."

"Oh." Doña Gloria reached for her tarot cards.

"He's exactly what I would like my boyfriend to be like. He's tall, handsome, hardworking, and really smart. Everyone at work likes him. All the guys want to be like him, and all the girls want to be with him."

Doña Gloria shuffled the cards. "A high-value man."

"I've tried to get his attention several times at work, but he doesn't even notice me. I feel so stupid. Everyone just looks at me and laughs. The last time I saw him, I fake-bumped into him. He excused himself and just walked right past me." Sella dropped her head. "My coworker said I should give up. Apparently, he only dates younger girls with no kids."

"I get a lot of women looking for high-value men." Doña Gloria placed the deck of cards on the table. "The problem is that there aren't enough of them."

Sella cut the cards. "I know we would make a great couple."

"Let's see what the cards tell us." She placed the cards face up on the table. "Very interesting."

"What? What is it?"

"Give me a second, Sella." She placed her finger on a card. "You see that card?"

"Yes. What does it mean?"

"It means that he's going to be rich." She looked up at Sella. "Millionaire rich." She traced her finger across several cards. "It says here that there are many women trying to seduce him."

"Of course they are." Sella crossed her arms.

Doña Gloria leaned back in her chair and stared at her.

"Well?" Sella said. "What do I have to do?"

Doña Gloria picked up her cards. "If you want this man, then here is what you have to do."

"Tell me. I'll do anything."

"Set an altar to *La Santa Muerte* in your home. Bring it fresh fruit, and every night kneel before the altar and pray to her."

"That's it?"

"That's it."

* * *

Afraid that her kids would freak out if they saw the idol, the following night, Sella waited until after bedtime before positioning a small altar at the back of her walk-in closet, flanked by two rows of newly purchased jeans, dresses, purses, and shoes. On the altar, she placed *La Santa Muerte*, two red candles, a glass of water, apples, oranges, and mangoes. This *Santa Muerte* wore a golden avarice hooded cloak, holding a scythe with her right skeletal hand and a small globe with the other.

After pinning several pesos to its cloak for good luck, Sella laid down on her bed and began flicking through her streaming services, when her boyfriend, Jorge, came home, who, after taking a quick shower, walked into the room wearing nothing but a towel around his midsection.

Heading straight for the closet, he asked, "Anything interesting?"

"Not really."

Head turned toward the television, gripping the closet's doorknob, he said, "Good, change it to the sports channel." He pulled the door open, and when he caught the idol out of the corner of his eye he jumped in a panic. Terrified and scrambling to cover himself, he backpedalled away from the closet, then lost his balance, arms windmilling, and landed hard on his back.

Sella laughed and leaned over to see Jorge on the floor. "What's the matter?"

Reaching for the towel, he said, "What the hell is that?"

"It's *La Santa Muerte*."

Jorge looked at her wide-eyed, then looked at the closet and back at her. "I don't want that thing here."

She shrugged.

"Get rid of it."

She sat back on the bed. "No."

He picked himself up off the floor. "I said, get rid of it, Sella," he demanded.

"And I said no."

He headed for the closet. "Well, if you don't, I will."

"Don't even think about it, Jorge."

"Watch me."

"Jorge, this is my house."

Jorge stopped. "Is that so?"

"That *is* so. The house is under my name and I'm paying all the bills. So you leave her right where she is."

"Are you mad?" Jorge said.

Sella's muscles tensed up.

He pointed at the closet. "That thing is evil. It's from the devil."

"It's not from the devil. She was here for me when you were gone."

He made a double take, and there was a pause.

"So, that's how you managed to—"

He didn't have to finish the sentence.

"Managed to what, Jorge? Deal with the mess you left me with?"

He took a step back. "You're a witch."

"I'm not a witch. Don't you call me a witch."

He stared at her, mouth gaping.

"What? Don't look at me that way."

"Does your mom know about this?"

"Don't even think about telling her. If you do, I swear I will make your life a living hell."

Jorge went into the closet and pulled some of his clothes out as quickly as he could.

"What are you doing?"

"Getting the hell out of here. What the hell does it look like I'm doing?"

"Okay. Fine." Sella shrugged. "Leave."

He put his clothes on. "You're making a huge mistake." He grabbed his keys. "Your mother is going to freak out when she finds out."

"Are you going to tell her?"

He opened the door. Paused. "I'll come back for my stuff tomorrow while the kids are at your mom's."

"Are you going to tell her?"

He closed the door behind him.

Grabbing the remote, she flung it at the door. "Jorge!"

* * *

The following day after work, Sella came home to find all of Jorge's stuff gone. On the kitchen table was his set of keys to the house. She grabbed them and placed them in a drawer. She opened the refrigerator and prepared dinner. *Some enchiladas would be nice.*

"*Mija*, we're here." Sella's mom walked in.

"Mommy!" The kids gave her a big hug. "Look what I did at school today," Little Maria said.

"Oh, that's really nice." Sella gave her a big kiss. "And you, Javier? What did you do?"

"Nothing."

Sella looked at him. "Nothing?"

Javier rolled his eyes. "Just the normal stuff."

"Okay, well, make sure you do your homework."

"We already did it at Grandma's."

"Yeah, I did my homework too," Little Maria said.

"Okay, kids, go to your room and play. I need to talk to your mother," Sella's mom said.

Sella's muscles tensed up.

The kids ran off. Sella's mother waited till they closed the door. "Sella, Jorge called me and told me you guys split up because you have *La Santa Muerte* in your closet."

"Shhh. The kids don't know that he left."

"Sella, for the love of God. Tell me that's not true."

"It's not. He's crazy."

"Let me see your closet."

"What? No."

Sella's mother headed for her bedroom.

"Mama!" Sella got in front of her.

"*Mija*, get out of the way."

Sella spread her arms out. "No."

"Sella, get out of my way and let me see your closet."

"No, Mom."

"You have that thing. I know you have that thing."

"No, I don't. He's crazy. You know how he is."

"So then why don't you let me look in your closet?"

"Because it's an invasion of my privacy. I shouldn't have to show you. You should believe me because I'm your daughter."

"Because you're my daughter is exactly why I *don't* believe you."

"Mom! I can't believe you right now."

Sella's mom closed her eyes tight and clenched her fists. "*Mija*, that thing is evil. You have no idea. Get rid of it right now and get a priest down here to bless the house."

"I'm not going to get no priest."

"*Mija*. Look at me." She held Sella by her shoulders. "Whatever you've done, God will forgive you. Just go to confession right now. We'll go to the priest, and we can have him absolve you of your sins."

Sella looked at her mom. "Okay, I'll go tomorrow."

"Promise me you'll go."

"Yes, I promise."

"You swear?"

"Yes, I swear."

"And you'll get rid of that thing?"

"There's nothing to get rid of."

Sella's mom tensed up, studied her, and then did the sign of the cross. And for a moment, Sella felt a bit of anger.

"What am I going to do with you, *mija*?" she said.

Chapter X

Most members of Pastor Ed's congregation didn't know what to make of their pastor performing exorcisms. A few were against the idea, believing that Pastor Ed was turning his ministry into a freak show, saying it brought embarrassment to the church. Amongst these was Albert. He gave Pastor Ed a piece of his mind, but Pastor Ed had enough sway over his congregation to dismiss his objections. A few others were very excited and showed their support, saying that he was doing the Lord's work.

Pastor Ed invited his supporting members to witness his upcoming exorcism. He set the event for Friday night and instructed them to keep it a secret from the others. Most arrived at the church early, eager to help with whatever they could. They sat chatting in the choir room. Pastor Ed sat at the front of the room, facing the members. To his left were Patricia and Joe. To his right was Derek, along with his father and two brothers. Mike was in the middle of the room, setting up his equipment.

Derek's father, who was a bald man with blond eyebrows and deep-set eyes, wearing an arctic blue button-up shirt with light blue jeans, turned to Pastor Ed and said, "Thank you for helping my son."

Pastor Ed looked into his brown eyes. "My pleasure." Then he turned his attention to Mike. "Is everything ready, Mike?"

Mike nodded. "Yes. We're all set."

Pastor Ed stood up and, holding his mic, he took several steps forward. "Everyone, I want to thank you for coming out tonight. As you know, I recently began performing exorcisms on people suffering from demonic influence."

He paused.

"I know what some have been saying, and I'm sure you do too. But make no mistake about it, the devil is real."

"Amen," the members said.

He turned to the three men and gestured for them to stand up. The father towered about three inches over his two oldest sons. Henry, his oldest, had dark peppered gray hair, a heavily receding hairline, and wore a dark green flannel with navy blue jeans. His other son, Josh, was clean shaven, with dark hair and no sign of a receding hairline. He wore a teal button-up shirt and black slacks. Derek was two inches shorter than his two older brothers and five inches shorter than his father. His hair was black, short, buzz-cut style. He wore a green sweater and black jeans.

"Everyone, meet Derek, Derek's father Scott, and Derek's two brothers, Henry and Josh. Now, Derek's father reached out to us because he's afraid that his son might end up in prison or worse."

The attendants murmured.

Pastor Ed raised his hand for a few moments, waiting for the murmuring to cease. "Now, we are not going to let that happen. Are we?"

"No," they cheered.

"Scott and Derek, why don't you two come up here?"

They walked up to Pastor Ed.

"Scott, why don't you tell everyone why you reached out to us?"

Scott stood still and observed the room.

"Go ahead. Relax. We're here to help. Aren't we, folks?"

They nodded. "Amen."

Scott cleared his throat. "My son Derek has a real problem with anger. He is always angry and, because of that, he's constantly getting into all sorts of problems."

"What kind of problems?" Pastor Ed asked.

"He gets into fistfights. He sometimes takes on two or three folks at the same time."

Gasps.

"Two or three at the same time? Wow!" Pastor Ed said. "When does he get like this?"

"Different times. At the house, the bar, on the road, and even at work."

The congregation muttered.

"Has he attacked you or his brothers?"

"Oh, yes. It's like we are living a nightmare every day," Scott said.

Pastor Ed turned to Henry and Josh. "Guys, come up here."

The men walked up.

"Has Derek attacked either of you before?"

"Yes, sir," they both answered.

"Why?"

"Various reasons," Henry said. "It's hard to tell what will set him off."

"Can you give us an example?"

"Sure. One time I was sitting at the kitchen table daydreaming, and I guess he thought I was staring at him or something because the next thing I know, the ketchup bottle smacked me in the head. Before I could even react, he was already lunging himself at me."

Gasps.

"Is this true, Josh?" Pastor Ed asked.

"Yes, sir. We have to be very careful when we're around him. It's like walking on a minefield."

"Must be hard to live your life like that every day." Pastor Ed turned to the crowd. "Imagine yourself as Josh, Henry, or Scott. Can you imagine if this was happening to one of your loved ones? A son? A daughter?"

Pastor Ed paused.

"I guess we should ask Derek why he is doing these things?"

The members nodded.

Pastor Ed turned toward him. "Derek, is what they're telling us true?"

Derek's cheeks turned red. "Unfortunately, it is true. Sir."

"I've gotten to know you before tonight's event, and I'm getting the feeling that you're actually a good person." Pastor Ed turned to the crowd. "What do you all think?"

"Amen," they said.

"I can tell that your parents raised you to be a fine young man by the way you speak."

"They did, sir. They're the best parents anyone can have," Derek said.

"So why are you attacking them?"

"Honestly, I don't know." Derek stared at the floor. "It's like one minute I'm fine, but then the next I'm just filled with uncontrollable rage."

"I'm guessing this rage has gotten you into a lot of trouble?"

"Yes. I've been to jail several times. I've also ended up in the hospital," he said. "Broken bones, bruises, and cuts."

The members shook their head.

Tears welled up in Derek's father's eyes.

"Scott, I see that you're getting a little emotional. What's running through your mind?"

"I'm just scared that if we don't do something, he's going to end up dead or going away to prison for a very long time."

Silence.

Pastor Ed held up his Bible. "Well, we aren't going to let that happen."

"Amen," the crowd said.

"Jesus heals," one member said.

Applause.

"Amen."

Pastor Ed stood facing Derek, making sure that the crowd could see him and Derek face off. "Scott and Josh, why don't you two stand on one side of Derek, and Joe and Henry on the other side? Patricia, stand behind me."

They all took position. The air was tense. Pastor Ed placed his hand on Derek's shoulders. He began uttering a prayer when Derek swung his arm, narrowly missing Pastor Ed. Pastor Ed jumped back while Derek darted toward him like a football player, dragging Joe, Henry, and Josh behind him. Scott got himself between Derek and Pastor Ed. All the while, Pastor Ed and Patricia attempted to get out of his way and avoid falling.

Eyes bulging, teeth grinding, and biceps curled, the men wrestled Derek to the floor. Pastor Ed balanced himself. "Okay. Settle down, Derek," he said. "Everyone, let's just calm down and wait for Derek to relax."

It startled the members of the church. They'd never seen violence in their place of worship before. After several minutes, Derek stopped struggling. "I'm okay. I'm sorry, everyone," he said.

"Okay, get him up. Make sure he's okay," Pastor Ed said.

Luckily, Derek wasn't injured and seemed to be his old self again. Pastor Ed took a good look at Derek. "Put your hands out in front of you. Cross them at the wrist."

Derek did as he was told.

"I take a cord of three strands from Ecclesiastes four twelve, and I bind those hands." Pastor Ed took his Bible and waved it around Derek's hands as if he was binding them with an invisible cord.

Derek's calm demeanor was gone, and in its place was pure anger.

"Your name, spirit?" Pastor Ed placed his microphone up to Derek.

Derek gnashed his teeth and growled.

Pastor Ed jerked his microphone back and raised his voice. "Your name?"

Pastor Ed shoved the microphone up to Derek.

Derek breathed deep into it.

"Well, you're pure hate," Pastor Ed said. "Anger? Rage? Let's get specific here. I command you to tell me your name."

Derek breathed deep into the microphone.

"Tell me," Pastor Ed said.

"Rrraaa...." he said in a deep raspy voice.

"What?"

Derek closed his eyes and turned his face to the left. "Rrraaage."

Pastor Ed leaned forward. "Rage," he said, peering into Derek's eyes. "Judgment has come."

Derek squeezed his eyes shut and crouched down.

"Judgment," Pastor Ed chastised.

Derek moaned.

"Get up, Rage," Pastor Ed commanded.

Derek stood up, his hands still invisibly bound together.

"How many years have you been there?" Pastor Ed said.

Derek stared into space.

"Answer me!" Pastor Ed smacked his Bible up against Derek's stomach.

"Five," he said in a raspy voice.

"Five? For five years, you've been tormenting this young man?"

Derek released a deep breath.

Pastor Ed took a step forward. "What happened five years ago?"

He turned the microphone to Derek, who moaned, "I killed his mother."

Gasps.

"Someone killed his mother," Pastor Ed said to the crowd. "Five years ago, and now we've got this."

He paused.

He pointed at Derek and then pointed to the ground. "Go down, spirit," he commanded. "I want to speak to Derek."

Fists clenched, eyes shut tight, the young man lowered his face for a few seconds before raising it, revealing a calm, benevolent face.

"Quickly, Derek, I want you to say," Pastor Ed pointed his microphone at Derek, "In the name of Jesus."

"In the name of Jesus," he said in his normal voice.

Pastor Ed took the microphone. "I break this curse of murder."

"I break this curse," he cleared his throat, "of murder."

Pastor Ed took a breath. "To the young man that murdered my mother."

Derek jerked back. "To the young man that murdered my mother."

"In Jesus's name, that curse is broken," Pastor Ed nodded.

Derek's eye twitched. "In Jesus's name, that curse is broken."

Pastor Ed clenched his Bible. "This evil spirit of rage has to obey me."

Derek coughed. "This evil spirit of rage has to obey me."

"And leave me."

"And leave me."

Pastor Ed took several steps back. He pulled out his cross and directed it at Derek. "Rage, come forth."

Derek stood before the cross, shaking. His eyes were full of fear.

"Stand at attention, Rage," Pastor Ed commanded. He took small steps toward Derek, holding up his cross. Derek, still bound by his hands, tried to walk away but couldn't lift his legs. He hunched over before the cross and couldn't bring himself to look at it.

Pastor Ed held the cross less than one foot away from Derek. "Were you inhabiting the man who killed Derek's mother?"

"Yyyeeeessss," Derek hissed.

"How did he kill her?"

"Sssaaa ssssaaa ssstabbed herrr."

Pastor Ed leaned forward and looked into his eyes. "Why?"

Derek leaned back, squeezing his eyes shut, jaw locked.

"What did she do?"

Derek swayed back and forth. "She left his father."

Gasps.

"Then what happened?"

Derek smiled. "He hanged himself."

"Was that you? Did you do that?"

Derek let out a prideful smirk.

Pastor Ed brought his cross closer. "Tell me."

"Yesssss."

"And when Derek was filled with rage, that's when you jumped into him? Was that it?"

"Aaaaaah."

"Of course it was," Pastor Ed said. "Go down, demon."

Derek stood up, tears flowing down his cheeks.

Pastor Ed placed his cross on his head. "Derek, I want you to forgive your step-brother for murdering your mother."

Derek closed his eyes. He opened his mouth and let out a small cry.

"Derek, you need to forgive your step-brother. It's what your mother would have wanted. It's what you need in order to be at peace."

Derek nodded. "I forgive him."

Pastor Ed took two steps back. The crowd was moved to tears.

Pastor Ed clenched his cross and walked toward Derek. "Come out and face me, Rage."

Rage resurfaced.

"Repeat after me, Rage," Pastor Ed said. "I, Rage."

"I, Rage," Derek said in the raspy voice.

"Renounce."

Derek's nostrils flared like a bull.

"Renounce!" Pastor Ed repeated.

Derek's jaw locked.

"Say renounce."

"Re — nounce."

"My right."

"My — right." Derek lowered his head.

"To this man."

"To this man."

"I lift the curse."

"I — lift — the — curse."

"Of rage."

"Of — rage."

Pastor Ed lifted his cross. He let the full weight of it fall on Derek's head, pressing down on it. "I command it to be lifted now through Christ."

Derek moaned.

"For what you've done to this man, his step-brother, and his entire family," Pastor Ed brought his cross to his side and swung it like a sword, "the wrath of God comes down on you seven times!"

Derek hunched over, moaning. He fell to his knees and hyperventilated.

Pastor Ed took several deep breaths. "In the name of Christ, I command you to leave and go back to the depths of hell from which you came."

Derek began to gag.

"Begone, Rage!"

Gagging, Derek's face turned red.

"Depart now!" Pastor Ed turned to his congregation. "Come on, let's help him."

"Leave, demon!" they shouted.

Derek gave off a long gag reflex.

"It's gone," Pastor Ed said.

The members cheered.

Derek stood up.

Pastor Ed placed his microphone up to him. "Do you accept our Lord Jesus Christ as your personal Lord and Savior?"

"I do." Derek took several deep breaths. The color on his face had returned. He raised his arms out. "I accept you, Jesus!"

Sounds of hallelujah rang up.

Scott, Josh, and Henry hugged Derek. Pastor Ed signaled to Mike to get a closeup of the family. He placed his microphone up to Scott. "What's going through your mind right now, Scott?"

Scott lifted his head. "I want to thank you from the bottom of my heart." He wiped his tears. "I just wish more pastors would take up the ministry of exorcism."

Pastor Ed cleared his throat.

"Amen," said the members.

"Amen indeed." Pastor Ed adjusted his tie.

* * *

The following week, Pastor Ed and Patricia headed to the University of Colorado to take part in their onboarding program. They toured the campus, learning about the various programs the school offered. Afterward, they visited several apartment complexes. Pastor Ed didn't want his daughter staying in the dorms; too much partying and bad influences, not to mention too expensive. Patricia didn't object. The thought of having to share a small room with another girl didn't appeal to her. She would much rather have a place to herself, even if it meant commuting to school every day.

On their way home, they stopped at a burger joint. Pastor Ed ordered a heart attack, while Patricia ordered a lettuce burger.

"I've been thinking." Pastor Ed took a bite of his burger.

Patricia lifted her lettuce-wrapped patty. "About?"

"About the YouTube channel." He wiped his mouth. "I want to commercialize it."

"Commercialize it?" Patricia struggled to get a good grip on her burger.

"The ads aren't bringing in much money, and the church is low on funds."

"True." She took a bite. "You need a huge following in order to really make money on ads."

"How do those famous kids make money on YouTube?"

"Companies hire them to promote their products," she said, "but even they pay based on the number of followers you have."

Pastor Ed looked up. "So either way you look at it, you need a lot of followers?"

"Pretty much. You're going to need at least a million followers."

"We're at 500 thousand subscribers right now, and I'm afraid that if all we keep doing is exorcisms, it's going to get stagnant." He dipped his fries in the ketchup.

"I don't think so," Patricia said. "I find that it's more about the families and what they're dealing with. Their backstories." She took a sip of her Diet Coke. "Everyone loves a good story."

"Yes, but I just saw another pastor start a similar channel. It's only a matter of time before more start doing it too."

"Like gamers," she said. "It's almost impossible to stand out now."

She leaned back. "The good thing is that you're the first one to do it. That's a huge advantage."

"Only if I secure my subscriber share." He chewed his fries. "We've got to drive up the subscriber count."

"Yeah, something that'll make our subscriber count go up big time. We need to go viral." she leaned forward, "like viral *viral*."

Pastor Ed smirked. "Viral *viral*?"

Patricia laughed. "Stop it, Dad."

He winked at her.

Patricia crumbled up her wrapping paper.

"You didn't even finish your food," he said.

"I'm not that hungry."

"You hardly ate all day."

She shrugged.

"You need to eat. You don't want to get too skinny."

"I'll eat when we get home."

"Okay, well, how about you look through the messages while I finish my food? See if you can find an excellent case for us."

"Okay." She pulled out her phone and started scrolling through the messages.

Pastor Ed took a sip of his Coke. *How can we go viral?*

"Oh, how about this one," she said. "Man claims the demon of lust got him addicted to porn and his wife threatens to leave him."

Pastor Ed shook his head. "No way. You saw the reaction we got from viewers after the Jezebel spirit case."

"But, Dad, that's what we want. The YouTube algorithm promotes videos that get a lot of interaction from viewers — likes, dislikes, good comments, and bad comments. That's why it's the video with the most views."

Pastor Ed rubbed his chin. "I don't want the channel to turn into a daytime talk show with demons."

"Now *that* would go viral," she said.

Pastor Ed frowned. "Okay, let's put that one on the maybe list and see what else came in."

Patricia scrolled through more messages while Pastor Ed finished his burger.

She paused, then looked up at Pastor Ed and held the phone to him. "That one."

Pastor Ed looked at the screen. The title read: *Possessed ex convicted murderer.* "Looks dangerous," he said.

"He looks like he's in a biker gang." She tapped on the screen. "Check out his picture."

Pastor Ed looked at the man's picture. He had to be at least six feet tall in his mid-thirties, covered in tattoos, and a lot of muscles. "I would hate to bump into him in an alley," he said. He took one last look at the menacing man, then looked back at Patricia.

"I've got it," he said.

CHAPTER XI

The day after Sella brought *La Santa Muerte* home, Hector asked her out to lunch. She was the envy of the office. Things seemed to go well in their relationship, and after two weeks of dating, she introduced him to her kids.

"Thank you for another wonderful night," she said.

"*De nada,*" he responded.

Little Maria tugged at Hector's pants. "Mr. Hector?" she said in a low voice. "Next time you take us to the theaters, can I pick the movie?"

Hector squatted down to her level. "Of course you can."

"No. She's going to pick a boring movie," Javier protested.

"No I'm not. Your movies are boring."

"Okay, kids, say good night to Mr. Hector."

"Good night, Mr. Hector," they shouted with a big smile on their faces.

"Good night, kids." He smiled back, then turned to Sella. "I'll see you tomorrow night?"

"Yes, I'm looking forward to it," she said.

He kissed her goodnight and left.

"Ooooo," the kids laughed.

"Shhhhh, it's late. Time for bed."

"But it's Friday."

"It doesn't matter. It's late and tomorrow you'll be going to Grandma's."

"Are we spending the night at Grandma's tomorrow?"

Sella nodded.

"Awesome," said Javier.

"Okay, off you go, and I better not catch you two on your iPads."

The kids closed the door to their room. Sella headed straight for the restroom and got herself ready for bed. She laid in bed for a while, scrolling through the comment section on her social media posts of her and Hector and, after a moment, she was fast asleep.

That night, sounds of someone dragging something awakened Sella.

Sella opened her eyes. *What time is it?* She grabbed her phone. *Three in the morning?*

More dragging sounds came from outside her bedroom.

"Javier, go to bed," she cried out.

Silence.

She cried out once more. "Javier, go to your room."

Silence.

An icy shiver ran down her spine. She raised herself out of bed and inched her way to the living room. The moonlight pierced through the living room window and splattered shadows throughout. She braced herself and flicked the light switch on. Squinting her eyes, she looked around.

Nothing.

She froze.

She went into the kitchen and grabbed a knife before heading for the kids' room. *They were asleep in their beds.* She gripped the knife tight and walked between their beds. She checked the windows. Sella moved back to the living room and checked the doors and windows. *There were no signs of an entry.* She took a deep breath. *Old house.* She put the knife away and headed back to bed. She laid in bed and closed her eyes.

Slap

Sella jerked up, eyes wide-open. She clenched the bed covers and scoured the room. Nothing. She rubbed her behind. Controlled her breathing. *Must have been a nightmare.* She got out of bed and checked the windows and doors once again. She laid in bed and checked the time. 3:20 AM. She took a deep breath and fell asleep.

Once again, Sella awoke to the dragging sounds emanating from the kitchen. *Again? What time is it?* She tried to reach for her phone but found that she couldn't move. Her body was completely paralyzed. The dragging sounds stopped, as if whatever was out there had noticed she was awake. Sella thought about Javier and Little Maria. She tried to call out to them, but her lips refused to move. Her jaw was clamped shut. All she could do was listen to her heart race as the dragging sounds began once more.

She lay staring at the ceiling, the dragging sounds drawing closer. Sella could only see the top of the door. It was closed. The dragging sounds drew ever closer to her room. She tried raising her head to get a better view, but her neck would not budge an inch. The dragging sounds came to a rest right outside her door. A torturous silence filled the room. She tensed her muscles as hard as she could in an effort to let out a cry, but all she could manage was a few weak moans.

The doorknob clicked and clacked. The room turned ice cold. She could see her breath in the air. They were sharp bursts of air. The door squeaked. Sella relaxed her body and directed all her attention to her neck muscles. With all her strength, she lifted her shaky head only to find a shadowy figure raise half its torso up by the entrance. It stared at her for a brief second and dropped to the floor. It slithered and hissed its way to the foot of the bed. The bed covers tightened. Sella let out another faint moan. She felt an indent form on the mattress by her feet. She tightened her neck muscles so hard that her head quivered as she tilted it further. Her feet blurred out of focus as she turned her attention to the shadowy figure rearing its head. She heaved. It extended its arm over her leg and hoisted itself on the bed. Sella closed her eyes tight. Her legs were pressed down by its weight. It placed its hand on her waist and yanked itself up closer to her. She felt its body press down against hers. A tear flowed down the side of her face as it began to military crawl its way up. Its elbows dug deep into her abdomen and up her chest. She felt its face hovering over hers.

She opened her eyes. A head made of charcoal gray ash looked down at her. It placed its hands in her mouth and opened it wide. Sella let out a moan and attempted to shake her head from side to side in a desperate attempt to get its hands out of her mouth, but her paralysis wouldn't let her. It stretched her mouth so wide that the sides felt like they were about to tear apart. Placing its head between her teeth, it pressed itself in. She let out a screech as it slid down her throat. She gagged as it slithered its way down the inside of her chest, suffocating her. Her vision became blurry. The further down her throat the creature went, the more her stomach expanded until finally she lost consciousness.

Chapter xii

Photos of Sella's kids decorated her cubicle, which was right next to Alicia's — the one who got her the job at the company. Alicia didn't have kids. She was a dog mom and, true to form, her cubicle was mostly covered in pictures of her and her two canines with a smidgen of pictures of her and her friends enjoying the nightlife.

Sella and Alicia had become good friends, and although Sella suspected Alicia might be a little jealous of her new relationship with Hector, it didn't bother her one bit. She knew it was only normal for girls to be jealous of her. To Sella, it really didn't matter since it would only be a matter of time before Hector proposed to her and she would no longer have to work.

"Psst!" Alicia raised her head over the cubicle. "You're daydreaming again."

Sella jerked up. "You scared me."

"Oh, sorry." Alicia stared at her face. "You look like you could use a drink. Happy hour after work? Or do you and Mr. Unreachable have plans?"

"I'm freaking out."

"What? Why?"

"Every time I close my eyes, I see my dog."

"You have a dog?" Alicia's face lit up. "You never told me you had a dog. Show me a picture."

"I got him yesterday because I keep hearing noises in my house."

"Oh my gosh, girl. Do you think someone is trying to break into your house?"

"I don't know." She shook her head. "I'm not so sure. I've been having these nightmares that seem so real."

"Oh, well, it's a good thing you got a dog then."

"That's what I thought, but he barks all night. The kids and I barely get any sleep."

"You should bring him inside."

"He was inside. He kept barking at the walls."

"He's just getting used to the place. Don't worry. He'll calm down."

"My kids looked like zombies this morning."

"I'd say they aren't the only ones."

Sella frowned. "I'm telling you, something is going on. Every time I close my eyes, I see the dog in the living room."

Alicia arched her eyebrows. "What do you mean?"

"I mean exactly what I said. I can see him in the kitchen as if I was standing right there."

Alicia looked around to see if anyone was listening. "What is he doing?"

"He's running around as if something is chasing him. He barks and then he jumps as if someone's kicking him or something."

"That's kinda creepy."

"I'm worried about him. He's scratching at the door, desperately trying to get out. His paws have blood on them and he's getting it on the door."

Alicia lowered her head behind her cubicle, her face turning pallid. "You're scaring me, Sella."

"I'm sure it's the lack of sleep," Sella said.

"Yeah, I'm sure it is." Alicia got back on her computer.

* * *

After work, Sella hurried home to check up on her dog. She parked her car in the driveway and sat for a second. Her house, what used to be a source of pride, now looked run-down and naked, ugly, its purple paint chipping away, stained and cracked. She got out of her car and, looking across the street, it surprised her to see someone else peddling drugs in Marco's spot.

"Hey!" she yelled at the young man.

The man turned toward her, nodding his head. "What you want?"

"What happened to Marco?"

He looked at her for a split second before responding, "He got promoted. I'm taking his spot. You want something or what?"

"Must have been Doña Gloria," Sella murmured to herself.

"What?" the man asked.

Sella wagged her fingers from side to side. "No," she responded. Walking up to the door, she inserted her key and took a deep breath before turning it.

The dog, Scooby, was waiting for her, wagging his tail. She stuck out her hand, and he licked it. Sella smiled and scratched his head.

"That's a good boy," she said.

Relieved at seeing the dog in a cheerful mood, she placed her purse on the table. *I think I'll make Javier's favorite dish tonight.*

She pulled a scrunchy from her purse and put her hair up. She turned her head to the side in order to tighten her scrunchy and glanced at the blood-stained door. Her soul shivered. She looked at Scooby. He cocked his head at her. She bent down and grabbed one of his paws, turning it slowly to reveal dried-up blood clenched between his paws.

Chapter xiii

The following morning, Sella woke up so late that she didn't have time to pack lunch. She gave the kids a couple of pesos and told them to purchase something from the lunch lady. At work, the day dragged. Normally, she ate at her desk, but since she didn't pack anything to eat, she invited Alicia out for tacos.

"I turned his paws over and they had blood on them. Just like in my vision," she said.

"Oh my God! Poor baby," Alicia said.

There was an uncomfortable silence.

"Maybe you're psychic," Alicia said.

"You think?"

"I don't know." Alicia shrugged. "What am I thinking about right now?"

Sella raised an eyebrow. "Your dogs?"

"Yes!" Alicia's eyes widened. "You are psychic."

"Alicia, you're always thinking about your dogs."

"Oh, yeah. I guess anyone could have guessed that."

They laughed.

"So," Alicia said, in a tone suggesting a change of subject, "how are things between you and Mr. Unreachable?"

"They're good. He took me and the kids out to the movies on Friday."

"No way!"

Sella grinned a big smile.

"I'm so jealous. I still can't believe you're dating him."

Sella frowned.

"I didn't mean it like that," Alicia said. "I'm just surprised because you've tried to get his attention before and suddenly he's taking you and your kids out to the movies. Girl, you're going to have to tell me how you did it."

"I didn't do anything. He simply walked in one day and invited me out to lunch."

* * *

Sella and Alicia returned to the office. Sella opened the door and, walking down the hallway leading to their cubicles, they noticed there was more chatter than usual. When they turned the corner to where the staff was, a silence fell and everyone's heads turned toward them.

Arriving at a complete halt, Sella and Alicia looked at each other. "What's going on?"

No one answered. One girl dropped a manila folder.

A door slammed opened. "Sella!" The manager stomped out of his office. "Get in here. Now!"

Everyone buried their heads in their cubicles.

The manager's face burned red hot.

Click click clack. Keyboard strikes filled the air.

Sella edged her way into his office, his gaze gnawing at her spine. He slammed the door shut and walked right past her. "Take a seat."

Grasping the armrests tight and looking up at him, Sella slowly sat down.

Hands on his waist, jaw clenched shut, fuming, he stood behind his desk.

"What did I do?" she asked.

He placed his hand on the monitor and flipped the screen over. Her jaw dropped.

To: AccountsDPT

*From: Sella Casta*ñon

Title: Mr. Rodriguez is a cock sucking faggot.

She looked at Mr. Rodriguez and then looked back at the screen. "It wasn't me."

"I checked with the IT Dept. and they said that the email originated from your computer."

"I swear, Mr. Rodriguez. I would never do such a thing."

"No? Then why does it say from Sella Castañon?"

"I don't know. I was at lunch. I couldn't have sent it."

"You clocked out for lunch from your computer at noon, correct?"

"Yes, me and Alicia."

"Do you see the time stamp?"

11:55 AM.

Fear knotted inside her stomach. She leaned forward, staring at it. Her head was a swarming beehive.

Outside his office, the printer machines shuttled paper, and the phones rang.

"I'm sorry, Mr. Rodriguez." She sat up straight, folded her hands, and gently laid them on her lap. "It's my fault. I have a bad tendency to leave my computer unlocked when I make a trip to the restroom. I'm very grateful for everything this company has done for me. You took a chance on me when no one would, and for that, I'm very grateful." She met his eyes. "I'm sorry you had to see that. I'm sorry everyone had to see that. I understand if you want to fire me, but you should know that it wasn't me."

Squinting his eyes, he looked at her for a brief moment before nodding and sitting down. "I'm going to give you a written warning for leaving your computer unlocked."

"I understand."

"Don't let it happen again."

"Yes, sir."

* * *

Back home right before bedtime, Sella gave the kids their gummy vitamins A, B, C, and, because Hector was coming over, Melatonin. The rumor in the office was that Sella never got up to go to the restroom. Everyone in the office avoided making eye contact with her. Alicia was kind enough to tell her what people were saying. So, when Hector called saying he was coming over to check up on her, she felt a sense of relief.

Her legs were like jelly as she lay on the bed.

He handed her a towel. "What was that?"

She cleaned herself. "What was what?"

He said nothing. Instead, he tucked in his long sleeve shirt and shook his head.

"Hector, what was what?"

He buckled his belt. "Maybe we're not compatible."

She sat up. "What!? Sure we are. Why do you say we're not compatible?"

He grabbed his shoes. "Never mind. Forget it."

"Is everything okay?"

He slipped his shoes on. "Yes, it's fine."

"Hector, look at me. I didn't send that email. I swear."

Fear was written on his face. "I know."

"Then what's wrong?"

"It was like you were someone else."

"What?"

"I didn't like it. It was too much."

She shook her head. "It felt normal to me."

"You call that normal?" A pale dread hung over his face. "My God, Sella!" He lifted his shirt. "Look at my chest." Red bloody scratch marks ran across his chest.

Sella stood dumbfounded. She covered her mouth. "I don't... I... How?"

He looked at her. "You don't remember?"

She shook her head. "No"

He rubbed the back of his neck.

"Look, I'm sorry, I haven't been myself lately." She got up and went to the bathroom. "Let me put something on that."

"It's okay. I have to get going."

"No, give me a second." She rummaged through the bathroom and seconds later came back with disinfectant and a clean white cloth, but he was long gone.

Chapter XIV

La Santa Muerte standing behind Doña Gloria looked different from the one Sella took home. She wondered if they were manufactured in a factory or handcrafted by a local artist. It was apparent to her that they were handcrafted, since the difference between them was too much to be caused by machines, but they could've been produced by two different factories. Maybe even made in China.

"He's not returning my text messages," Sella said.

"And you've been praying every night?" Doña Gloria asked.

"Yes, and I make sure she's got fresh offerings."

"Let's see what the cards have to say." She shuffled the cards. "But I will say that it doesn't sound good. The nightmares, in particular, are troublesome."

Sella split the cards. "That's what I was afraid of."

Doña Gloria placed the cards on the table. "Oh, dear."

"What is it?"

Doña Gloria held up her hand. "This is bad."

Sella frowned.

"People are jealous of your newfound success."

"Go figure."

"A witch has placed a hex on you." She looked up. "It doesn't say who, but it's evil. Very evil."

"A witch? Do you think it's Hector's ex-girlfriend?"

Doña Gloria studied the tarot. "No, definitely not an ex."

"Then who?"

"I don't know. She's warded herself very well."

"But you can break the curse, right? Like you did before."

Doña Gloria shook her head. "This is an experienced witch. Last time, it was an amateur. This witch knows exactly what she's doing. She could end your life right now if she wanted to."

Cold terror gripped Sella in its icy embrace.

Doña Gloria looked up. "But she's toying with you like a cat playing with its prey."

Sella looked around.

"I can't protect you, Sella."

"What!?" Sella jolted.

"Don't worry. I can't protect you, but I know who can. *La Santa Muerte*. No witch is more powerful than her."

"What do I have to do?"

"I'll give you one of my chickens."

"A chicken?" Sella asked in a quizzical voice.

"Yes, take it home with you. Place it on the altar and slit its throat. It will make a lot of noise and try to run off, but hold it still. Its blood must run down the altar."

She took out pen and paper. "Say this prayer right before you kill it, and be quick about it."

"And she'll protect me from the witch?"

"Has she failed you before?"

Sella shook her head. A sense of relief flowed throughout her body. "Where's the chicken?"

* * *

Sella rushed straight home; picking up her kids from her mother's house would have to wait. The last thing she needed was her mother asking her what on earth was she doing with a chicken. No, the more sensible thing to do was to go home, kill the chicken, clean up the mess, and then go pick up the kids.

Sella parked her car in the driveway, but her nosy neighbor was outside. *She'll see the chicken.* In the passenger seat, the chicken clucked in its cage. *I could get a box from the house and then place the chicken in it. No, too obvious.*

The neighbor waved. Sella waved back. *Go home, you crazy old cook.* She made her way toward her car. *Crap.* Sella jumped out of her car and met her halfway.

"Hello, Sella," she said.

"Hola, Doña Maria. How are you?"

Placing her hands on her hips, lifting her chin up, and looking at Sella through her black-framed glasses, she asked, "Where's your dog?"

"He ran away."

She nodded toward her house. "It was in my yard this morning."

"I'm so sorry. Call me next time you see him. The kids have been worried—"

"It left a little present behind."

Sella frowned. "I'll pick up the mess. Give me an hour, tops."

"It's been there all day. The entire neighborhood has seen it."

"I'm truly sorry, Doña Maria. I'll get to it as soon as I can."

"Uh-huh." She looked at her car. "What do you got there?"

"Oh, nothing. It's nothing."

"Is that a cage?"

"Uh." Sella glanced at her car. "Yes, I got the kids a bird. They miss Scooby, but I didn't want to get them another dog."

"And you shouldn't. It's obvious that they can't take care of one dog. This neighborhood is already filled with strays."

"And that's why I got them a bird."

"What kind of bird is it?"

"It's a brown bird."

"A brown bird?"

"Yes, a brown bird."

"I love birds. I have a parrot. Let me see it and I'll tell you what breed it is."

"Ah, you know what, Doña Maria? The sooner I get inside the house, the sooner I can go pick up the kids and the sooner I can clean up the mess Scooby left behind."

"You should have your kids clean it. Teach them to look after their dog."

"That's an excellent idea."

She turned and headed back. "Okay. Have fun with your bird, Sella."

"Goodbye, Doña Maria."

Sella scrambled to her car, opened the passenger side door, and pulled out the cage. Resting the cage on the side of her body, facing away from her neighbor, she darted for the door.

"That's a chicken!" she yelped.

Sella stood by the door. *Mind your damn business!* She opened the door and ran inside.

* * *

Placing the cage on the sofa and locking the door, Sella checked her phone. Text message from Mom ten minutes ago: *Mija, we're on our way to your house.*

What!? Why? She grabbed the cage, ran to her room, then opened the closet door and placed the cage inside. *La Santa Muerte* stood on the altar at the back of the closet, flanked by the two rows of clothing.

My clothes! Grabbing stacks of clothing from the hanger, she threw them onto her bed when her mom's car drove up.

They're here! She pulled the paper out of her bag. *The knife!* She ran to the kitchen and, glancing out the window, she found her mother talking to Doña Maria. *Crap.* Sella grabbed a knife and ran back to her closet. Placing the paper on the floor in front of the altar, she opened the cage and pulled the chicken out. Holding it by its neck, she read the prayer and, placing the knife up against its throat, she took a deep breath and *SLICE.*

She cut hard. The chicken's head flew off. Blood bubbled up like a small bloody spring, and muffled gurgling clucking sounds came out of its neck, its legs kicking non-stop.

Sella squeezed its neck as hard as she could until it stopped kicking. She tipped it over like a limp vase and poured the blood on the altar.

"*Mom?*" Little Maria stood by the door. "What are you doing?"

"Hey, *mija*." Sella put the chicken's corpse down. "Let's go with your grandma, okay?"

"What's that?" She pointed to *La Santa Muerte*, wide-eyed, jaw open. "Is it the Day of the Dead?"

"No, but… I'll tell you later." She nudged her toward the door. "Tell your grandma I'll be right there, okay? If she asks you what I'm doing, tell her I'm in the bathroom. Got it?"

"Got it." Little Maria ran off.

Sella washed the blood off her hands in the restroom and headed to the living room.

Her mother was unpacking groceries. "I brought you some groceries."

"Thanks, Mama."

"The neighbor told me Scooby left her a surprise in her front yard."

Sella laughed.

"She's so nosy. I tell you, the Holy Ghost kept me from giving her a piece of my mind."

"She's a lot. Did she tell you anything else?"

"She said that a man's been coming over and staying until inappropriate hours."

Sella smiled. "Hector."

Her mother finished unpacking the groceries. Turning toward Sella, she sighed and placed her hands on her daughter's shoulders. "Why don't you come to church with me—"

She flinched. "What's that smell?"

"Yuk! Mom, you smell." The kids pinched their noses.

Her mother leaned forward. "*Mija*, you smell like roadkill." She recoiled. "Go take a shower."

Chapter XV

At night, Sella dreamed she rested on a floating device out on the ocean, rising and falling with the waves, a calm she hadn't experienced in a while, gently rising and gently descending, smooth, rhythmic, in sync with her breathing. Sella took a deep breath, pausing at the wave's peak, then slowly released her breath, pausing at its valley. Her lips curled.

There came a rasping, a rhythmic tapping. *From where?* Sella looked around. More tapping. She found herself alone in the vast ocean. More rasping. The wave rose. *Tap... tap... tap*. The wave descended. *Tap... tap... tap*. She looked into the ocean: blue, endless blue.

Tap ... tap ... tap.

She opened her eyes. In sync with her breathing, the furniture rose. *Tap... tap... tap*. Then descended. *Tap... tap... tap*.

She shook her head. *The bed is moving.*

The mattress was rising and falling beneath her.

It's breathing!

She scurried to the edge of the bed. Sharp, electrifying pain shot up her spine. Her head jolted back. Falling on her bed, she stared at the ceiling. Stiff and paralyzed, invisible hands grabbed her shoulders, pulling her mid-air, pausing, then pinning her to the mattress hard, again, and again, and again, faster, more violent, her body going limp, slamming up and down. Hoisted mid-air, she let out a cry, kicking and screaming.

Javier and Little Maria opened the door. Her body came crashing to the floor. Little Maria screamed, and Javier ran out of the room.

"Mommy!" Little Maria cried.

Sella sat up and reached out for her daughter, who curled herself in terror, when a stabbing pain ran up Sella's spine and burrowed itself into her skull. She arched her back, Little Maria's screams bouncing off the walls. Sella fell on her back, her eyes rolled to the back of her head.

The invisible hands choked her. Clawing at her neck, she gasped for air until her face turned red and she passed out.

* * *

Javier, Little Maria, and Sella's mother stood around the hospital bed. The television played a telenovela Sella had never heard of. She stopped watching them years ago. It's always the same story: a poor woman marries a rich man.

The doctor walked in. "So you're the brave little boy that dialed 911?"

Javier looked up at the doctor and nodded.

The doctor raised his clipboard. "Sella, looks like you had a seizure." Taking out a pen, he scribbled. "I'm going to give you a prescription for Valium, but you're going to want to see your family practitioner for follow-up treatment."

"Is she going to be okay?" Sella's mother asked.

"Yes, she should be okay. In fact," he turned to Sella, "Sella, you can go home."

"Doctor," Sella's mother interrupted, "she lives alone with the children. Should she have someone with her in case it happens again?"

"That's really up to her. The medication should prevent another seizure from happening, but it's not a refillable prescription. She'll need to check up with her doctor for continued treatment."

Sella got up. "Thank you, Doctor."

"Make sure to check out with the front desk. They'll transmit your prescription to your local pharmacy," he said before stepping out.

Sella signaled to her mother. "Let's go."

"*Mija*, let's go to church first thing in the morning."

"I have to work tomorrow, Mama."

"Then during your lunch."

"I really just want to go home right now, Mama."

"Then let me stay with you and help with the kids."

"Mama, you heard the doctor. I'll be fine."

Sella's mother shook her head.

Chapter XVI

Sella sat in Doña Gloria's waiting room. The woman with the child that she first encountered there sat across from her.

"You've come back," she said.

Sella nodded, staring at the floor.

"Once you become a customer, it's hard to stop coming."

Sella looked up at her. "How long have you been coming?"

Doña Gloria's door opened, and Marco exited the room, wearing a cowboy hat, leather belt, expensive jeans, and really nice-looking boots. On his wrist flashed a Rolex watch. Rumor had it he'd risen in the ranks to *capo* of the Juarez cartel. He made his way to the exit and didn't even notice the women sitting in the waiting room.

"Come in, Sella," Doña Gloria said.

Sella got up, and before heading to the room, she noticed that both the woman and her son were staring at her midsection.

"Sella," Doña Gloria said.

"Yes?"

"Are you coming in?"

"Right." Sella made her way into the cold room. Taking her seat, the candles flickered, and Sella could see her breath.

"What's bothering you?" Doña Gloria asked.

"Yesterday, I did as you told me, but then I was attacked at night."

"What kind of attack?"

"I was asleep and the bed…" She paused. "It was as if it was breathing."

"Breathing?"

"Yes, then I felt a shock go up my spine. I began to shake violently, as if someone were shaking me. Picking me up and slamming into the bed over and over. Then it choked me and I passed out. Before I knew it, I was at the hospital."

Doña Gloria tapped her fingers on the table. "I was afraid of this."

"What is going on with me?" Hot tears welled behind her eyes.

"Sella, this witch is extremely powerful. She must have sensed that you performed the sacrifice."

A wave of apprehension washed over Sella.

"This witch must have unleashed a demon on you."

Fear gnawed at her spine. "What?"

"If you want to live, you're going to have to perform a human sacrifice."

Sella shot up. "A human sacrifice?" She shook her head. "No. no. I can't kill anyone."

"You don't have to kill anyone."

"I don't want anyone to die," she sobbed.

"Sella, calm down. It's not what you think."

"Then what is it?" She placed her head in her hands.

"All you have to do is have an abortion and dedicate the fetus to *La Santa Muerte*."

She looked up. "What?"

"It's the highest form of worship anyone can do to her."

"I can't do that. I'm not even pregnant."

"You are pregnant, Sella."

Sella jerked her head.

"It's your ex's. It'll just get in the way of your relationship with Hector. He's not going to accept you once he finds out you're pregnant with another man's child."

Sella looked down at her stomach. "I'll tell him it's his."

"Men like him don't get to the top by being stupid. He's going to demand a DNA test and then he'll leave you for sure. You have to abort it."

Sella's throat closed in grief.

"It's your right as a woman to choose," she said. "Modern science says it's not even a real human. It's just a blob of cells."

"No. I can't kill my baby." Sella looked up and wiped her tears away, then jumped out of her chair. "It moved."

"Don't be silly. It's too early for it to move."

"No, *it*!" Sella pointed at *La Santa Muerte*. "The statue, it moved."

Sella did a double-take on Doña Gloria. She looked calm. Too calm for someone who was just told that an inanimate object moved. *It's you! You're doing this.*

"My mom was right," Sella muttered.

"You have to do it, Sella," Doña Gloria said. "I know a doctor who can perform the procedure."

Sella shook her head and dashed out the door. The woman with the child stared at her with a grim smile, the child cackling on her lap, exposing its over-sized, heavily stained adult teeth. It had facial hair and wrinkles around its eyes and forehead.

"Do it," the woman said.

Sella ran out the door, the child's cackling following her all the way to her car. She jumped in and then drove off, pressing on the steering wheel's phone button. "Call Mama."

"Calling Mama," the car's speakers reiterated.

Pick up. Pick up. Pick up.

"*Mija*."

"Mama!"

"What's wrong?"

"Mama, you were right. That thing is evil."

"What thing?"

"*La Santa Muerte!* I need you to help me get it out of my house."

"*Si, mija*. I'll head to your house right now."

* * *

Sella and her mother both arrived at the house at the same time.

"Mommy," the kids yelled from the back seat of their grandma's car.

Sella ran up to the car window. "Stay in the car while your grandma and I go inside the house, and don't come inside until we tell you to."

"Yes, Mama," the kids said.

Sella's mom jumped out of the car. "*Mija*, let's go quick."

"*Si*, Mama."

They ran into the house, Sella leading the way.

"I called the priest. He's on his way to bless the house."

Sella inserted her key into her bedroom door. "*Si,* Mama." She turned the key and stepped inside. Standing before the closet door, Sella turned to her mother.

"Go ahead, *mija*," her mother said. "Open the door and let's get rid of that thing."

Sella placed her hands on the doorknob and swung it open.

Her mother gasped. "*Dios mio!*"

Sella marched straight up to it and reached out to grab it by the head, but some invisible force sent her flying in the air.

"*Mija!*"

Sella fell to the ground, her hands clamped up, and her pregnant belly heaved as something kicked her in her stomach.

My baby. "Maaaaa-maaaaa!"

"*Mija!*"

Sella's throat bulged up, gasping for air like a fish out of water, and her face turned crimson red. Then it rained down a flurry of blows on her, striking hard on her back, her chest, her stomach, her head, over and over in an endless barrage so hard that her ears rang.

"*Dios mio!*" her mother shouted.

Turning toward her mother, she pleaded, "Heeeelp meeeeee!" as her hair rose slowly. Then it yanked her head up, nearly snapping her neck.

Sella's mother shouted in horror as she watched her daughter get hoisted up by her hair, kicking her legs in mid-air. "Pleeeeease," Sella begged, desperately trying to free herself.

Sella's mom covered her mouth and took a step back.

The kids ran in. "Mommy!"

Sella's mom pulled the kids behind her. "Get behind me."

Sella stood hanging by her hair. Her eyes rolled down into their sockets. She swayed back and forth like a cobra. "Yesssssss," she hissed, hugging herself. "You're mine," she said in a demonic voice. "My little whore. You're all mine." Sticking her tongue out and twirling it around her lips, she pressed down hard on her breasts as she slowly descended, her feet touching the floor.

Her mother made the sign of the cross.

Sella's neck whipped sideways toward her mother. "That won't help you!"

CHAPTER XVII

Filling the church's parking lot in two columns, the Warlocks biker gang drove their Harley Davidsons, making the distinctive low, deep-throated vibrations the bikes are best known for. They came to show their love and support for their long-time member, Eduardo Mejia.

There were two types of men from two types of worlds making their way into the church. There were clean-shaven, Bible-thumping Christians with their tucked-in long sleeve shirts and ties, and there were long-bearded, bar-crashing bikers with their leather jackets and rough worn-down boots.

On the stage were four seats arranged in traditional daytime TV talk show manner. Patricia sat on the far left, followed by Pastor Ed, Eduardo, and Joe. Mike, as usual, was behind the camera.

Pastor Ed raised his hand and waited for the chatter to quiet down. "Today we are gathered here to help a poor soul in distress. Everyone, I would like for you to meet Eduardo. I don't have to tell you that he's one tough guy. You can tell just by looking at him that he is not someone you want to mess with. In fact, Eduardo served 20 years in Colorado's own ADMAX prison facility. For those of you who don't know, ADMAX is the only federal supermax prison in the country, and is known for holding some of the worst criminals in American history." He read the room. "But he's turned his life around, and today he works with several local Christian communities."

"Amen," said the crowd.

Pastor Ed got up from his seat and took a few steps forward.

"Eduardo, I want you to step forward and show everyone your tattoos."

All eyes were on Eduardo as he got up from his chair. He was six feet four inches tall, had a shaved head, tan skin, athletic body, and the strongest jawline on planet Earth. The man practically oozed testosterone as he stepped forward and extended his arms. The Virgin Mary was tattooed on one arm, and a rosary wrapped around the other.

"Did you get those tattoos in prison, Eduardo?" Pastor Ed asked.

"Yes, I did. I was one bad dude, but then I met a priest who gave me a copy of the Bible and I fell in love with the scriptures."

"Amen," said the bikers.

"It's good that you fell in love with the scriptures, Eduardo, but the priest didn't turn your life around, and neither did Mary nor any beads." Pastor Ed took his cross and placed it on Eduardo's left arm. "I cancel these Catholic tattoos."

"Amen," said the congregation.

The bikers looked a little confused.

Pastor Ed took his cross and placed it over Eduardo's other arm. "I cancel this idol image. In the name of Jesus Christ, I cancel all Catholic idolatry that you have tattooed on your body." He waved his cross all over Eduardo's body. "The second commandment says thou shall not make unto thee any graven images."

"Amen." The congregation broke out in chatter.

Pastor Ed raised his hand once more. "Eduardo, you seem to have turned your life around, but obviously you're here for a reason. Tell us what troubles you."

Eduardo shrugged. "Addiction."

"What kind of addiction?"

"Ah, cocaine, marijuana, heroin, anything I can get my hands on."

Pastor Ed nodded. "So you've been able to help others, but you haven't been able to help yourself?"

"I feel like a fraud," he said.

"No!" the bikers yelled out.

"What are you running from, Eduardo?"

"What?"

"Come on. I know you're running from something."

Eduardo's face turned red. "Abuse."

"What kind of abuse? Emotional? Sexual?"

A hot tear of shame ran down his cheek. "Both."

"I get a feeling that you're one of those guys that no one picks on, not just because of your stature, but because they know that once you cut loose…" Pastor Ed shook his head, "Look out, because Eduardo doesn't stop once he gets started."

The bikers laughed.

"Is that right?" Pastor Ed asked with a smile.

"Yeah," Eduardo grinned.

Pastor Ed turned to Joe. "Why don't you come here and stand next to Eduardo."

Joe got up and stood next to Eduardo. Eduardo towered over Joe, so Joe made an effort to straighten out his back and make himself look as tall as he could.

"Yeah, that ain't going to work," the pastor said as the crowd broke out in laughter. "Can we get two of Eduardo's biggest biker friends to come up on stage and give us a hand?"

Two big men in leather jackets, jeans, and biker boots made their way to the stage.

"That's better." Pastor Ed then turned to the crowd. "I know you came here to watch me take on this 6' 4" demonically possessed ex-convict, but I'm here to tell you that that's not going to happen." He canvased the room. "No. Instead, I want you to meet," he paused for effect and then turned toward Patricia, "the teenage exorcist!"

The congregation gasped. The bikers made an uproar. "He'll kill her!" one of them yelled. The congregation chanted Patricia's name as she made her way toward Eduardo with her Bible in one hand and a cross in her back jeans pocket.

Patricia walked right up to him and tilted her head up. "Put your hands out, Eduardo."

Eduardo looked around in disbelief.

"Hey! I said, put your hands out in front of you."

Eduardo slowly placed his arms out.

"I take a cord of three strands from Ecclesiastes four twelve, and I bind those hands." Patricia took her Bible and waved it as if she was binding Eduardo's hands with an invisible cord.

Pastor Ed nodded at the two bikers. They wrapped their arms around Eduardo's arms.

"Repeat after me, Eduardo," Patricia said. "I renounce all evil."

"I renounce all evil," he said.

"In the name of Jesus Christ."

"In the name of Jesus Christ," he repeated.

Patricia gazed into Eduardo's eyes. "I want to talk to the part of Eduardo that can bust the head of anybody, at the drop of a hat, that would dare cross him."

Eduardo snarled.

"I want to talk to the part of Eduardo that is filled with rage," she said.

He groaned.

"You're a tough guy, aren't you?"

He flashed his canine tooth.

"Eduardo, I want you to turn this rage over and hand it over to God."

Eduardo turned his face away and slumped over a bit.

Raising her hand, Patricia placed it on his shoulder. "Eduardo, we're going to banish this demon together. You want that?"

He turned toward her. "I want to banish it to hell."

"Yeah!" the bikers shouted.

The members clapped.

"Banish it to hell, Patricia!" one member said.

"Stand up straight, demon," she said. "I'm calling you to attention."

His face turned red.

"Who are you?" she asked.

"You should know." He glared.

"I sense murder. I sense hate. Did I miss one?"

He smiled.

Patricia reached up with her Bible and placed it on his forehead. "Your name?"

He groaned. "Murderrrrr."

She took a step back.

Pastor Ed tugged at Mike, who was getting a close-up of the two. "Record from this angle."

"Say, 'I, Eduardo,'" Patricia said.

"I, Eduardo."

"Break the curse of murder."

"No!" Eduardo's voice fell deeper.

"I break the covenant of blood," Patricia said.

"I said no!"

"Say, 'I, murder.'"

"No."

Patricia slammed her Bible on his chest. "I command you!"

"Aaaah." Eduardo clenched his fists.

"Say, 'I, murder.'"

"I, murder."

"Now say, 'I lift the curse.'"

"Aaaah." He waved his two invisibly bound arms up. "I lift the curse."

"On this man."

"On this man," he repeated.

Patricia gazed deep into his eyes. "Come on, demon," she taunted him, and slapped the Bible across her chest.

"You don't want that."

"Yes, I do. Come on. Bring it!" she gibed him.

Leaning toward her, veins bulging, Eduardo Mejia took one step forward, then another, dragging the bikers behind him. Joe got in front of him, but was unsuccessful in pushing him back.

Patricia walked to the far edge of the stage. "Come on, demon. Come and get me. What are you afraid of, a little girl?"

"Aaaaaaah!" he yelled. His hamstring muscles stretched his jeans to the max as he dragged the three men, inching his way forward.

"Release him," she said.

Pastor Ed's eyes widened.

"No!" Joe said.

"I said release him now!" She stood up straight like a soldier, arms to her side, shoulders arched back, chin up, taunting, "Come on, demon. What are you? Scared?"

Eduardo yelled and, shaking the two men off him, they fell to the ground, exhausted. He then grabbed Joe and tossed him toward the crowd. They jumped and gasped in disbelief. Pastor Ed's heart dropped to his stomach as Eduardo rushed toward Patricia like a great white shark. The crowd was on their feet. Patricia stood her ground, clenching her Bible close to her chest, and she thrust it toward him. Eduardo's eyes widened, and much like a great white shark that had never been confronted before, he panicked and came crashing down on his back with a loud thump. The crowd went wild. Joe and the two bikers jumped on him, while Eduardo lay stunned.

"Stand him up," she said.

Joe and the two bikers helped Eduardo up, his face turning red, grinding his teeth. Inching his way toward Patricia, he dragged the three men with him once again.

"Say, 'we go'!" she commanded.

"Aaaaaah." The vein on his forehead bulged.

"I command you to say, 'we go'!"

Eduardo inched his trembling body closer to her.

"Say, 'we go'!"

"Aaaaaah."

"Say it!"

"We go," he moaned.

"To the."

"To the." He was within arm's length, the two bikers hanging off each arm, Joe desperately trying to push him away from Patricia.

"Pit," she said.

His face came within inches of hers. "Pit," he groaned.

"Come out." She placed her Bible on his head. "Come out in the name of Jesus."

Pastor Ed turned to the crowd. "Come on, everyone," he said, waving his hands up.

"Come out in the name of Jesus!" they all shouted.

Eduardo dropped to his knees.

"Come out. Come out," the crowed continued.

Eduardo lifted his head and let out a cry.

"Yes!" Pastor Ed shouted.

Patricia unclipped her microphone and moved it toward him.

"Eduardo, do you accept Jesus as your personal Lord and Savior?"

"Yes. Yes. Yes. I do," he said.

"Hallelujah," the crowd shouted, both bikers and church members cheering.

Pastor Ed spun Mike around toward the crowd. "Get the crowd on tape."

Mike captured the scene. "Would you look at that."

Patricia hugged Eduardo. "You're free," she said.

He placed his arm around her, closing his eyes. "Thank you."

Pastor Ed spun Mike back around. "Make sure to get Patricia and Eduardo too."

The bikers rushed to their friend. Pastor Ed grabbed Patricia's arm and held it up in front of the camera. "We did it!"

Nancy stepped onto the stage with a stack of t-shirts. Pastor Ed grabbed one and displayed it in front of the camera. "Folks, help us in our upcoming evangelical mission to Juarez, Mexico, by purchasing one of our many exorcist t-shirts. The link is in the description below." He wrapped his arm around Patricia and gave her a big kiss on the forehead.

She grabbed a large shirt and put it on over her clothes. "We are desperately short on funds, but you can help by purchasing our merchandise, or by simply donating to our Patreon account," she said.

"Help us spread the gospel," Pastor Ed said.

Chapter xviii

The colonial Spanish Cathedral of Our Lady of Guadalupe towered above the city of Juarez. Policemen in black SWAT uniforms patrolled the neighborhood as the sun pounded the streets. By day, Pastor Ed's volunteers set up tables at street corners and passed out bags filled with canned food, clothing, and Bibles. They told the passersby to attend a free sermon by the famous American Pastor Ed, handing out pamphlets with a map to the convention center and depicting pictures of him preaching from the pulpit and performing exorcisms.

In the evening, the volunteers ushered the curious to Pastor Ed's sermon, where Patricia stood behind an orange podium. She didn't know any Spanish, but she knew how to introduce her father. Leaning her head toward the microphone, and in a thick Spanish accent, she said, *"Presentando al pastor Ed."*

Pastor Ed made his way to the small stage amongst the applause. The room had a modern corporate feel to it. Except for the wall behind him, which was a nice cream color, the walls were the same orange as the podium. Most years, the church had a hard time filling half the seats, but this year the volunteers had to bring in additional chairs. The room was at max capacity, and no matter how much Pastor Ed tried to convince the manager, they stopped letting people in. Pastor Ed looked out at the number of people looking up at him and wondered if his idol, Billy Graham, was just as nervous the first time he stood in front of a large crowd.

He covered the microphone with his hand and cleared his throat before speaking. "I know most of you were brought up Catholic," he said in Spanish. "Really quick, raise your hand if you were brought up Catholic."

Pastor Ed made a quick mental note of the percentage of hands that went up. "Okay, thank you. So, you've been told your whole life that you must go to a priest to have your sins forgiven. Is that right?"

The attendants nodded.

"Well, I'm here to tell you the truth. A priest can't forgive your sins, only God can." He raised his Bible. "Nowhere in the Bible does it say to go to a priest to have your sins forgiven."

The attendants sat silently.

"You're all children of God and can go directly to Him whenever you want. Going to a priest won't help because they can't forgive your sins. If you want your sins forgiven, you must go straight to Jesus. Only he can forgive your sins."

Silence.

"The Catholic Church places all these obstacles between you and Jesus because it wants you to believe that you need the church to be saved, but the gift of salvation is offered to everyone. Do you know what you must do to be saved?"

He paused.

"You just have to accept Jesus as your personal Lord and Savior. John 3:16 says, '**For God so loved the world that he gave his only Son, so that everyone who believes in him may not die but have eternal life.**'"

Pausing once more, he continued, "You can simply remove the word 'world' and replace it with your name." Pastor Ed noticed one attendant in the front row was paying more attention to the free sandwich he received than to his sermon. "Young man, what's your name?"

The man pointed at himself, eyebrows raised, mouth full.

"Yes, you. What's your name?"

He swallowed and then let out a faint, "Francisco."

"Francisco?"

"Yes."

"Francisco, I want you to replace the word 'world' with your name." Pastor Ed opened his Bible and pretended to read from it. "For God so loved Francisco that he gave his only Son, so that if Francisco believes in him, he may not die but have eternal life."

Emotional tears welled behind the young man's eyes.

"This is the gospel truth. God's salvation is eternal, and no one can take it away from you. The Catholic Church teaches that you must continue to go back and be re-saved through their sacraments, but the Bible teaches otherwise. **'My sheep hear my voice,'** the Lord said, **'and I know them, and they follow me. I give them eternal life, and they will never perish, and no one will snatch them out of my hand. My Father, who has given them to me, is greater than all, and no one is able to snatch them out of the Father's hand. I and the Father are one.'** John 27:30. Once saved, always saved. You can't lose your salvation."

The attendants clapped. Pastor Ed beamed at Francisco. "Francisco, are you ready to give your life to Jesus?"

The lights in the room dimmed and soothing music played. All eyes were on the wide-eyed Francisco, who nodded.

"Come up here, young man."

Francisco made his way to the stage. Pastor Ed placed his hand on his bony shoulder. "Francisco, do you recognize that you are a sinner?"

Leaning into the microphone, "Yes," he said in a nervous tone.

"Do you believe that Jesus died for your sins and rose from the dead?"

"Yes."

"Francisco, I want you to confess with your mouth in front of everyone that you accept Jesus as your personal Lord and Savior."

"How do I do that?"

Pastor Ed pulled out a card from his coat pocket and flashed it to the attendants. "This is called the sinner's prayer. You should each have one in the gift bag you all received." He handed the card to Francisco. "Take it and read it out loud to everyone."

Francisco took the card with his trembling hands. "Okay," he said. "'Heavenly Father, I come to you in prayer asking for the forgiveness of my sins. I confess with my mouth and believe with my heart that Jesus is your Son, and that He died on the cross at Calvary that I might be forgiven and have eternal life in the Kingdom of Heaven. Father, I believe that Jesus rose from the dead and I ask you right now to come into my life and be my personal Lord and Savior. I repent of my sins and will worship you all the days of my life. Because your word is truth, I confess with my mouth that I am born again and cleansed by the blood of Jesus. In Jesus' name, Amen.'"

The volunteers clapped, followed by the rest of the attendants.

* * *

Pastor Ed's sermon touched many of the attendants, and many of them answered the altar call. Pastor Ed stayed on stage to answer questions the attendants might have. Afterward, when the attendants had left, he gathered his team around him.

"Alright," he said, "time to call it a day. Everyone, gather around me."

Joe was the first to reach him, delivering a fist bump. "Great job, Pastor Ed, and congrats on your YouTube channel success. 1.5 million subscribers. Wow! That's amazing."

"Thanks, Joe," Pastor Ed said, "but it's our success. You played a big part in it."

Joe smiled. "They're calling you the demon slayer."

Pastor Ed grinned. "Demon slayer. That's cool."

With the rest of the team gathered around him, he said, "Great job, everyone. This year's mission is going to be a success. I want each and every one of you to be proud of yourselves for doing the Lord's work."

The volunteers looked at him with glowing wide rounded eyes

and enormous smiles, and whispered in hushed, excitable tones. To many of them, he'd become a hero.

"Let's clean this place up. Afterward, you can head back to your rooms or meet up with some of us at the pool. It's hot and we could use a little r&r."

"It is hot," Patricia said.

"One more day, guys. Hang in there," Joe said.

Pastor Ed turned to Mike. "You don't have to stick around and help us clean. I want you to edit today's video. Make sure to include our street evangelization along with the sermon."

"Yes, sir." Mike grabbed his gear and headed for the exit.

"Meet us at the pool when you're done. I want to see the video before uploading it."

"You got it."

Nancy made her way to Pastor Ed. "I need to talk to you."

Noticing her stern face, he told the group, "Okay, everyone, let's clean up."

The team dispersed and began cleaning.

"What's going on?" Pastor Ed said.

"There's a lady here who says her daughter's possessed," Nancy said.

Pastor Ed stretched his back. "I don't have time for an exorcism. Tell her to give you her number and we'll call her back." He took a chair and folded it up. "And make sure to come back and help us."

"Okay, sir, I will, but before I do, I think you're going to want to hear this lady out."

Carrying two foldable chairs, he made his way to the side wall. "Oh yeah? Why?"

Nancy trailed behind him. "Well, the thing is, she says that she's taken her daughter to the Catholic Church and they haven't been able to expel the demon."

Pastor Ed froze. He turned to her. "Really?"

"Yes, she's waiting in the lobby."

"How's her English?"

Nancy thought for a second. "It's broken, but you can totally understand her. Why?"

"Patricia!"

Patricia raised her head from picking up the trash.

"Go get Mike. Tell him to come back quick."

Patricia made her way to the lobby. "Okay."

"And tell him to bring his equipment."

Patricia gave him a thumbs up on her way out.

"Nancy, tell the lady that I'm really busy and don't have time."

"But I thought you would be interested."

"I am, but I don't want her to know that. When she insists, tell her that you think you can convince me to change my schedule if she's willing to tell her story to the public and have the exorcism recorded."

"Oh, I see. Okay, you got it." Nancy headed for the lobby.

"Okay, team, change of plans."

Chapter xix

The conference room was completely empty, and since there were no more bookings for that evening, management had no issues with Pastor Ed using the room a little longer. The volunteers were told that Pastor Ed had some business to attend to so he wouldn't be able to make the pool gathering. Mike had set up his tripod in front of two chairs. Patricia dimmed the lights for effect and stood behind Mike, while Nancy led Sella's mother into the room, the bags under her eyes revealing a mother in distress.

"Have a seat on this chair," Pastor Ed said.

Sella's mother slowly rested her tired body on the chair, folding her hands in her lap and fingering a tissue. "Thank you."

Pastor Ed sat in the other chair. "Just act normal, and before you know it, the camera will fade into the background."

She nodded.

Patricia raised her hand up, fingers extended. Closing her fingers, she started the countdown. "Ready in 5.4.3.2—"

Pastor Ed rested his eyes on the camera lens. "Hello, everyone. As you know, we are out here in Juarez, Mexico, evangelizing for the

Lord." He paused for a brief second. "Beside me is a woman who, having heard about our ministry of exorcism, came to us for help."

He turned to Sella's mother. "Can you tell everyone your name?"

"My name is Lurdes Castañon."

"And how long have you been living in Juarez, Mrs. Castañon?"

"Always."

"And do you attend church?"

"Yes, I go to church at the cathedral."

"I see. So you are Catholic?"

"Yes."

"And you say your daughter is possessed?"

"Yes, she is possessed by a demon." She shook her head. "There is no evil like it. No. no. no."

"Yes, indeed. Demons are pure evil."

"Every time I look into her eyes, I see pure hate, an evil unlike anything."

Pastor Ed turned to the camera. "You guys only get to see the demons behind a screen, but as Mrs. Castañon says, it's extremely frightening to go face to face with the most hateful of all beings."

Sella's mother wiped her eyes with her tissue, then shook her head. "Señor, please help my daughter."

"I will, Mrs. Castañon. I'll cast that demon out even if it's the last thing I do."

Sella's mother grabbed his hand and kissed it. "Gracias, señor."

"Okay. Okay," Pastor Ed said. "I'm not the pope now."

Patricia and the gang laughed.

"Mrs. Castañon, when did this all start? How was your daughter possessed?"

"She went to see a witch."

"A witch? Well, that's new. Where is this witch now?"

"She ran away."

"She fled? From who?"

"From the Federales."

Pastor Ed raised an eyebrow. "Why was she running from the Mexican authorities?"

"I don't know. The people in the neighborhood say she was performing spells for the Mexican cartel."

Pastor Ed looked at Patricia.

"The cartels will ask witches to place a spell on their drug cargos to ensure they reach the other side of the border. Sort of like a blessing, but with evil intent," Patricia said.

She must have seen it in a documentary. "Oh, I see," Pastor Ed said. "Well, I hope they catch her and put her behind bars."

Sella's mother nodded.

"Have you sought help, Mrs. Castañon?"

"On the night of my daughter's possession, I had asked the priest to come and bless the house. He arrived minutes after the demon took possession of her body."

"Did he perform an exorcism?"

"No, he restrained her from attacking me and my grandchildren, and said he had to report it to the bishop."

"Did the bishop visit your daughter?"

"No."

"Then what happened?"

"The bishop said we need to see a doctor."

"Well, that's good advice, but did they even attempt to expel the demon?"

She stared at the ground. "No."

Pastor Ed shook his head. "What did the doctor say?"

"The church sent a psychiatrist and he—" She paused, unsure of herself. "I don't know how to say it in English."

"Go ahead and say it in Spanish. I'll translate."

"*Prescribió* medicamentos para un raro caso de trastorno de identidad disociativo," she said.

"He prescribed medication for a rare instance of dissociative identity disorder," Pastor Ed said. "I'm guessing the medication didn't work, otherwise you wouldn't be here with us tonight."

"No, it didn't work. So I went to the priest and asked if they would now perform an exorcism."

"Did he perform the exorcism?"

She shook her head. "He sent his report to the Vatican, and says he's waiting for a response."

"The Vatican!? That could take forever." Pastor Ed turned to the camera. "This is what I'm talking about. The Catholic Church always places so many barriers between people and Jesus. Why won't they just perform the exorcism? I'll tell you why. Because they can't cast out demons. They turn to Mary and the saints instead of turning to Jesus. Well, Mary and the saints can't cast out demons because they're dead."

Looking directly into her eyes, he placed his hand on her shoulder. "Here's what I'm going to do, Mrs. Castañon. Tomorrow, after my sermon, I will head over to your house with my team and we will expel that demon in the name of Jesus Christ."

"Amen," said the crew.

Sella's mom wiped away her tears, nodded, and with a faint smile said, "*Gracias, muchas gracias.*"

Pastor Ed turned his attention to the camera. "For the first time in this channel's history, we are going to perform an exorcism live, tomorrow at eight p.m. central time. You don't want to miss it."

CHAPTER XX

The following evening, the sun set on the run-down city of Juarez. Pastor Ed sat on the passenger side of the SUV — Mike, Joe, and Patricia sat in the back — while the Uber driver drove down a street flanked on both sides by beat-up old cars parked in front of brightly colored houses.

Pastor Ed's phone rang. "That reminds me," he said. "Make sure to silence your devices." Glancing at his phone's screen, he noticed the international number. "Must be the old lady," he said before answering.

"Hello?"

"Pastor Ed?" came a man's voice.

"Who's this?"

"This is Father Ortiz, the exorcist assigned to Sella's case. I've called to warn you not to perform an exorcism on Sella. You don't know what you're getting yourself into."

"How did you get my number?"

"From Sella's mother," he said. "I'm on my way. Whatever you do, don't—"

Pastor Ed ended the call.

"Who was it?" Patricia asked.

"The priest." He looked at the driver. "Step on it."

"I'm not allowed to drive past the speed limit."

"I'll give you a hundred American dollars."

"A hundred?"

"Make it two hundred."

Without hesitation, the driver stomped on the gas pedal, sending everyone jolting back.

Placing his phone on silent, he looked back at the crew. "The priest is trying to stop us, or worse. He's going to try to step in at the last minute and claim credit for our exorcism. Well, I won't have it."

"But what exactly did he say?" Patricia asked.

"I don't know, I think he was trying to scare us," he said, then gazed at the GPS screen. "Looks like we're almost there. Start streaming, Mike. Let's give the audience the complete experience."

Mike attached his phone to the stabilizer and clicked on the screen several times. "Okay, we're live."

Pastor Ed turned his head back to the camera. "Okay, everyone, we're almost at the victim's residence."

The driver pulled up in front of Sella's house, and the team stepped out of the car.

Mike panned his phone across the house, landing on Scooby standing on the sidewalk, growling and barking non-stop. "Wow, that's freaky," he said.

"What's he barking at?" Patricia asked.

"Looks like he's barking at the house."

"Guys, come on," Pastor Ed said.

With his team following right behind him, Pastor Ed made his way to the house. Knowing that the priest was on his way, Pastor Ed knocked on the door repeatedly. It didn't take long before Sella's mother opened the door. An incessant cursing came bellowing from the back of the house, deep with anger, hate, and frustration.

"Thank God you're here," she said. "Come in. I'll take you to her."

She led the team across the living room, lighted only by the setting sun. They made their way to the back of the house and stood before the bedroom door, from where the cursing voice changed to domesticated animal sounds. First something of a steer, then the sound of swine. That's when Pastor Ed felt a chill, tugging deep inside him, an ice-cold warning flowing through his veins.

Another door opened slightly, revealing two little children sticking their heads out, the boy's head stacked above the little girl's, eyes fraught with fear.

"Maria, Javier," their grandmother said, "go back inside and lock the door."

The little boy closed the door, but not before getting one last look at Pastor Ed.

Sella's mother pulled out her cell phone and scrolled through her photo album. "This is my daughter." It was a video of a young beautiful Latina celebrating her birthday.

Pastor Ed took the cell phone and looked at it. "She's very beautiful," he said, tilting the phone so that Mike could capture the video.

"Let me see." Patricia leaned over from behind. "She's really pretty."

He handed the phone back to Sella's mother, who looked down at it, tears filling her eyes. "I took this video three months ago." She made a smacking sound with her lips and put the phone away, then placed her hand on the doorknob. The sounds stopped and a cold silence filled the air. "Now look at what that thing's done to my *mija*."

"Who's in there with her?" Pastor Ed asked.

She opened the door. "No one."

He held her haunted gaze. In the stinging silence, Pastor Ed turned his eyes to the door creaking open to reveal Sella's bedroom, flinching at the pungent stench that blasted his face. Reining in their revulsion, the team gagged.

"My God." Patricia retreated. "I think I'm going to vomit."

"The restroom's over there," Sella's mother said.

Patricia retreated, and the rest of the team stared at Pastor Ed, pinching their noses shut, brows drawn together, expressing concern. He shifted his gaze to the front of the house, the front door, and then back to the phone's camera. "Come on," he said.

Pastor Ed inched his way into the room and laid eyes on the thing that was Sella. She was lying upon white sheets stained in red with her head propped up against a pillow. Her eyes laid in hollowed sockets. She wore a loose gown. He turned his eyes onto her thickly tangled hair, her cracked and peeled lips, her bony shoulders, arms, and legs, her bloated stomach like that of a starving child, then back to her eyes. Her wild, fully dilated, bulging eyes filled with malevolence, piercing deep into his soul. She was watching him, analyzing him.

Pastor Ed walked to the foot of the bed. "Hello, Sella."

Yellowish saliva dripped from the corner of her mouth down to her chin. "Well, well, well," she gloated. "She sent for you." She crowed. "Why, you're not even a real exorcist. No. I have nothing to fear from you."

Pastor Ed's eyes narrowed. "I am a real exorcist. I've cast out more demons than you can count."

"Well then, if you're a real exorcist, you have nothing to fear from me."

"That's right, demon. I'm a servant of God, and God is more powerful than any demon."

She jerked up from the pillow. "Then you wouldn't mind unstrapping these straps." She pulled her arms, revealing her wrists, scratched and bleeding, heavily restrained by leather straps embossed and embroidered with Christian crosses.

Mike swung around to a flanking position to get a better view of both of them. Sella turned her head to him. "Oh, what's this?" She settled back into her pillow. "Are we live? Oh yes. Yes, we are."

"You don't mind, do you?" Pastor Ed asked.

"Not at all." She grinned. "But you'll find that I can't give an excellent performance while bound with these straps," she said, drooling a little from the corners of her mouth. "Now, John Henry Edwards, kindly undo these straps and I promise your audience a show to die for."

"You know my full name?"

"I know just about everything."

"Oh, really?"

"Yes indeed. In fact, I know your wife very well. Would you like to talk to her? Oh, wait… No, you can't because she's too busy sucking demon cock in hell."

Pastor Ed's face burned iron hot. He clenched his fists, his knuckles turning white.

"Oh, poor Edwards couldn't even save his own wife, so now he goes around trying to make up for it." Sella raised her head. "She wasn't saved, Edwards! She never accepted the Nazarene," she jeered.

Patricia emerged from behind Pastor Ed. Sella stopped laughing and stared deep into Patricia. Pastor Ed snapped his fingers at her. "Hey, eyes over here."

Sella ignored his hand gestures, eyes on his daughter. "Tell you what, Edwards. You give me your daughter and I'll make sure you go viral, like viral *viral.*"

Pastor Ed and Patricia looked at each other, and hairs prickled up on the back of his neck.

"Okay, that's it." Pastor Ed grabbed his Bible.

"You're going to exorcise me with my hands tied? Whoa! Some demon slayer."

Pastor Ed's nose flared. He grabbed the strap. "Joe, unstrap the other strap."

"No! Señor, no!" Sella's mother dashed to the bedside and vigorously yanked back the pastor's arm. "Very bad, señor! Don't do it."

Patricia grabbed her by the shoulders and pulled her away. "It's okay, we're professionals."

Pastor Ed gave Joe the nod to go ahead. They unstrapped Sella, and she slowly sat up while Pastor Ed made his way to the side of the bed, placing his Bible on Sella's head.

She smacked Pastor Ed's arm away. "Get your mutilated word of shit off of me."

Mutilated? "Okay, that does it." Pastor Ed gripped his Bible. "Place your arms together in front of yoooouuuuuuuu…"

Sella squeezed his scrotum in an iron grip. Pastor Ed screamed in excruciating pain, struggling to free himself. "Joe! Joe! Help!"

Joe and Patricia rushed forward, wrestling with her, all four of them a tangled pile of limbs. Sella howled and cackled until Pastor Ed lifted his fist and rammed her in the face, hitting fast and hard. "I command you back to hell."

Her skeletal face flinched to the side. Sella turned her ash-gray face toward him, eyes radiating with anger and hate. Releasing her grip, pulling her arms back, she struck hard.

Pastor Ed was airborne, timeless, his body suspended in mid-air. Patricia and Joe flanked his sides, moving in slow motion through the air, their bodies crashing against the wall. Patricia landed face-down, Joe landed sideways. Pastor Ed, still reeling from his pain, too hurt to move, took the fetal position. "Joe, pin her down," he groaned.

Joe got up and rushed Sella. She pulled a spring from the mattress and, raising it high, she swung it down, full force, slashing his arm. Crimson rain flowed from his open wound. He grasped his arm, mouth open, speechless, wide-eyed in terror, desperately trying to stop the bleeding. He fell back against the wall, blood dripping down his arm.

Sella wasted no time in crawling to the edge of the bed, looking down on Patricia, who was getting herself up. She jumped on Patricia's back, pinning her to the ground. Grasping Patricia's hair tight, she lifted her head, suspended it horizontally in mid-air, and slammed it savagely against the floor, again and again, before turning her around and clasping down on her neck.

Pastor Ed jumped on Sella's back and pulled as hard as he could. Patricia opened her mouth wide, yet no sound came out. Air was everywhere except in her lungs.

"Mike, help!" Pastor Ed shouted.

Mike dropped the phone and pulled on Sella. Both men couldn't move her a quarter of an inch away from Patricia.

"Let us in," Sella shouted in Patricia's face, yellowish saliva dripping from her cracked lips.

Under Sella's relentless attack, Patricia's face turned purple, and her eyes turned toward her father. His chest an airless vacuum, filled with icy-hot pins, he watched in horror as she closed her eyes, feeling her body go limp.

Pastor Ed felt dizzy, the ground tilting underneath him, a withering motion sickness rolling through him, the world spinning around him. Scooby barked from the sidewalk, his barks bouncing off the walls and ranging deep in Pastor Ed's ears.

Water drops splashed Pastor Ed's face. Sella fell to the ground and rolled around, crying, groaning, twitching, arching her back as water continued to pour down on her.

"In the name of the Father... And of the Son... And of the Holy Spirit."

"It burns! It burns!" Sella said in a guttural voice. "Stop it, priest bastard."

Walking past everyone, the priest picked up the phone and ended the live stream

* * *

The room was a battle scene: Joe pressing down on his bloody arm, the fear in his face raw; Sella on the ground, reeling; Pastor Ed hunched over, holding his daughter's head; Patricia coughing as air once more filled her lungs.

"When did you get here?" asked Pastor Ed.

"Just now. The kids let me in," said the priest, scouring the room. "Get those two to a hospital."

"We don't have a car," said Pastor Ed.

"I can drive." Sella's mom stepped forward. "But we won't all fit. Someone's going to have to stay behind with the children."

"Just lend us the car. We can use the GPS to get there," Pastor Ed said.

"Guys, I'm bleeding really bad," Joe groaned, blood dripping down his arm and forming a small puddle beneath his feet.

Distracted, the sound of the window sliding open caught everyone off guard.

Taking one step forward, extending his arm toward the window, the priest shouted, "No!" as Sella made her escape.

Turning toward the group, he said, "I'll go after Sella. The rest of you, get to the hospital."

"I'm coming with you." Pastor Ed got up and followed the priest through the living room, past Javier and Little Maria, who were standing by the front door, and out into the front yard, where Scooby was jumping around aggressively, barking down the street.

"St. Francis," the priest said, looking up at the sky as he ran past Scooby, "tell the dog to guide us to Sella."

Pastor Ed was amazed at this; no sooner than he said this, the dog darted past the priest, making his way down the block and coming to a complete stop at the corner, then looking back at the priest, impatiently waiting for him to catch up.

As he and the priest caught up to the dog, Pastor Ed turned his head and was relieved to see the car drive out of Sella's driveway. The dog sped off and the two men followed.

"We have to catch her," the priest said. "She's extremely dangerous."

Turning the corner, the two men ran a mile through another residential neighborhood. Huffing and puffing, Pastor Ed slowed down his pace. The priest turned his head back and said, "Come on. You must keep up." Finding it difficult to keep up, Pastor Ed nevertheless picked up the pace for about half a mile until his calves burned and he once again fell behind the priest, who was steadily keeping up with Scooby.

Pastor Ed hadn't yet caught his breath when a loud, blood-curdling scream came from ahead. He raised his head and sprinted toward the scream. A short distance ahead, Scooby barked at the base of a driveway, where two parked trucks blocked Pastor Ed's view. The priest caught up to the dog, turning his head toward the gap between the two trucks, and a cold moonlight of fear shone in his face.

Pastor Ed caught up to the priest, who was staring speechless at Sella, who stood between the two trucks, holding up a woman, whom she then slammed to the ground. The back of her head struck the concrete, making a loud fracturing sound like that of coconut cracking open. Adrenaline shot through Pastor Ed's veins as Sella rained blow after blow on the woman's head.

Pastor Ed and the priest made their way up the driveway between the two trucks. Sella leaped off the woman and crept toward them, a black curtain of hate over her morbid eyes. The priest pulled the holy water from his pocket, raised it in the air, and swung it, releasing the flask of holy water as she struck him across the side of the head.

Two thunderous claps rang as both the priest and Sella hit the concrete, Sella rocking back and forth, spewing profanities, the priest holding the side of his head with bloody hands. Blood was everywhere: his head, his shoulders, and the pavement, where a bloody shard of glass lay. Pastor Ed attended to the priest and saw a deep cut running across from his head to his neck and all the way to his back. He had five puncture points from the one blow Sella dealt him.

Scooby ceased barking and made his way to the priest, whimpering. Pastor Ed swung his arm around the priest and hoisted him up. Twisted fingers of fear clawed his guts, and Scooby began to growl at Sella slowly rising behind him. He pulled with all his strength. "Get up. Get up. Get up," he said frantically. All three of them ran to the house across the street, not knowing if Sella was hot on their trails. He banged repeatedly as hard as he could on the door. A man let them in before locking the door behind them.

Pastor Ed laid the priest on the couch. "Call 911."

The man ran into the kitchen and Scooby jumped on the couch and placed his head on the priest's lap, whimpering.

"I already did." The man returned from the kitchen with a clean towel and placed it on the priest's head. "The police should be here any moment."

Leaning toward the window and pulling the curtain to the side, Pastor Ed prayed that Sella had run off, but his hopes were dashed when loud animalistic grunting sounds came from across the street, followed by someone screaming at the top of their lungs. The screams came nonstop, indistinguishable between one person or two people, male or female. Neck stiffened, forearms strained, fingers twitching, Pastor Ed compulsively reached for the door, wavered, then in a flash unlocked it and ran out.

"No!" the priest yelled.

Pastor Ed scurried across the street seconds before a police car arrived. The police officer jumped out of his car. Pastor Ed pointed at the space between the two pickup trucks, then swung around one of them as the police officer, who was crouched down with his gun drawn, made his way up the driveway now filled with a stream of blood.

Pastor Ed walked up the side of the driveway slowly, coming around the front of the truck. The police officer aimed his gun down at a man laying on his back, staring up at the cop, then at Pastor Ed, eyes wide, frightened; it was more than fright, it was a freezing of the soul.

"Please help me," the man said.

Sella was laying sideways on the man's chest, holding him in place with her left arm, which was wrapped around his neck, and with her right arm she was doing something to his face, but Pastor Ed couldn't tell what. Turning his attention to the woman laying on the ground, Pastor Ed placed his fingers on her neck and, not feeling a pulse, he began administering CPR.

The police officer, meanwhile, walked around Sella, pointing his gun down at her, but from his angle he couldn't safely release a round. It was clear that the officer risked killing them both.

"Hold on. I'm going to tase her," the police officer said. Then, getting himself into position behind Sella, he pulled his taser gun out and pointed it at her back.

Pastor Ed continued administrating CPR on the woman and, expecting the sound of the taser gun to go off, he turned his head and noticed that the police officer had frozen. He shouted at him, "What are you waiting for? Tase her—" A cold terror gripped Pastor Ed. From his new angle he could see exactly what Sella was doing.

Sella had her right hand reaching into the man's mouth, pulling his cheek out like a fishhook as far as she could, biting into his flesh, ripping out pieces at a time, chewing, and swallowing them. The man's face had chunks of flesh missing, like an incomplete jigsaw puzzle.

Pastor Ed couldn't believe his eyes and, like the policeman, froze for a second or two, his hands resting on the woman's breastplate, which grew cold, her life slipping beneath his hands. *Oh God!... Oh God!... Don't die!... Don't you die on me!* He continued giving chest compressions, harder and faster, in a desperate attempt at reviving her.

The police officer, snapping out of it, fired his taser into Sella's back. She didn't even flinch. She was entirely focused on biting the man's face. The officer ran around to the other side in front of Sella. Getting himself into position, he planted his heels to the ground and kicked Sella square in the face, knocking her head off the man's face. But no sooner had she come off the man than she jumped back down, getting a deeper grip on him and plunging her mouth back into his face, tearing and chewing his flesh. Astonished, the officer wound up his boot and delivered a power kick right in her face, knocking her head back, but again she got right back down on the man's face and continued her cannibalistic onslaught.

In complete shock, the police officer looked back at Pastor Ed for a split second, who by now was completely exhausted, drenched in sweat, and out of breath. The woman was dead. She was dead, it was all his fault, and there was nothing he could do about it. But there, right there underneath one of the trucks, was the flask of holy water. Pastor Ed got up and, darting underneath the truck, he began to crawl his way to the flask.

At the same time, a K-9 unit arrived on the scene. Its officer made his way up the driveway and, seeing the situation, he ran back and released the K-9. The dog flew out of the car, ran up the driveway, and bit Sella on the arm, pulling her arm way from the victim. Sella swung her arm away from the dog, ripping her flesh, then repositioned herself and went back to biting the man's face. The dog grabbed another bite onto Sella's arm, yanking it back. Sella, once more unfazed, yanked her arm away from the dog's teeth, shredding the muscles of her arm, and continued her assault. Finally, the dog got one more bite of her arm, and this time the police officer timed it and kicked her in the face just as the dog pulled her away from the victim, sending Sella flying back and landing right next to the shard of glass.

Pastor Ed emerged from the side of the truck. Sella picked up the shard of glass and rushed toward the police officer. Pastor Ed swung the flask, releasing the holy water, striking Sella.

Boom! Boom!

Hands drawn together, finger on the trigger, the barrel smoking, the police officer released two rounds. The first bullet crunched her rib cage, while the second tore a hole through her heart. Her body hit the concrete, and Sella lay dead, eyes wide open, with a Cheshire grin on her face.

Chapter XXI

"This is CTTV Live News. I'm David Hunter."

"And I'm Margaret Thomas."

"In tonight's news, Colorado's very own Pastor Ed was arrested and later released in Juarez, Mexico, after a botched exorcism that resulted in three gruesome deaths."

"That's right, David. Pastor Ed, who's become famous for performing exorcisms online, was streaming his latest exorcism live to an audience of almost one million of his followers when the so-called possessed woman managed to escape, but not before nearly killing his daughter and seriously wounding one of his crew members."

"Well, it's not the first time Pastor Ed places his daughter's life in danger for the sake of garnering views. Just a month ago, he had her perform an exorcism on a convicted murderer."

"That's right, David. After fleeing from Pastor Ed's archaic ritual, the possessed woman attacked another woman in front of her house, beating her to death. The husband, who was out on a walk and returned to find his wife under brutal assault, was himself attacked in a vicious, gruesome manner."

"Cannibalism. You heard right. Police reports from Mexico explain that the woman severely beat the husband and then, get this, began to eat his face."

"Gives me the chills just thinking about it, David."

"Me too, Margaret. Here to help us explain how things got so out of control is Dr. Winston."

"Welcome to the show, Doctor."

"Thank you, David. I would like to say that it's a pleasure to be here, but given the reasons you'd understand why I can't."

"Indeed. Doctor, how did things escalate out of control?"

"Well, the thing is, we have a pastor who doesn't seem to understand mental illness, or who simply decides to ignore it."

"I believe he performed his first exorcism on a boy who was suffering from schizophrenia."

"Well, I'm not the boy's doctor, so I can't say for certain whether or not he was suffering from schizophrenia."

"Yes, but if you scroll down in the comment section of the video, you'll see comments from the boy's schoolmates saying that he had stopped taking his medication, and was known for taking serious illegal substances."

"From my professional point of view, all of these cases can be easily explained away, from a boy who refuses to take his medication, to a woman who refuses to take responsibility for her promiscuity, to men who are troubled by a violent and abusive past."

"Yes, but what do you make of his latest exorcism? In particular, the fact that the police report states she continued to bite the man's face even after she was threatened with a gun, tased, kicked in the face repeatedly, and the k-9 dog bit chunks of flesh off her arm? Wouldn't a person, even under the influence, retain a basic survival instinct to protect themselves?"

"Well, the toxicology report came back negative for flaka, bath salt, or any other illegal narcotic that could explain her behavior, so the only thing I can conclude is that she was suffering from psychosis."

"But her friends and coworkers all say that she didn't show any signs of mental illness. They're all baffled by what occurred."

"If she were still alive, I could diagnose her, but since she's no longer with us, this will remain a mystery."

"A tragic mystery."

Chapter XXII

Pastor Ed stood quiet behind the pulpit, looking down, uneasy, arms stretched out, hands gripping tightly on the wooden edges, his Bible open before him. He raised his head slowly, scanning the half-empty pews. His members stared at him, long-faced, quiet, awkwardly waiting for him to say something.

He cleared his throat. "Any questions or comments?"

A blonde woman with an A-line haircut in her mid-30s stood up.

Pastor Ed pointed in her direction. "State your name, please."

She tugged at her blouse and pulled strands of hair away from her face. "My name is Lisa, and I think I speak for everyone when I say that I am horrified and sadden by what occurred in Mexico." She looked around the congregation. "I also feel like I speak for everyone when I say that I thought twice about attending today's church service."

"Amen!" came the cries.

"Our church is constantly on the news," Lisa continued. "The kids at my son's school are calling him names, and everyone at work avoids me because they think I'm some kind of religious nut. And it's not just the news stations. Everyone on social media is posting the video of Pastor Ed's exorcism." An awkward silence filled the church. "I'm sorry, but I don't think I'll be attending this church any longer." She sat back down, and a man sitting close to her squeezed her shoulder and whispered in her ear. She turned toward him and smiled.

Norma stood up. Pastor Ed signaled to her.

"My name is Norma," she said, "and I understand that what happened in Mexico was tragic, but we shouldn't forget that Pastor Ed was only trying to help—"

"He was trying to get subscribers," someone yelled out.

Pastor Ed leaned into the microphone. "Please let her speak."

Norma nodded. "Look, everyone here knows Pastor Ed. You know how zealous he can be about spreading the gospels. I am here as a Bible-believing Christian because of him. I ask how many of you today are Christian because of him?"

Clapping.

Albert stood up. Pastor Ed's stomach rolled.

"My name is Albert," he said. "Most of you already know that I thought this was a bad idea from the beginning. I made my thoughts on the matter known. I always felt like Pastor Ed was turning this ministry into a reality TV show. The worst part of all this is that he made the Catholic priest look like the hero and made us look like religious freaks. I tell you that demon knew exactly what it was doing. They were probably working together. They set the whole thing up."

"Really? Albert!" Frank shouted from across the aisles. "Three people are dead, and all you can think about is how bad the Catholic Church is? Are you crazy? Everyone should be glad that the priest was there to save Patricia's life, not to mention Joe's. The whole thing could have been a lot worse."

Albert's face turned crimson red. "We should be glad?" He clenched his fist. "I'm telling you, the priest and the demon were in it together. They're part of the same church." He paused and turned his attention to Pastor Ed. "This is all his fault."

Here it comes.

"I move that Pastor Ed step down immediately."

The congregation erupted into a shouting match between yeses and nos.

John Barrett stood up, and the room fell silent. "My name is John Barrett. I was the pastor at this church before retiring. I want to start off by saying that I am saddened by the events that occurred in Mexico…"

Pastor Ed shook his head. *Get your mutilated word of shit off me.*

"…resignation is not warranted. I do not, for a split second, believe that Pastor Ed was acting for selfish reasons."

Mutilated?

"…I want to be clear about this. There will be no more exorcisms…"

Why did it call it mutilated?

"…then I too will move that Pastor Ed step down…"

What did it mean by mutilated?

"Pastor Ed? Pastor Ed?!" John was looking at him with a bewildered look. "Do you agree with what I said?"

"Yes. I agree."

* * *

Pastor Ed closed the door to his office and sat behind his desk, re-watching the video of Sella's exorcism, reliving the events — Patricia, Joe, the priest, the two victims, Sella — all of it running through his mind in stop-motion, a series a life-sized still photographs.

Nancy knocked on the door before opening it and leaning against it. "You should really go home. You know?"

Pastor Ed looked up at her. "I'll go home soon."

She put her head down. "How's she doing?"

"She's not talking to me."

"Have you tried calling her?"

"I call her every day, but she's not returning my phone calls. She just texts me back saying she's busy getting her apartment ready for the school year."

"It's always hard to see your kids go off to college." Her eyes narrowed. "She'll come around. You just have to give her space."

Pastor Ed took a deep breath. "I hope you're right."

"Leave it to God."

"I always do."

"Well, if you need anything, call me. Okay?"

"Will do."

She closed the door and left.

Pastor Ed turned his attention to the video for several minutes before navigating to his YouTube channel's settings page, hovering over the delete button. Noticing his subscriber count had dropped to 20 thousand, he pressed down on the mouse pad.

Seconds later, there was a knock on the door. "Go home, Nancy," he said.

There was another knock.

Pastor Ed looked up. "Norma?" He straightened himself up. "Come in."

Norma walked in holding a casserole. "I brought you some food."

Pastor Ed got up. "Oh, you shouldn't have." He took the casserole from her hands. "Smells good. What is it?"

She shrugged her shoulders. "Oh, just a little something my mother taught me." Her eyes met his. "I'm so sorry for what happened."

"I am too," he said.

Chapter xxiii

Before leaving for the day, Pastor Ed picked up the phone and dialed the priest in Mexico.

"You're going to have to excuse me, but I just can't call you 'Father.'"

"That's fine. You can just call me Jose or Mr. Ortiz. But if you don't mind me asking, why does it bother you?"

"Well, the Bible says not to call any man on earth 'father.'"

"So does that mean you don't call anyone 'teacher'?"

"I don't follow."

"You're referring to Matthew, chapter 23 verse 9, but verse 8 says not to call anyone a teacher. If verse 9 forbids us from calling any man on earth 'father,' then it's only logical that verse 8 forbids us from calling any man a teacher."

Pastor Ed thumbed through his Bible. He placed his finger on verse 8. *It says rabbi. Rabbi means teacher.*

The priest continued, "If we are not to call any man on earth 'father,' then why does St. Paul refer himself as a spiritual father in 1 Corinthians, chapter 4 verse 15? **'For though you have countless guides**

in Christ, you do not have many fathers. For I became your father in Christ Jesus through the gospel.' If Matthew 23:9 forbade calling any man 'father,' then St. Paul would be disobeying Christ's express command. But St. Paul's words in 1 Corinthians 4:15 are divinely inspired, and therefore can't contradict what Jesus said."

Pastor Ed mumbled 1 Corinthians 4:15 to himself.

"There are other examples where the word 'father' is used for people other than God in reverential ways. For example, Isaac is called 'father' in Romans 9:10. Jacob is called 'father' in John 4:12, David is called 'father' in Acts 4:25, the Jewish elders are referred to as fathers in Acts 7:2, and we can't forget about Abraham, who is called 'father' in Luke 16:24, Acts 7:2, Romans 4:12, and James 2:21."

The verses ran through Pastor Ed's mind. "I guess it is okay to call someone father."

"What else would you call your biological father?"

The two let out a laugh.

Pastor Ed leaned back on the couch, and after a brief pause asked, "How are you feeling?"

"I'm still in a lot of pain, but the doctor said I should be fine soon."

"Good. That's good." Pastor Ed ran his fingers through his hair. "There's something that Sella said to me that's been bothering me."

"Don't pay any attention to the demon. He's a liar and a trickster."

"No. It wasn't anything like that. It was more of a comment. When I placed my Bible on its forehead, it smacked my arm away and called my Bible 'mutilated.' Do you have any idea why the demon would call my Bible mutilated?"

The priest paused for a moment. "Do you have your Bible with you?"

"Yes, I have it in my hand right now."

"Can you tell me the number of books that are in your Bible?"

"Sixty-six."

"Then that's what the demon was referring to. During the Protestant Reformation, Martin Luther removed seven books from the Bible and declared them to be uninspired. The seven books that he removed from the Bible are Baruch, Tobit, Judith, Wisdom, Sirach, and 1 & 2

Maccabees. He also removed the book of Revelation and the book of James, but other Protestants convinced him to put them back in the New Testament."

Pastor Ed shook his head. "I was always told that the Catholics added those books to the Bible during the Council of Trent as a response to Luther."

"No, the Catholic Church reaffirmed those books as a response to the Protestant Reformation to make it clear to every Christian that they are divinely inspired. Those seven Old Testament books were in the Septuagint, which is the collection of Old Testament books the Apostles used."

There was a brief pause.

"Pastor Ed, can I ask you a simple question?"

"Sure, go ahead."

"How do you know that the books in your Bible are divinely inspired?"

"Because they're in the Bible."

"Okay, but who decided what books belong in the Bible?"

"Christians, in general."

"I'm afraid that's not true. Between the years 30 and 393, there was no official collection of New Testament writings. In fact, there were other writings that Christians considered inspired that are not in the New Testament today. For example, the Epistle of Barnabas, the Shepherd of Hermas, and the Acts of Paul. There were also several books that Christians back then didn't consider inspired that are in the New Testament today, like Second Peter, Jude, and the book of Revelation. So who made the final decision as to what books belong in the New Testament and which books don't?"

Pastor Ed drew a blank.

"Church historians all agree that we got the New Testament from the council of Hippo in 393 and the Council of Carthage in 397, both of which sent off their judgment to Rome for the pope's approval."

"The pope's approval? I don't know if I can trust that."

"Oh, I see," the priest said. "I don't have time to go over the pope right now. But let me ask you a simple question. What would you say is the pillar and foundation of the truth, the Bible or the Church?"

"That's easy, the Bible."

"Well, that's not what the Bible says. 1 Timothy 3:15 says that the pillar and foundation of the truth is the Church and, for the first 1500 years, there was only the Catholic Church. Protestant churches didn't exist before the Protestant Reformation in the year 1516. In fact, the Baptist Church didn't exist until John Smyth founded it 100 years later in 1612."

"I don't believe it."

"Go ahead. Look it up yourself."

Chapter XXIV

Walking through the university campus, surrounded by school buildings — science, business, engineering — Patricia looked down at her phone, pinching and zooming in on the screen's map, trying to decipher which direction to head to next. "Okay, where is this building?" she asked herself.

"Patricia!"

Patricia looked up and found a blonde girl with a round face and dark brown eyes, wearing a red headband and a pink t-shirt, prancing toward her.

"Hey, Rebecca," Patricia said.

"Hey, do you know where the—"

"I don't know where anything is," Patricia countered. "I'm just as lost as you."

"Gosh, this place is so big," she said, catching her breath.

"Yup."

"How are things with you and your dad? Mom says you guys aren't talking."

"Peachy."

"Come on, he's your dad."

"And?"

"Aaaannd. You should talk to him. He needs you right now. Things got serious at church. They were actually calling for him to step down."

"God, I wish."

"You can't be serious."

"I am serious."

"Patricia!"

"I'm serious, Rebecca. Life was so much better when he wasn't a religious zealot."

"You can't say that. Mom said he was drinking a lot after your mom's accident. She said the gospel saved him."

"The gospel did nothing a psychiatrist and a couple of AA meetings wouldn't have done for him. If Barrett would have minded his own business, Dad wouldn't have turned into an over-zealous, over-protective jerk."

"He's not a jerk, and you've always done whatever you wanted to do."

"He's not a jerk? He totally used me. All he's ever cared about is becoming a famous televangelist. And he is too overprotective. He never let me go out unless someone from church accompanied me. I couldn't have a boyfriend because everyone knew me as the pastor's daughter, and the second I started dating someone, everyone at church knew about it."

"It couldn't have been that bad."

"Look, I'm late for class. I'll talk to you later." Patricia walked away.

"Hey! Can I come over to your apartment? Maybe we can do our homework together?"

"It's the first day of class. They never hand out homework on the first day," Patricia yelled back.

"Oh, Okay!"

* * *

Patricia was late, and tardiness beckoned her forward. Pacing through the hallway, scanning the door signs, she paused before door A-02. Gripping the doorknob, she slowly opened it, the professor's muffled voice becoming clearer. He was going over the syllabus when she stepped inside. The whiteboard had *Intro to Criminal Justice* written in blue marker. Looking for a place to sit, she scouted the room. Everyone's eyes were on her. Patricia paused and glanced at the professor, who stopped the lecture and stared at her too.

Coming in late must be a big deal in college.

The awkward silence was broken when one student yelled, "It's the teenage exorcist, everyone!"

The room erupted in laughter. Patricia was dumbfounded. She turned toward the professor, and her heart dropped. He was laughing too. She lowered her head and sank into the first available seat.

What the hell?

"Okay, everyone, settle down," the professor said.

After a brief moment, the class fell silent.

"Before your heads spin," he chuckled, and the students followed suit.

Patricia glared at the professor, and after a few seconds he turned toward her, raising his hands up. "I'm kidding."

Chapter XXV

The following week, the students marched disorderly across campus, and amongst them was Patricia, sitting on a bench, having lunch, watching them scurrying to-and-fro, the wind blowing her hair across her face. She took the last few bites of her cold sandwich, then crumpled up the wrapping paper and tossed it into the bin. Picking up her book bag, she headed to her next class.

"Hey, Exorcist girl!"

Patricia's body tensed up. She pivoted and saw a tall guy with brownish wavy hair, thick eyebrows, and a square jaw approaching her.

"Hey," he said.

"What did you call me?"

"Exorcist girl. I didn't know what else to call you."

"Don't call me that."

"Oh, sorry." He rubbed the back of his neck. "My name is Jesse. What's your name?"

"Patricia."

"Hi, Patricia."

Patricia crossed her arms. "What do you want?"

He shifted his body. "I just wanted to invite you to our frat party this Friday."

Patricia focused her sights on the four guys standing ten feet behind him, all wearing the same colored blazers and ties, staring at them, childishly laughing.

"Why are they laughing?"

He turned his head toward them. "Oh, they thought it was a bad idea to invite you."

"Why?"

"Because, you know?" He shrugged. "You're a pastor's kid. They think you're too prudish to come."

Patricia tapped her foot. "Oh yeah?"

"Uh, yeah, I told them that—"

"Okay, I'll go."

* * *

Small groups of students lingered outside as Patricia and Rebecca arrived at the party. Strobe lights pulsated in sync with the music. Patricia could feel their stares as they made their way in. The place smelled of beer, marijuana, and hairspray. Cans, shooters, and shots lined the counter tops. There were skimpily dressed girls bunched up together, posing and taking selfies, couples making out on the couch, and groups of students playing drinking games around the tables. Patricia tried to strike up conversations with other girls, but they avoided her, and with the exception of the two guys that tried to hit on Rebecca, no one approached them.

"Maybe he had an emergency," Rebecca said.

Patricia took another sip of her drink. It was her fifth one, and the effects were taking place. "Maybe," she said.

"Do you want to leave?" Rebecca asked.

Patricia looked around. "No," she responded, lifting her cup and shaking the ice. "I'm going to get another one."

Rebecca grabbed her by the arm. "Hey, you've had enough," she said.

"Relax, Rebecca."

"I don't want to relax, and you should stop drinking. You've had too much already."

Patricia made a smacking sound with her mouth. "If you don't want to—"

"If I don't want to what?"

Patricia perked up. "There he is. He's coming this way."

"Hey, Patricia," Jesse said.

Patricia smiled. "Much better."

"Yeah, sorry about that."

"Sorry about what?" Rebecca asked.

"He called me 'Exorcist girl.'"

Jesse looked at Rebecca. "I'm Jesse."

"Hi. I'm Rebecca. Nice to meet you."

"She's my friend from church," Patricia interjected.

"Oh, cool." He turned to Patricia. "So what's it like growing up as a pastor's kid?"

"Oh God. It sucked. You have to live up to everyone's expectations of a perfect little girl, and God forbid you sin."

"It wasn't that bad," Rebecca said.

"She wouldn't know. She's not a pastor's kid. She's my dad's assistant's daughter."

"Oh, okay. Cool."

A flush crept across Rebecca's cheeks. "Yeah. Cool," she mumbled.

Jesse took a sip from his cup. "I saw that video that went viral. The one you guys recorded in Mexico. It looked like you got hurt pretty bad."

Patricia shook her head. "I seriously thought I was going to die."

Rebecca raised her cup. "She prefers not to talk about it."

"Oh, okay. Yeah, I get it." He pointed at Rebecca's cup. "What are you drinking?"

"Coke."

"Coke?" He smirked, raising an eyebrow. "I don't know if I can trust someone who doesn't drink."

"Oh, you can't," Patricia said, slurring her words. "She'll totally rat you out. She's ratted me out to her mom a bunch of times."

"Your dad's assistant?"

"Yeah, and her mom's just like her. She rats me out to my dad." She leaned over to him. "You can't trust her."

"Patricia!" Rebecca protested.

Patricia shrugged.

Jesse's mouth dropped.

Rebecca turned to Jesse. "She's usually not like this. She's just had a little too much to drink."

"She's being…ridicu-lush… I'm not that drunk…"

Jesse placed his hand on Patricia's lower back. "Hey, why don't you and I go somewhere private and talk?"

Patricia leaned toward him. "Yea, I'd like that."

"Uh, no," Rebecca said, pulling Patricia toward her. "She's had too much to drink."

"See what I mean?" Patricia yanked her arm away. "She's a narc."

Rebecca's mouth dropped.

"Go home, Rebecca. I don't need you to be my babysitter." She turned to Jesse. "Let's go."

He grabbed her hand and guided her to one of the rooms.

Chapter XXVII

The following day, Pastor Ed spent his afternoon in his office reading *Where We Got the Bible,* by Henry G. Graham, and was about to read *Why Catholic Bibles Are Bigger,* by Gary Michuta, when Nancy walked up to his door. "Okay, I'm heading out. Did you need anything before I leave?"

He glanced at the clock and was surprised to find that it was time to go home. "No. Have fun."

"Will do."

She grabbed her bag and walked out of the office.

Seconds later, he received a text message from Norma: *Are we still on for tonight?*

He replied: *I'm wrapping things up so, how's about we meet up in an hour?*

Her reply came quick: *Okay, see you then.*

Pastor Ed's phone rang. Glancing at the screen, he tapped the answer button before placing it to his ear.

"Hello?"

"Hello, Pastor Ed?"

"Hello, Father, how are things with Sella's family?"

"They're still in mourning. The kids are adjusting to living with their grandmother and not having their mother around anymore. Looks like their father isn't interested in raising them, which is sad."

"I just feel terrible."

"It's not your fault, Pastor Ed, you were just trying to help. What happened to Sella was completely the demon's doing. Which is why I'm calling you."

"Really?"

"Yes. You know, Pastor Ed, all this time, there's one thing that's been bothering me."

"What's that?"

"Why did Sella attack that couple? And why was she so focused on executing such a brutal murder?"

"You know, now that you mention it, it's been bothering me too. We must have run past a half-dozen people that night chasing her. Why did she specifically target this couple?"

"Exactly. So I did some investigating, and it turns out that the man she killed was an undercover Mexican federal agent."

"A *federali*?"

"Yes, he and his wife were both agents."

"Wait, why would the demon attack two federal agents?"

"That's the interesting part. It turns out that the couple were investigating the occult and its ties to the cartels."

"The cartels?" Pastor Ed paused for a moment. "That's right. Sella's mother mentioned something about a witch."

"Right. The witch that was responsible for Sella's possession was under investigation. My guess is that the demon exacted revenge, and it used Sella to perform the horrific act."

Pastor Ed leaned back in his chair, running his hands through his hair, dumbstruck.

"Dear Lord." Pausing to reflect, he leaned forward in his chair, placing his elbows on the table. "Wait, does this mean that any person that becomes possessed can be made to commit murder?"

"It depends. Contrary to popular belief, when a person becomes possessed, the person's free will isn't removed, but instead severely compromised by the emotional, mental, physical, and spiritual attacks, allowing the demon to temporarily seize control of the person's actions. However, if the person remains under demonic possession for too long without receiving help from the church, then they enter what is called 'complete possession.' This is where the person's free will becomes nonexistent, at which point the demon takes complete control of a person's body. In these cases, the person becomes constantly possessed, and is like a demon walking the earth."

Ice shivered down Pastor Ed's back. "Is that what happened to Sella?"

"Yes, we believe that's what happened to Sella."

Pastor Ed shook his head. "No, wait. That doesn't make any sense. Her mother told us that Sella first became possessed about a month before we got there. I don't think a month qualifies as a long time."

"That's because most cases of possession are what we call 'involuntary possession.' It comes about when a person unknowingly invites a demon in, say by playing the Ouija board or tarot cards. Basically, any attempt at contacting the dead or divination opens the person up to the possibility of demonic possession. In these cases, the demon has to work hard in a long, dragged-out battle between the demon and the victim to achieve complete possession, and in most cases it never achieves it. Unlike most cases where the person's intentions were never to invite a demon into their life, Sella actively sought the help of demons by engaging in witchcraft, and further sealed her fate when she engaged in satanic rituals and demonic worship."

Pastor Ed let out a slow, disbelieving shake of the head. The events in Juarez were running through his mind. Sweat formed on his forehead, and he leaned back into his chair, which creaked beneath him, and pressed his hands on his abdomen.

"Thank you for keeping me informed, Father, and please let me know if you learn anything else."

"Woooah, hold on there, Pastor Ed. Not so quick."

"Look, Father, no offense, but I'm not so sure I want to talk about exorcisms anymore."

"Let's talk theology then."

CHAPTER XXVII

Pastor Ed let out short breaths, feeling lighter, more relaxed. "Yeah, sure. Let's do that. What exactly do you want to talk about?"

"Well, last time we spoke, you mentioned something about not believing in the pope's authority. Do you mind if I ask why?"

"Well, there's no biblical support for the pope. In fact, he's never mentioned in the Bible."

"The pope is most definitely in the Bible."

"Where? I've read the Bible several times and have never come across the word 'pope.'"

"Well, yes, that's true. The word 'pope' isn't in the Bible. Neither is the word 'Trinity,' but that doesn't mean that the Trinity isn't true."

Pastor Ed rubbed his chin. "Even so, I don't see anything remotely resembling the pope in the Bible."

"What about Matthew 16:18? There we see Jesus establishing his church and the papacy when he changed Simon's name to Peter, which means rock. Jesus said: '**And I tell you, you are Peter (which means rock), and on this rock I will build my church, and the gates of hell shall not prevail against it. I will give you the keys of the kingdom**

of heaven, and whatever you bind on earth shall be bound in heaven, and whatever you loose on earth shall be loosed in heaven.' Here we can see that Jesus made Peter the rock on which he would build his church. Peter, as you know, was the first pope."

"Peter doesn't mean rock, it means small pebble. The New Testament was written in Greek, and there Jesus used the word Petra for Peter, which means small pebble in Greek. What Jesus is saying is that Peter is a small pebble, but that he is going to build his church on himself. He's referring to himself as the rock, not Peter. If Jesus meant for Peter to be the rock, then he would have changed his name to Petros, not Petra."

"Pastor Ed, while in Mexico, you spoke to me in Spanish. Can you tell me how to say Peter in Spanish?"

"Pedro."

"And would you call someone by that name Pedra?"

"No, of course not. It would be an insult."

"Exactly. Petra is a feminine word. Jesus could not have called Simon 'Petra' because he is a man. It's like calling Stephen 'Stephanie.' Protestant scholars agree Jesus was referring to Peter as the rock on which he would build his church. Protestant scholars like J.N.D. Kelly and D.A. Carson."

"D.A. Carson said that?"

"He wrote about it in a book called *The Expositor's Bible Commentary*. In fact, the New Testament makes it unquestionable that Jesus was referring to Peter as the rock because John 1:42 explains that the Aramaic equivalent of the Greek word *petros* is *cephas*, which means rock. John quotes Jesus as saying to Simon, **'You shall be called Cephas'** and then St. John interjects, **'which means Peter.'** Pastor Ed, did Jesus speak Greek or Aramaic?"

"Aramaic."

"Which means?"

"He would have said you are Cephas and on this Cephas I will build my church."

"Exactly! In fact, Petros doesn't mean small pebble in Greek, it means rock. You will, however, find it used as a small pebble, but this is only confined to earlier Ancient Greek and only within poetry."

"Okay, well, maybe Jesus founded his church on Peter, so what?"

"Don't forget that he also gave him the keys to the Kingdom of Heaven and the power to bind and loose both heaven and earth. The other Apostles who witnessed this would have instantly known that Jesus was quoting scripture."

"What scripture?"

"Isaiah 22:20, where God gives Eliakim the keys to David's kingdom and entrusts its government in his hands. He says that he will be a father to the inhabitants of both Jerusalem and the house of Judah. God also says that whatever doors he opens, none shall shut, and whatever doors he shuts, none shall open. Just like when Jesus gave Peter the keys to his kingdom, he said to him whatever you bind on earth shall be bound in heaven and what you loose on earth shall be loosed in heaven. Notice the similarities in the wording that Jesus and Isaiah use."

"That just tells me that Peter and Eliakim had been entrusted with special authority. It says nothing about the pope today having that kind of power."

"Jesus is the Davidic king, correct?"

"Yes, that's correct," Pastor Ed responded. "He's the eternal Davidic king, and his kingdom will know no end."

"Right, and all throughout the Davidic kingdom there was a group of ministers that administered the kingdom on behalf of the king. One of these ministers was placed as the overseer, or prime minister, above the rest. Everyone knew who he was because he carried a big visible key. The key that Isaiah in verse 22:20 was referring to. When the king was away, the prime minister was in charge. When this prime minister died, the key did not go back to the king, it was handed down to another minister. Just like we see today with the popes. When one pope dies, another takes his place, just like the New Testament says in Acts 1:20. After the Apostle Judas hanged himself for betraying Jesus, the rest of the Apostles replaced him with Matthias. They quoted scripture and said, **'let another take his office.'** Here we see the Apostles held offices and when an Apostle dies, another had to take his office. Which means?"

"Which means that when Peter died, another had to take his office."

"That's right. Pope Francis replaced Pope Benedict XVI, who in turn replaced Pope John Paul II, and on and on all the way back to Pope Cletus, Pope Linus, and Pope Peter himself, the first pope, the one whom Jesus built his church on."

There was an odd silence in Pastor Ed's office.

Pastor Ed shook his head. "I don't know, Father Ortiz. I just don't see a need for a pope when we have the Bible."

"You're talking about *Sola Scriptura*, the belief that the only thing a Christian needs is the Bible, correct?"

"Not just the only thing we need, but the belief that the Bible has authority, and not a church or a pope."

"Right, but can you tell me where in the Bible it says that?"

"Well, much like you pointed out with the pope, you're not going to find it taught explicitly in the Bible, but we can derive from what the Bible says that it is true."

"Okay, I'm willing to accept that. Can you show me how we can derive *Sola Scriptura* from the Bible?"

Pastor Ed smiled. "Absolutely. 1 Timothy 3:16 says that '**all scripture is inspired by God and profitable for teaching, for reproof, for correction, and for training in righteousness, that the man of God may be complete, equipped for every good work.**' As you can see, the New Testament makes it clear that scripture is sufficient. It's all we need."

"Sufficient?"

"Yes, sufficient."

"I don't see the word 'sufficient' there. I see the word 'profitable,' but I don't see the word 'sufficient.'"

Pastor Ed reread the passage. "But that's clearly the meaning of the text."

"No, I don't think so, but perhaps an analogy would help. If I were to tell you that my college math book is profitable for teaching, for reproof, for correction, and for training in mathematics, does that mean that it's the only thing we need for teaching, for reproof, for correction, and for training in mathematics?"

There was a long pause. "No, I guess it wouldn't."

"Likewise, studying a handbook on how to be a police officer is profitable to becoming a complete, thoroughly equipped police officer. But there's a lot of other stuff we'd also need to undergo. For example, firearm training, physical training, and real-world experience. Profitable doesn't equal sufficient."

"I have to tell you, Father, I still see the word complete and read it to mean that it's sufficient."

"That doesn't follow. Let's take a collector, for example. The collector might say that he needs a certain piece to complete his collection, but no one would take that to mean that the one piece by itself results in a complete collection, because we understand that other pieces are also needed to make the collection complete. Likewise, the scriptures may lead to the end of Christian perfection, but that doesn't mean that the Bible alone is sufficient to achieve that end."

"Okay, Father. The fact remains that I don't need anyone to explain the faith to me. All I need is the scriptures. I can simply read the Word of God."

"The New Testament says otherwise, Pastor Ed."

"Where? Where does the New Testament say otherwise?"

"Acts, Chapter 8 verses 26 through 40 tells us that the evangelist Phillip ran into an Ethiopian eunuch who was reading scripture. Phillip asked him if he understood what he was reading. The Ethiopian eunuch answered him by saying, 'How can I unless someone explains it to me?' Furthermore, 2 Peter 3:16 says that there are things in Paul's letters that are hard to understand, which the ignorant and unstable twist to their own destruction, as they do other scriptures. The Bible is the inspired Word of God, but to say that it's all we need or that it's our only authority goes against the Bible."

Pastor Ed leaned back in his chair, glancing at the time. "Oh, no! I'm late for my date."

Chapter xxviii

The following Monday morning, on her way to her criminal justice class, Patricia was passing through the crowded campus courtyard when she noticed a group of guys standing in a horseshoe formation. The guy at the center looked like Jesse, but with his back toward her and so many students obstructing her view, she wasn't sure it was him. They hadn't spoken since the night of the party, and Patricia wondered if she should go say hi.

What the hell, what's the worst that could happen?

Adjusting the strap of her book bag, she aimed her steps toward the group, drawing closer to them. She could see that, indeed, it was Jesse and his friends. They were all smiling.

Perfect. I'm catching him at a good time.

Patricia came within arm's reach of the group.

"I can't believe you banged the exorcist girl," one of them commented.

"The entire time I was like, if this chick's head spins around, I'm out of here," Jesse said, breaking out in uncontrollable laughter.

Her blood boiled and her body tensed up. "You jerk!"

Jesse's friends broke their horseshoe formation. "Oh snap," one of them cried out.

Patricia grinded her teeth. "You're such an asshole!"

He stared at her wide-eyed. "Hey, I was only kidding."

Her hand landed hard across his face. "No you weren't." She continued her assault.

Trying to catch her arms, retreating, Jesse said, "Get off me."

One of his friends swung his arm around Patricia's waist and pulled her back. "Hey, back off, he was only joking."

A bunch of students pointed their cell phones at her. Jesse was hunched over with his hands over his face.

"Is that the exorcist girl?" someone asked.

"I'm not an exorcist," she shot back. "Stop calling me that."

Jesse straightened up and turned toward her. His friends gasped. He had deep scratch marks running across his face.

"She's crazy," someone commented.

Patricia's eyes burned. "I'm not crazy!" She picked up her book bag and headed back to her apartment. No way was she going to her criminal justice class after that.

* * *

Patricia's one-bedroom apartment rested on the second floor. Her living room was small, but her bedroom was even smaller, a queen-sized bed and computer desk taking up most of the space. She sat in front of her computer screen in her warm pajamas, focusing on her class assignment. Although most nights in Colorado are chilly, she didn't expect it to be this cold, but she took advantage of it by making herself a warm cup of hot chocolate. Taking small sips of her hot drink, she worked leisurely on her paper when she noticed tapping sounds coming from the walls. She did her best to ignore it, thinking they'd stop soon. After finishing her drink, she went into the kitchen to wash her empty mug. The tapping sounds seemed to follow her there. Turning her head around, she wondered where the sounds were coming from.

It's coming from the neighbor.

She put her cup away and went into the bedroom. She propped her pillows up and laid back on them.

Argggh! Enough already.

Patricia grabbed her phone and browsed her social media page. She laughed at a couple short videos, and after a while she seemed to not notice the tapping sounds anymore and felt drowsy. Until she came across the video. *Exorcist girl says she's not crazy. What do you think?* It had over a hundred comments.

Great! Just what I needed.

She thought about reading the comments, but decided it was best to put it behind her.

I'm going to have to keep a low profile until people forget about me.

She put her phone down and laid on her side. Doing her best to ignore the tapping sounds, she closed her eyes, but after thirty minutes, she decided she'd had enough. She put tennis shoes on and walked out of the apartment.

Odd, it's not as cold outside.

She took a couple steps down the hall and banged on the neighbor's door. There was no answer.

They must have gotten the message.

She pivoted and went back to her apartment. Apparently the neighbors didn't get the message, because shortly after getting beneath the covers, there came three hard knocks on her wall.

Today is not the day to mess with me.

She marched out and banged hard on her neighbor's door.

A door opened behind her. "No one's there."

Patricia turned around. A young chubby guy stuck his head out of the apartment from across.

"I can hear them from my room," she said.

"That's not possible. They moved out over the summer," he said.

"Then there's got to be someone in there."

"Call the maintenance guy. He lives one complex over."

"Good idea," she said. "Do you have his number?"

"I think the number is in the pamphlet they gave you when you moved in."

She nodded and went back to her room.

* * *

Thirty minutes later, the maintenance guy showed up at the door. "You call?"

"Yes, the people next door are knocking on the walls and they're not letting me sleep."

He headed over to the other neighbor's door.

"No, not that apartment. The other one."

He gave her a bewildered look. "That one's vacant."

"Well, there's someone in there. I can hear them tapping on the walls."

He grunted and opened the door to the vacated room. He walked inside, and after a minute or two he came back out. "It's empty."

"Did you hear anything?"

"No, is it still happening?"

"Come check for yourself," she said.

He stepped inside. "Damn, it's cold in here," he said. He looked around and headed toward the wall. "You probably got rats."

"Gross."

He raised his eyebrow. "The little critters sure have rhythm," he said. "I'll put an order in to have them removed."

"Can you fix my A.C. while you're at it?"

"I'll have the A.C. guy look into it."

Chapter xxix

The following week, after his usual walk to the coffee shop, Pastor Ed returned to his office with a freshly brewed cup of coffee. On his desk sat a small pile of books he'd ordered over the internet: *The Early Church Was the Catholic Church*, by Joe Heschmeyer, *Why We're Catholic*, by Trent Horn, and *Twisted Unto Destruction*, by Donald J. Johnson. Leaning back in his chair, having finished reading *Pope Peter*, by Joe Heschmeyer, he put the book down and reflected on it, his muscles tensing up right before throwing the book across the room.

The book's violent crash spooked Nancy. "Everything okay?"

Pastor Ed rubbed his face. "Yes, everything is fine." *Not really.*

"Okay," she said. "I'm leaving early today because Rebecca is spending the weekend with us."

"Oh, that's nice," he said. "Tell her I said hi."

"Will do." She gathered her stuff and stood by his office door. "It's Friday," she said. "Are you and Norma doing anything special?"

"She's making dinner for us."

"That's nice." She rubbed her elbow. "Okay. Well, I'll see you tomorrow."

"Okay, bye."

Pastor Ed looked up, wondering if he was being tested. He reflected on Job and how his friends believed he was being punished because he had committed a sin. They implored him to confess his sin. Pastor Ed snapped his fingers. *That's it!* He dialed the priest.

"Hello?" the priest answered.

"Hello, Father Ortiz. Am I catching you at a bad time?"

"Not at all. I just finished giving mass."

"You have mass on Fridays?"

"We hold mass every day. It's important that our parishioners have access to communion every day, and eat the new manna from heaven, which is the body of Christ, the lamb that takes away our sins. Which reminds me, Pastor Ed. I've been meaning to ask you—"

"Hold that thought, Father Ortiz, because I actually have a question for you this time."

"A question for me? Alright then. Go ahead."

"The reason I'm calling is that I've been thinking about the differences between our religions, and one thing just stuck out to me."

"What's that?"

"Forgiveness of sin," Pastor Ed said. "In Catholicism, a person is told to confess their sins to a priest, whereas in my religion we simply tell the person to confess their sins to Jesus."

"Where in the New Testament does it say to do that?"

"What?" The question caught Pastor Ed off-guard.

"Where in the New Testament does it say to confess your sins to Jesus?"

Pastor Ed drew a blank. "Well, only Jesus can forgive sin."

"I'm going to have to repeat my question. Where does it say that in the New Testament?"

Again, the question caught him off-guard. "Well, where does it say that men can forgive sins?"

"John 20:21," came the quick reply. "Jesus said to his apostles, **'Peace be with you. As the Father has sent me, even so I am sending you. And when he had said this, he breathed on them and said to them, Receive the Holy Spirit. If you forgive the sins of any, they are**

forgiven them; if you withhold forgiveness from any, it is withheld.'"

Opening his Bible and quickly navigating to John 20:21, Pastor Ed ran his finger across the verse.

"We also see this in Matthew, Chapter 1 verses 1 through 9, where Jesus cured a paralyzed man and forgave his sins. The Bible says that the people marveled and glorified God for giving the power to forgive sins to men." The priest continued, "Jesus delegated his authority to forgive and retain sin to his church. However, the Catholic Church teaches that priests can't forgive sin by their own authority, but only through the authority invested in them by our Lord and Savior, Jesus Christ."

"I must have read through those verses a hundred times. I can't believe I'm just noticing the significance of them."

"Can I ask my question now?" asked the priest.

"Sure, go on."

"Pastor Ed, you believe that the bread that is given during communion is merely a symbol, correct?"

"Yes. That's right. We reject the idea that the bread really becomes the body of Christ."

"Well, the Bible tells us in the gospel of John, chapter 6, that the day after Jesus multiplied the loaves and fish, his followers demanded more food. Jesus said that he would give them bread that would sustain them forever. They clamored, 'Lord, give us this bread.' He said to them, 'The bread that I give is my body, for my body is food indeed.' To which they recoiled and asked, 'How can this man give us his flesh to eat?' Jesus then told them that his flesh was food indeed and that unless they eat the flesh of the son of man, they would not have everlasting life. The Bible then says that they all left him and stopped believing in him. In fact, the Bible tells us that even the Apostles murmured amongst themselves, to which the Lord turned to them and asked, 'Will you leave me too?' Fortunately, Peter replied, 'Lord, to whom shall we go? You have the words of eternal life; and we have believed, and have come to know, that you are the Holy One of God.'"

"But Jesus was only speaking symbolically," said Pastor Ed. "The bread that he was referring to was his words, not his actual flesh."

"So you're saying that his followers misunderstood him?"

"Yes, that's exactly what I'm saying, because the people took him to mean it literally, but Christ meant it symbolically. They failed to understand him and so they stopped believing in him."

"But if they stopped believing in him because of a misunderstanding, then at that point, Jesus had a moral obligation to stop them from leaving and explain their misunderstanding. However, he doesn't do that. He simply lets them walk away."

"Okay," said Pastor Ed, "but there are instances when the people misunderstand Jesus and he doesn't correct them. For example, when he told the Jews that if they tore down the temple, he would raise it in three days. The people thought he was referring to the temple building, but the Bible tells us he was referring to his body."

"That's true, but the Bible clarifies the misunderstanding. In all cases, when anyone misunderstands Jesus, either Jesus himself clarifies the misunderstanding or the Bible clarifies what Jesus meant. However, this would be the only instance in the entire gospel where both Jesus and the Bible fail to clarify the misunderstanding."

Pastor Ed rubbed the back of his neck.

"Paul tells us in 1 Corinthians, chapter 11 verse 24, that whoever eats and drinks of the bread and wine in an unworthy manner will be guilty of profaning the body and blood of the Lord. If the bread and wine are just symbols, then why does Paul tell the Corinthians that the reason some of them are sick and dying is because they are partaking of the bread and wine in an unworthy manner? In the Catholic Church, we are not allowed to partake of the bread or wine unless we are in a state of grace. Is that the case in your church?"

"No, it's not."

"If you'd like to learn more on the subject, Pastor Ed, I recommend this wonderful book by Brant Pitre. It's called *Jesus and the Jewish Roots of the Eucharist: Unlocking the Secrets of the Last Supper.*"

* * *

Norma placed two plates of sopes on the kitchen table. Pastor

Ed had never even heard of sopes, although his deceased wife was Hispanic. He was eager to try them out. He sat looking down at his plate. On it was a small round disk made of corn that almost resembled a squished bowl. It held beef, beans, sour cream, and white crumbly cheese called *queso fresco*, topped off with red salsa.

"Looks good," he said.

"I hope you like it," Norma said.

"What's the difference between sopes and poppusas?"

"I've never had poppusas, so I wouldn't know," she replied.

Pastor Ed took a bite. His taste buds lit up. "Wow, that's really good."

Norma smiled and took a bite of hers.

He couldn't help but think about his conversations with Father Ortiz earlier that day.

"What's the matter? Are you still thinking about what happened in Mexico?"

"Yes, but it's not just that."

"What else is it?"

"It's Father Ortiz. I have to admit, he's been able to answer all of my objections to Catholicism. I've never met a Catholic that could explain his faith before."

"That's because the mass is different from church services."

"What do you mean? Do they not preach at mass on the Bible?"

"The priest goes over New and Old Testament verses, but not like we do at our church."

"That's a pity," he said, wiping sour cream off his face. "You know, I didn't know that for the first 1,500 years, everyone believed that the bread and wine truly became the body and blood of Christ. I had no clue that it was until the Protestant Reformation that all changed."

Norma raised an eyebrow, a concerned look on her face.

"What?"

"Are you thinking of becoming Catholic?"

"What!? No!"

"Good, because I like our church. I'm not going back to the Catholic Church."

"Oh, yeah, for sure. I would never pray to Mary. That's crazy!"

Norma smiled and nodded.

Pastor Ed took another bite of his sopes when a text notification came in. Pastor Ed picked the phone up to read the message: *Pastor Ed, this is Mrs. Barrett. Please call back.*

Pastor Ed returned the call. "Hello, Mrs. Barrett. Is everything okay?"

"I'm afraid not, Pastor Ed," she said with a cracked voice. "John suffered a stroke today and passed away."

Chapter XXX

The maintenance guy must have been incompetent, because the tapping sounds continued to torment Patricia to no end. Every time she called the maintenance guy over, the sounds would stop, causing him to look at her quizzically.

"Arrg! I'm not crazy," she'd say.

"There are no more mice. My traps caught them all. See, the traps are empty," he'd say, holding up empty mouse traps.

"You said that it was rats."

"No rats. Just mice."

"Use better bait."

He'd grudgingly replace the traps.

"Maybe it's the pipes."

"No, the plumber says the pipes are fine."

"Tell him to check again."

He'd nod, but of course, the plumber never showed up.

At school, Patricia kept to herself, maintaining a low profile, avoiding Jesse and everyone else, including Rebecca, whom she hadn't heard from since the night of the party, which was fine with her.

Patricia sat in the third row of class behind a pretty girl with brunette wavy hair. It was a small classroom, about four rows deep, with no more than twenty students attending the class. The professor was a middle-aged, kind woman, wearing the type of glasses you see in a 1960s yearbook. She was going over *The Epic of Gilgamesh*, an extremely ancient, not to mention boring, story about some guy who couldn't deal with the fact that he was mortal, or something like that. Patricia stopped paying attention and instead shifted her gaze to the back of the head of the girl in front of her, admiring her hair for a moment before turning her attention out the window.

Blinking twice, she couldn't understand why it was so bright outside, and it seemed to get brighter by the second. The colors were much more vivid than normal. They seemed to sing to her. She could taste the colors in her mouth. Seeing hues she'd never seen before, Patricia couldn't believe the incredible beauty she was witnessing. But after a few moments, she became disappointed when the bright vivid colors dissipated into their bland colors again. She'd hoped it would have lasted longer.

She turned her attention to the girl in front of her once again, only to find her curled up against her desk, leaning away from Patricia, her eyes filled with fright. Patricia looked around to find everyone staring at her with the same scared look as the girl in front of her, including the professor.

"Are you okay, Patricia?" the professor asked.

"Yes, why is everyone looking at me?"

"You contorted your face," she responded. "And your hands were curled up, and you were waving them around in front of you."

The girl in front of her looked her up and down. "It was all very frightening."

The professor leaned closer. "Patricia, weren't your eyes green?" she asked.

"They are green," she responded.

"They look…brown."

"What?" Patricia asked, opening her purse and pulling out a makeup container. She looked into the small mirror, shrieking at the sight of herself. It was her with brown eyes, almost like looking at someone else.

"I'm not feeling well." Patricia got up. "Do you mind if I excuse myself?"

"Yes, go ahead. Get better," the professor said with a worried look on her face.

* * *

By the time Patricia reached her apartment, her eyes were once again their original green color. Half-past eight, and Patricia's apartment was an icebox. She rested her back against a stack of pillows, her body underneath two layers of blankets, a mug of hot chocolate by the nightstand and her literature book resting next to it. She took a sip of her hot cocoa and opened *The Epic of Gilgamesh*. Reading through the story, she felt bad for the story's protagonist. Relating to his fear of dying, she wondered how far anyone would go for the chance of immortality.

The room was quiet. There were no tappings on the walls. Losing her focus, the incident at school ran through her mind. Putting her book down and pulling out her phone, she scrolled through social media to see if anyone in class had recorded that day's incident. After scrolling for several minutes, she found nothing. Relieved, she relaxed and switched back to reading her book.

Several chapters into the story, Patricia realized that she'd dozed off. She found herself slumping forward, looking down on her book that had fallen from her hand and was now resting on her lap. Patricia attempted to pick it up, but her arms were too heavy to lift. She felt a sharp pain in the back of her shoulder blade. She turned her head to the side and saw Sella in her peripheral vision with demented eyes, sitting right behind her, her cold dead left hand grasping Patricia's left shoulder, her right hand holding a needle. A grin ran across her face, and she released short bouts of laughter as she scraped Patricia's back with the needle.

Shortly after sunrise, Patricia's alarm went off. Hitting the snooze button and laying in bed, she thought about her nightmare until the alarm went off a second time. She got up and headed to the restroom. She turned the shower on and brushed her teeth while the water warmed up. After rinsing her mouth, she stuck her hand in the shower. The warm water felt good, and she jumped in. The water fell on her forehead and ran down her body, washing away her goosebumps. She turned around, and as soon as the water hit her back, she jumped. The water stung her back. She slid her fingers across her right shoulder blade and felt thin scratch marks. She got out of the shower. Leaving a trail of water behind her, she walked to the mirror and turned around to catch her back's reflection. There were thin red scratches across her shoulder blade that looked like letters, but they made no sense.

LAPUERTAESTAABIERTA

Chapter XXXI

Patricia sat on a clinic bed, the thin white paper making noises every time she shifted her body. The room smelled sterile. The hazard box filled with needles made her feel uncomfortable. She wondered if any of the medical assistants had ever accidentally pricked themselves with one. The doctor listened to her as she described the odd occurrences she'd been experiencing before sitting down in the chair. He was a typical middle-aged white male.

"Have you had any gaps in memory?" he asked.

"Aside from the incident that occurred in class last week?"

"Yes, besides that one."

"No, I haven't."

"And when your bed shakes, does it happen when you're awake or asleep?"

"When I'm asleep. It wakes me up, and it continues for ten, maybe fifteen seconds."

He put his clipboard down. "Can you take off your shoes and scoot all the way back? I want to do a quick test."

Patricia took her shoes off and pulled herself back until her feet dangled off the floor.

"Relax your right leg, please." He picked up her right foot with both his hands, flexing it toward her ankle, holding it there in tension, before releasing it, her foot relaxing into normal position. He repeated the procedure several times, always with the same result.

"Well, what do you think?" she asked.

"I suspect that the shaking of the bed is due to clonic seizure contractions. It's an alternating tensing and relaxing of the muscles. It usually indicates a lesion in the brain. Perhaps you got it from your head injury, but if it were that, then," he looked at the corner, "the alternating flexing and releasing of the foot would have triggered a run of clonic contractions." He wrote on his clipboard. "Probably best to order a CT scan. I'm also going to have you get an EEG."

"What about the scratch marks on my back?"

He looked up at her. "I wouldn't worry about that. It's not uncommon to scratch oneself when asleep."

"But they looked like letters."

He ignored her last comment. "Let's wait and see what the CT scan and EEG tell us. We'll have a clearer picture of what we are dealing with." He got up and headed for the door. "Wait right here. My MA will come and get you when they're ready to run the tests."

After the tests, the medical assistant lead Patricia back to the doctor's room. She waited for what felt like an eternity, but was more like 45 minutes.

Finally, the doctor walked in. "Thank God for modern science," the doctor said. He held up the CT scan results. "You have a small lesion on your frontal cortex." He pointed to a dark spot with his pen. "Right here. It's really small."

"Is it dangerous?"

"Lesions in the brain can be totally harmless or fatal," he said. "I'm going to have you see a specialist who will provide you with the proper treatment. I wouldn't worry about it too much. You're probably suffering from seizures, which are treatable with medicine."

* * *

The campus security guard yanked Patricia by the arm.

"Let me go," she protested.

The guard opened the door to the main office and lead Patricia in. He sat her down on one of the chairs. "Give me your campus ID," he said.

"Why? I did nothing wrong."

"That's not necessary, Jeffrey," the dean's assistant said. "I know who she is. She's Patricia Edwards."

The security guard let out a grunt. "Wait here," he said.

Patricia crossed her arms while the security guard briefly chatted with the dean's assistant. She nodded and walked into the dean's office. The guard stood next to Patricia for what seemed like an hour, but was something more like fifteen minutes.

The assistant stepped out. "Okay, Jeffrey, the dean will see Ms. Edwards."

"Okay, let's go." The guard grabbed Patricia by the arm.

Patricia yanked her arm away. "I can see my way in," she said, and stepped into the office.

The dean wore a two-piece brown suit. He had ice-blue eyes and no facial hair, and except for the streaks of brown that ran across the sides of his head, his hair was mostly gray.

The dean leaned forward. "I think you're lying."

"I'm not lying," Patricia said.

"Jeffrey saw the whole thing." He nodded his head toward the security guard standing behind Patricia. "Tell us what you saw, Jeffrey."

The security guard cleared his throat and looked straight ahead. "Patricia was walking across campus when she came across the victim."

"The victim!?" Patricia protested.

"Don't interrupt. Let him finish." The dean signaled to the guard. "Continue."

"Patricia hissed and shouted profanities at the vi— uh…the other student. She then yanked the crucifix from her neck and hurled it. When the girl protested, Patricia slapped her across the face. That's when I grabbed her and brought her here, sir."

The dean bit his lips and shifted his gaze from the guard to Patricia.

"I didn't do that," Patricia protested. "Why would I do that? I don't even know the girl."

The dean opened his mouth, but before he could say anything, the phone rang. He picked it up. "Okay," he said. "Have two or three campus volunteers comb through the area. Hopefully, they'll find it."

He hung up. "That was my assistant. She says the crucifix belonged to the girl's deceased grandmother," the dean said. "I'm having volunteer students search for it. That's time you've taken away from them. These students didn't pay tuition to comb through our campus."

Patricia shook her head.

The dean sat up straight. "Apparently you have a problem keeping your hands to yourself, because my assistant showed me a video where you attacked one of our male students. We have zero tolerance for violence at this university."

"Can I say something?"

He looked at her. "Go ahead," he said in a low voice.

"This isn't easy for me to say, but given the situation, I feel compelled to tell you that I suffered a head injury that left a lesion on my brain. It's causing me seizures, and they even think it might have something to do with my odd behavior. It's a medical problem for which I'm receiving medical care."

The dean nodded. He interlocked his hands and leaned back in his chair. He looked up at Jeffrey and then turned his attention to her. "I'm going to have to suspend you from the university."

"What!? You can't do that!"

He lifted his hand up. "You can appeal your case and reapply for admission next semester. Given this is your one and only incident, and given your unique situation, I have no doubt that you'll be readmitted the following semester, but for now, you must leave campus and not return until your appeal has been approved." He leaned forward. "You should use this time to focus on your treatment." He turned his attention to the guard. "Can you escort Miss Edwards off campus?"

The guard nodded. "Yes, sir."

CHAPTER XXXII

Shortly after sunrise, Pastor Ed woke up extra cheery. He'd spent the last month learning all he could about the Church Fathers. He was relieved to find out that there were other Protestants who had been transformed by their writings. People he could relate to, like Scott Hahn, Steve Ray, Marcus Grodi, Tim Staples, John Bergsma, Dr. David Anders, and many more. He'd read through their books and watched their presentations. He binged on YouTube channels like EWTN, Catholic Answers, Pints with Aquinas, Reason and Theology, and How to Be Christian.

Pastor Ed arrived at his office extra early. He hadn't been this fired up for a very long time.

Nancy knocked on his door.

"Come in," he said.

Nancy stuck her head in. "Albert wants to talk to you."

He stopped typing. "Let him in."

Albert walked into his office. He pointed at the chair across from Pastor Ed. "You mind if I sit?"

"Please, go ahead."

He sat down. "I'm going to make this quick," he said. "Some members of the congregation don't agree with your latest preaching."

"Oh?" Pastor Ed sat up. "What in particular do they disagree with?"

"All of it," Albert shot. "You're twisting the scriptures, Pastor Ed. The folks think you're coming across as Catholic."

"Oh, come on. You know I would never preach Catholicism."

Albert looked up and pointed. "Is that a picture of Jesus?"

Pastor Ed turned to the painting on the wall. "It's a replica of *The Calling of St. Matthew* by Caravaggio. I purchased it from a local artist. Norma and I like it a lot."

"That's exactly what I'm talking about. It's idolatry. God prohibits idols in Exodus chapter 20."

"No, Exodus chapter 20 prohibits the worshiping of statues and images. It doesn't prohibit images or statues because, five chapters later, God orders the Israelites to build two statues of cherubim and place them on the ark of the covenant. And don't forget that God ordered the Israelites to build two twenty-foot statues of angels and place them in the holy of holies in the temple. He also ordered cherubim images to be carved on the walls and doors of the temple. Jesus taught at the temple, and never once did he rebuke the Israelites for having statues and icons there."

Albert shook his head. "I'm not going to stand by and watch you tear this church apart."

"Tear the church apart? Albert, I'm simply trying to teach what the earliest Christians believed. Wasn't that the point of the Protestant Reformation? To take Christianity back to before the Catholic Church started adding stuff?"

"Yes! And we did. So why are you adding all this stuff?"

"I'm not adding anything. Look for yourself." He pointed at a stack of books. "There are all these Christian writings that date back to the time of the Apostles. We can learn from the Christians that were ordained by the Apostles themselves. People like Ignatius of Antioch, who was taught Christianity by the Apostle John and who probably knew Peter and Paul, and Polycarp, who was also a disciple of

John. Both of whom were martyred for the faith by the Romans. And Clement, who's named in the book of Acts and became the bishop of Rome."

"Bishop of Rome?" Albert's face turned red. "There were no bishops in Rome until the pagan emperor Constantine invented the papacy."

"Albert, take this book and read it." Pastor Ed handed him Jimmy Akin's book, *The Fathers Know Best*.

Albert slapped Pastor Ed's hand away. "I don't care what these books have to say. I have the Bible." Then he got up. "Ever since you came back from Mexico, your preaching hasn't been the same."

"If you truly care about the truth, you'd at least take the time to read what the Church Fathers have to say about what the Apostles taught them."

Albert shook his head and walked out.

* * *

"You've got to be careful," Norma said. "You can't just drop all this new information on them out of nowhere. They need time to digest the information."

"But it's the truth. Isn't that why people come to church? To hear the truth?" Pastor Ed said. "I mean, it worked with you."

"Yes, but that's different. I wasn't a devoted Catholic. I wasn't used to going to church every Sunday. It was boring for me. These people are devout Baptists. They've studied the Bible and have been ingrained in their beliefs. They're going to resist you."

Pastor Ed picked at his plate. "What have you heard?"

"You think they're going to tell me?"

"True," Pastor Ed said.

"All I'm saying is that you need to slow down."

Pastor Ed nodded. He was going to say something when his phone rang. He pulled it out and raised an eyebrow.

"What is it?" Norma asked.

"It's Rebecca," he said

"Who's Rebecca?"

"Nancy's daughter," he said before answering the phone. "Hello?"

"Pastor Ed? This is Rebecca."

"Hi, Rebecca. Is everything okay?"

"That's why I'm calling. Have you spoken to Patricia lately?"

"No, I've tried reaching out to her, but she always texts me back, saying she's busy with school."

"She was suspended from school over a month ago."

"What?"

"I thought you knew. She got into an altercation with a fellow student and got suspended for it."

"Oh my God. Was she hurt?"

"No. No. From what I hear, she wasn't hurt. It was mainly…"

"What?" Pastor Ed asked.

"Never mind. What's important is that you check up on her."

"Why? What's going on?"

"I don't know how to tell you this, but…"

"But what?"

"But Patricia and I are no longer friends. We haven't been friends for a while. When I heard she got suspended, I visited her at her apartment, but she wouldn't open the door, so I figured she was still not talking to me. A month passed by and I thought I should go check up on her. So last week I drove by her apartment and saw her walking around aimlessly, talking to herself. At first I wasn't sure it was her because she dropped a lot of weight. I figured it would be a good idea to bring her some food, so I picked up some Chinese food, but when I knocked on her door, I got no response. I heard movement behind the door, so I left the food on her doorstep and told her I would swing by to check up on her the next day. When I got there the following day, there was a small box where I had left the food. It was wrapped in a red bow and it had my name written on. I was thrilled, so I opened it and… and…"

"And what?"

"Pastor Ed, it had feces inside."

"What!?"

"I'm sorry to have to tell you this, but I really think you need to get her help."

* * *

Pastor Ed drove, his hands sweaty and hot on the wheel. The only thing on the highway going faster than him was his mind. He felt guilty, felt like slamming his fists into something. He felt like driving faster, and he did, shooting past yellow lights just as they turned red, and when he didn't make the yellow light, he'd rev the engine, pumping on the pedal impatiently.

Norma placed her hand on his arm. "Slow down. You're no good to her dead."

Pastor Ed ignored her and instead focused his attention on the truck in front of him driving the speed limit. He laid on the horn. "Step on it!"

Norma removed her hand from his arm and stared out the window the whole way there.

Pastor Ed and Norma pulled up to Patricia's apartment complex, jumping out of the car and dashing up the two flights of stairs. Pastor Ed knocked on the door, but there was no answer.

The door behind them opened. "Are you looking for Patricia?" the chubby kid asked from across the hall.

"Yes, have you seen her?"

He shook his head. "Not for a while. But there was a girl looking for her last week."

Pastor Ed looked at Norma. He turned and knocked repeatedly on Patricia's door. "Patricia! It's Dad! Open up!"

"Maybe we can get the office to open it for us," Norma said.

"No, it's closed," said the kid. "I can try the maintenance guy, if you'd like."

"Would you please?" Norma said.

"I have the number somewhere in the kitchen. Give me a second." He closed the door behind him.

Pastor Ed and Norma continued knocking on Patricia's door until the chubby kid reemerged. "He said he can't unlock the door without her permission."

"Damn it!" Pulling out his cell phone, Pastor Ed dialed 911.

"What did they say?" Norma asked.

"They're on their way. In the meantime, let's keep knocking."

Ten minutes later, two African American police officers arrived, a twenty-something-year-old and a middle-aged officer.

"We can't open the door, sir," the older cop said.

"Why not?" Pastor Ed protested.

"It's her apartment, and the law forbids us from doing so. We can knock and try to get her to come out, but that's as far as the law permits us."

"I can't believe it. I'm her father."

"You can file a missing person's report, but you're going to have to wait twenty-four hours."

"That's insane." He paused. "Wait, what about the fact that I'm paying for the apartment? I can show you email receipts on my phone."

The police officers shook their heads. "We just can't. Unless there's something suspicious that we can observe, we can't break in."

Pastor Ed walked up to the door. "Patricia, honey. It's Dad. Look, I'm sorry for what happened. I was a total jerk and selfish. I need you to forgive me. Please, please, please open the door."

Norma placed her hand on his shoulder.

Pastor Ed rested his head on the door's edge. "Patricia!"

There came no answer. Then it hit him. Striking his nose, he flinched back.

"What wrong?" Norma asked.

Pastor Ed shook his head. "Do you smell that?"

Norma placed her nose on the edge of the door. She made a face. "Oh my God."

The two police officers looked at each other. "Move aside," they said.

The older cop placed his nose up against the door. Looking at his younger partner, he nodded, then clicked on his communication device strapped to his shoulder and requested an ambulance.

Pastor Ed's heart sunk.

The other officer told them to move back, and the two policemen took turns kicking the door. The younger cop kicked first, followed by his older partner, taking turns until they finally broke the door open. One of the officers pushed an eager Pastor Ed back. "Stay back. We'll go in first."

The older officer went in and shouted from the living room. "She's alive." Pastor Ed stepped toward the door, but the younger officer held him back. "Hey. Stay here with me."

The older officer stepped out of the apartment. "You called for an ambulance, right?" he said to his partner.

"They're on their way," he responded.

"What's wrong?" Pastor Ed asked.

The police officer took him and Norma to the side. "Is your daughter anorexic?"

Pastor Ed looked into the police officer's eyes. "No."

The police officer placed his hands on his hips. "She's alive, but she's not looking too good. We're going to have the ambulance take her to the hospital."

Chapter XXXIII

Pastor Ed waited impatiently in the waiting room. Norma tried to calm him down, but he kept pacing back-and-forth, non-stop. The doctor walked out of the patient room and asked Pastor Ed to follow him to a small room where they could speak in private.

"So, that's what happened, Doc," Pastor Ed said. "Sella is the girl that we performed an exorcism on and the one who attacked her."

The doctor looked at him. "Do you know the name of the psychologist your daughter was seeing?"

"I didn't know she was seeing a psychologist."

"She claims her doctors diagnosed her with a lesion on her brain, and that she's been seeing a psychologist."

Pastor Ed stared at the floor. "I didn't know that either."

"Our tests confirm that she's suffered a lesion on her frontal cortex, but she refuses to tell us the name of the psychologist who's been treating her."

Pastor Ed shook his head. "The only doctor we've taken her to is her family practitioner. You can try calling him."

"No, their EMR system didn't have any records of such a visit.

Based on what you've told me and what I've been able to observe from your daughter, it seems likely that she's developed a dissociative disorder. It was believed that could only happen when someone experienced something traumatic in childhood. That is, until recently, when a 32-year-old man developed the disorder following a mild traumatic brain injury."

Pastor Ed turned his head.

"Are you sure there wasn't any childhood trauma?"

"Just her mother passing away."

"And she's shown no signs before?"

"No, Doc. Nothing at all."

The doctor leaned forward. "Mr. Edwards, your daughter's mind is very fragile right now. I advise you not to perform any rituals. It's very dangerous."

Pastor Ed nodded.

The doctor gazed at his eyes. "Your daughter believes she is possessed by Sella. You're going to have to pay no attention to that. Possession only happens in movies. You need to put your trust in medicine."

Pastor Ed didn't say a word, simply nodded.

"In the meantime, I'm going to put you in touch with a nutritionist, a psychotherapist, and a psychiatrist. It's important that you follow the dietitian's feeding advice, as it can be deadly—"

"Deadly?" Pastor Ed shot up.

"Yes, it's called re-feeding syndrome, and it is caused by the rapid re-feeding of someone in a state of starvation. That could be fatal. Although your daughter isn't at that stage yet, it's best to stay on the cautious side. My nurse will print out the instructions for you on your way out."

* * *

The clouds blotted out the moonlight as Pastor Ed and Norma helped the frail Patricia out of the car. It would be midnight soon, and Pastor Ed was desperate to call his priest friend. He opened the door to his house and flicked the light switch on. A small flicker of light flashed, small beams of light shooting out of the bulb. Walking up to the bulb, Pastor Ed noticed the strangest thing: flickers of light shone through and moved. Thinking perhaps the light bulb had come loose, he stretched to tighten it when a wave of flies hit his face. They had covered the bulb almost completely, and now the living room was completely lit up.

Pastor Ed and Norma looked at each other. Norma nodded toward Patricia's room. Placing his arm around his daughter's bony shoulder, Pastor Ed guided her to her room.

Norma went into the kitchen. "I'll fix something up quick."

"Make sure to follow the instructions," Pastor Ed said.

Pastor Ed sat Patricia down on the bed and took off her shoes. "I'll get some blankets. Let me know if you want me to adjust the temperature."

Turning her head and closing her eyes, Patricia didn't say a word. Norma walked in with a sandwich. "She needs to eat." Norma said.

Pastor Ed looked at his daughter and took a deep breath. He extended his hand toward Norma and wiggled his fingers. Norma handed him the plate. "Patricia," he said in a calm voice. "Wake up. You need to eat."

Patricia made a groaning sound. Pastor Ed shook her shoulder. "Eat," he said in a more demanding voice.

"No," she said.

"Patricia, you're too skinny. You need to eat. The doctor said that it's important."

Silence.

Pastor Ed looked at Norma. She shook her head.

* * *

Pastor Ed could not wait until morning. He felt bad calling the priest so late at night, but he had to get answers.

"I'm just as enthusiastic about theology as you are, Pastor Ed, but don't you think it's a little late to engage in theological discourse?"

"I'm sorry to bother you so late, Father, but something's happened."

"What's wrong?"

"It's my daughter. She and I had a breaking off shortly after our encounter with Sella, and today her friend called me saying that she was in trouble. My girlfriend and I went down to her apartment, and we found her very sick. She's so skinny. She's not herself. We took her to the hospital. She claims to be possessed by Sella."

"By Sella?"

"Yes."

There was a short pause.

"What did the doctor say?"

"He wrote her a prescription and referred her to a specialist. They found a lesion on her brain that must have been caused by Sella's attack. They believe it's caused her to develop a dissociative disorder."

"You're not thinking about doing an exorcism, are you?"

"I don't know, Father. A part of me wants to."

"I suggest you don't. It's too dangerous."

"Why?"

"In the first place," he said, "it could make things worse."

"Worse?"

"Yes, worse. Because the ritual of exorcism is dangerously suggestive. It could implant the notion of possession where it didn't exist before, or, in the case of your daughter, it could tend to fortify it."

"But—"

"Second, you said your daughter claims to be possessed by Sella, right?"

"Yes, that's right."

"Did she say anything about a demon possessing her?"

"No."

"Then that's proof that she's not possessed, because humans don't possess people. Demons do. Your daughter doesn't believe that she is possessed by a demon. She believes Sella is possessing her. Which is not possible."

Pastor Ed looked up to see Norma sitting at the kitchen table straight across from him. "I don't know," he said.

"The third reason that I will advise you to follow the doctor's advice is that demonic possession is extremely rare. A person can't just be possessed for no reason. The possessed must have done something to allow the demon in."

"Like what, Father?"

"Well, like playing with the Ouija board, tarots, witchcraft, seeking psychics, or dabbling in the occult."

"Father, there's something you should know about my daughter."

"What's that?"

"She's not a Christian. She's not really a believer in Christ."

"Even so, that doesn't give the demon permission to invade a person, and just so you know, Christians *can* be possessed by demons. In fact, they're what demons crave most."

"That's not all. During the summer, she and a few of her friends visited a medium. She said this medium was able to contact her mother."

"Oh, I see. That is cause for concern. But, unlike in the movies, one visit or one go at the Ouija board isn't necessarily going to result in demonic possession. If that were the case, then we'd be bombarded with demonically possessed people. Pastor Ed, in the end, no human spirit can possess someone. The best thing you can do for your daughter is pray and follow your doctor's advice."

Pastor Ed felt a sense of relief. "Thank you, Father. I'll do just that."

"Keep me posted, Pastor Ed, and know that I'll be praying for your daughter."

"Thank you."

He hung up the phone to find Norma staring at him.

"What did he say?"

"He agrees with the doctors. He says she's not possessed because humans can't possess people. Only demons can."

CHAPTER XXXIV

The following morning, after Norma made breakfast, Pastor Ed knocked on Patricia's door before turning the knob and entering her room. The smell of urine washed across his face.

"Patricia, did you wet yourself?"

Patricia stared at the ceiling. "It's been happening."

Pastor Ed sat on the bed next to her, placing his hand on her shoulder. "Why don't you wash up and come to the kitchen for breakfast?"

"I can't."

"Why not?"

"I can't bend my knees."

"What do you mean, you can't bend your knees? Do they hurt?"

"No, Sella won't let me. She paralyzed my legs."

"Patricia," he said in a strained voice. "Sella's dead."

She hadn't removed her gaze from the ceiling. "I know. The demon killed her."

"No, the police officer shot her."

"The demon killed her, and she says it's all my fault."

Pastor Ed let out a short breath. "Come, let me help you up." He grabbed her arm and pulled her up. Sure enough, Patricia never once bent her knees. He guided her to the restroom, and the whole time Patricia walked with a stilt.

Knowing full well that he couldn't undress her, he called out for Norma.

Norma came to the restroom. "Yes?"

Pastor Ed opened the door. "Can you help her undress?"

Norma looked into his eyes, gave him a faint smile, and nodded before entering the restroom.

"No, I can undress myself," Patricia said.

"Are you sure?" he asked.

"Yes, I'm sure."

Pastor Ed and Norma went into the kitchen. Several minutes later, Patricia came out of the restroom wearing pajamas. She grabbed onto furniture, pulling herself along. She walked that way to the kitchen. She sat with her legs extended, staring at her food, never once taking a bite.

"Go ahead, hun, eat," Norma said.

Patricia played with her food.

Pastor Ed took a spoon full of oatmeal and moved it toward Patricia's mouth. Her face contracted into a hideous, grimacing countenance that couldn't be described in detail. Her body became completely stiff. It took half an hour before the cramp disappeared.

Patricia didn't eat a thing. She got up and walked to her room. Pastor Ed was relieved to see her bend her knees. He looked at Norma. They locked eyes for a moment until Norma turned her attention away from him with a look of horror as she stared at something behind him. He turned around to find Patricia standing completely stiff before a crucifix hanging on the wall. She looked at it fixedly, and her gaze was full of hatred. She growled like an animal and gritted her teeth so hard that Pastor Ed was afraid that they were going to fall out. He started praying for her in thought, without making any indication of what he was doing.

"Stop praying," she said.

* * *

For the rest of the day, Patricia refused to eat. She spent all her time in her bedroom.

Norma turned to Pastor Ed. "She has to eat something."

"I've tried. I'm at my wit's end here."

"What if I try?" she said.

Pastor Ed nodded. "Please."

Norma got up and looked around the kitchen. "Something simple," she murmured, and turned her attention to a bowl of fruit. She grabbed an apple, raising it toward Pastor Ed. "What do you think?"

Pastor Ed shrugged. "Wouldn't hurt to try." He got up and followed her to Patricia's room.

Norma sat on the bed next to Patricia, who lay in her bed. "Patricia, I got you an apple."

Patricia looked up at Norma and extended her hand out from under the covers.

Pastor Ed felt relieved and nodded at Norma.

Norma handed her the apple. Patricia grabbed the apple and looked at it. Then she tensed her muscles, squeezing it so hard that it exploded like a grenade in her hand. The fragments splattered all over the room. Fast as lightning, she sat up and grabbed Norma, then threw her to the floor as if she were a rag doll. Stunned by what he had witnessed, Pastor Ed rushed to Norma's side.

"Are you hurt?"

Norma made a groaning sound. "I'll be fine."

Patricia chuckled in a low voice that sounded distinctly like Sella's.

Pastor Ed helped Norma get up and together they left the room.

"What are we going to do?" Norma asked.

Closing the door behind him, Pastor Ed said in a low voice, "I have an idea. Why don't you drive down to St. Michael's Catholic Church and retrieve some holy water for me?"

"You're not thinking about exorcising her, are you?"

Pastor Ed looked her in the eyes. "What just happened in there wasn't normal. The speed with which she moved and the strength with which she threw you. You can't tell me that wasn't paranormal."

"No, Ed! No way. You heard what the priest said. She's not possessed. She's got a psychological problem."

"What if he's wrong? Huh? What if humans *can* possess people?"

Norma shook her head. "God wouldn't allow it."

"There's one way to find out."

Norma's eyes shot open. "I see," she said. "Okay, but only to find out."

"Agreed."

* * *

As the sun was setting, Norma returned from St. Michael's Catholic Church with a flask filled with holy water.

"Here," she said, as she handed him the flask.

"Good." Pastor Ed took the flask and placed it in his pocket. Holding her hand, they made their way to Patricia's room. There was a heavy feeling of foreboding. It was extra quiet and, for a moment, Pastor Ed wondered if Patricia had fallen asleep. The two stood by the door, unsure of what to expect. Pastor Ed grasped the doorknob and slowly turned it. Taking a deep breath, he gently swung the door open and stepped inside.

Patricia sat on the edge of her bed. She stared at the floor and chuckled, turning her head toward him, an unnatural smile running across her face.

"You're going to exorcise me?" she said.

Pastor Ed pulled out his flask of holy water.

She stared at it.

He raised the flask high. Holding his breath, he swung his arm down, releasing the holy water and sending the droplets into trajectory, landing on Patricia's hair, forehead, and face.

She didn't so much as flinch. "Are you even a competent theologian?"

Stunned, Pastor Ed looked down at the flask in his hand.

Norma squeezed his arm. "There, you have your proof."

Still looking down at the flask, incredulous, he asked, "You're sure this is holy water and not just regular tap water?"

"Yes, I'm sure," she replied.

* * *

That night, Pastor Ed woke up to the sounds of movement in the garage. Thinking someone was trying to break into the house, he grabbed his phone to call the police, but quickly the thought of Patricia crossed his mind. He put his phone down and made his way to the garage. He found Patricia naked, squatting down in the corner. Pastor Ed walked up to her, and placed his hand on her shoulder. "Patricia," he said. Patricia turned around, and what Pastor Ed saw horrified him. There was a spider leg sticking out of her mouth. She crunched it with her teeth and swallowed it.

Chapter XXXV

The following day, Patricia walked around the house naked, complaining that the house was too hot. She walked to and from her bedroom and the kitchen, where she would take in large amounts of water. Every time Patricia stepped out of her bedroom, Pastor Ed would try to cover her up.

"No, no, it's too hot," she'd say. "It's hard enough to breathe."

She filled a twenty-ounce cup of water and ice and took it with her to her room, but not before walking up to the air conditioner. "Is this thing broken?"

Pastor Ed ran his fingers through his hair. "I think the Lord is punishing me for moving away from my fundamentalist beliefs," he said.

"You said God doesn't punish people," Norma said.

"I don't know what to believe anymore."

Norma was about to say something when they heard gasping sounds coming from Patricia's room. Pastor Ed got up and headed toward her room, followed by Norma. They found Patricia struggling to breathe, clawing at her neck with deadly desperation. She fell on her knees and pressed her nose to the floor repeatedly, flattening it, then raising her head and gulping for air. Norma placed a pillow down to save her face from injury, which made the struggle worse. Her father tried to hold her upright, but then she turned red as a lobster and choked.

"Just let me do what I must," she pleaded as soon as she could talk. "If you try to help me, I'll be forced to do something much worse."

* * *

Later that day, Norma helped Pastor Ed take his daughter to her 3:30 appointment with the psychiatrist. The door to her office said *Dr. Schmidt*. She was a blonde woman in her fifties who spoke with a strong German accent. Her office looked like a living room that someone decided to turn into a partial office. There was a long yellow sofa facing a white armchair and a brown recliner. Pastor Ed and Patricia sat on the yellow sofa. Norma took a seat in the white armchair. The doctor sat behind her desk from where she asked her questions.

"And that's what happened to her nose," Pastor Ed said.

"Has she tried to hurt herself in any other way?" Dr. Schmidt asked.

"No, no. Just that one time."

"Her weight is of grave concern. Has she eaten anything at all?"

"We've tried plenty of times, but so far only water and—" Pastor Ed didn't finish the sentence.

"And what?"

"Nothing, just water."

"Mr. Edwards, if your daughter is to be treated back to health, you mustn't keep anything from me."

Pastor Ed turned to Norma.

"Tell her," she said.

He turned to the doctor. "I caught her eating insects in the garage."

"I see." Dr. Schmidt leaned back. "Has she used the latrine?"

"She urinates the bed, and this morning she did the same, but when I found her she was," he paused briefly before continuing, "chewing on her urinated underwear."

The doctor jotted down her notes. "There is a specialist from Germany who will be in town," she said. "He's a good friend of mine, and it would be a good idea that he sees your daughter."

Pastor Ed nodded. "Okay, when will that be?"

"I'll set it up and call you with the details. In the meantime, I'm going to change her prescription. I'm also going to prescribe haloperidol as a sedative."

Chapter XXXVI

The following week, Albert had achieved enough support to force a meeting to discuss Pastor Ed's latest teachings.

Once again, it was Lisa who spoke up first. "I really don't know what to think. I was brought up to believe certain things about Christianity, and now I'm being told that what I've always believed to be true is a lie."

"Amen," said the congregation.

"And that's not all. I also heard that Pastor Ed's daughter might be possessed by a demon."

There was chatter amongst the members.

"No, no. My daughter is just going through a hard time, that's all. There is no demon, no possession, and no exorcisms."

"That's not what I heard," Lisa continued. "Someone told me she claims to be possessed by that Mexican girl."

The congregation stopped their chatter to gawk and listen.

Pastor Ed turned to look at Norma. *How could you?* Norma's face turned red.

"Some of the girls and I are afraid that the pastor is going to start uploading videos of him exorcising his daughter."

"Amen."

"I think that's it for me," Lisa continued. "I'm going to attend another church. And I know I'm not the only one of us girls that's fixing to leave."

"You're always leaving," someone shouted to a burst of laughter.

Frank stood up, and the laughter died down. "I think we should leave Pastor Ed's daughter out of this conversation. He's obviously been through a lot, and I don't think he wants to broadcast his daughter's illness for everyone to see."

"How do you know she's not faking it? I mean, she went along with it last time," Lisa said.

"I won't speculate about Patricia's condition, and I suggest no one else does either. It's not Christian-like," Frank said.

"Amen."

Albert stood up. "Unchristian-like? What's unchristian-like is what he's been preaching. He's teaching error and splitting the church apart."

"I don't know about that, Albert. Everything he's been saying checks out. I've gone through the historical records on my own and found them to be true."

"Are you crazy? Were you not here last Sunday when he said we are not saved by faith alone? *Sola fide* is the cornerstone of the Protestant Reformation."

"I was here, and it checks out. No one before Luther believed in salvation by faith alone as Protestants have come to believe."

"That's because the pope forbade anyone from reading the Bible, you fool!"

"Don't call me a fool." Frank stared him down. "And even if it were true, that doesn't account for the large swaths of Christians living outside the Roman Empire. Why is it that none of the Christians living in Russia, in Byzantine, in the sub-continent of India, in Africa, and in the Middle East ever write or teach about salvation being by faith alone? Iraq alone had the largest community of Christians in the world, yet there are no records of them ever teaching salvation by faith alone.

If Luther was the first one to derive that from the Bible, then it means that the Bible was incomprehensible for the vast majority of Christian history."

Albert's face turned red, and not being one to stand down, said, "That's because the pope ordered all those books burned."

"That's crazy! Your hate has blinded you."

"You're the one who's crazy. You crazy Catholic!"

"Don't call me that!" Frank shot back.

The church erupted into a large shouting match that lasted about five minutes.

Albert extended his arms. "See what I mean? He's tearing this church apart. I move that Pastor Ed step down immediately."

Three-fourths of the congregation shouted, "Amen," and less than a quarter shouted, "No."

Pastor Ed clenched his fist and slammed it down. "I'm not stepping down, Albert. If you don't like my preaching, then you're more than welcome to leave, but as for me, I'm staying right here."

There was a long silence.

Albert looked directly into Pastor Ed's eyes. "My grandparents grew up in this church, and they got married in this church. My parents met in this church, and they also got married in this church. I grew up in this church and met my wife in this church." Placing his hands over his two sons, he raised his voice. "And my children are right here." He raised his hand and pointed directly at Pastor Ed. "You've only been here for ten years. You leave!"

Pastor Ed realized at that moment the importance of authority. What could he say to Albert?

* * *

The following morning, Pastor Ed had great difficulty taking Patricia to Dr. Schmidt's office. The doctor had told him that she'd be out of the office that day but was looking forward to hearing what her colleague had to say about Patricia's condition. Pastor Ed sat in the waiting room, while the doctor evaluated his daughter. He wondered how he was going to afford her treatment now that he was unemployed. The church had provided him with excellent health coverage, but that coverage would end soon. He shook his head.

The German psychologist finished evaluating Patricia. He spoke in a much thicker German accent than Dr. Schmidt. "What happened to your face?" he asked.

Pastor Ed placed his finger just below his right eye. "I was attending to my daughter when she swung at me."

"She was very violent with us too," he replied. "Is this behavior new? Or was she this violent from the moment you discovered her in the apartment?"

"It's gotten worse. Fortunately, the sedatives Dr. Schmidt prescribed calm her down."

"She is taking her medicine?"

"It's been challenging, but yes, she has."

The psychiatrist looked perplexed. "What else can you tell me about her behavior?"

Pastor Ed paused to think. "There are so many things. Yesterday she did 400 squats, non-stop. Each time, her knees hit the floor."

The doctor jotted some notes down. "How did she get the cuts on her face?"

"I didn't see how she got those."

"Are you the only one attending to her? Do you have anyone helping you?"

"It's just me right now."

"I see. When her mother died, did your daughter display any odd behavior?"

"Like I told Dr. Schmidt, nothing you wouldn't expect from a grieving girl her age."

"Okay, Mr. Edwards, after evaluating your daughter and speaking with you, I recommend that she be placed in a psychiatric ward. Patr—"

"What!?" Pastor Ed shot up. "No. I will never place my daughter in—"

"Mr. Edwards, please understand that your daughter's weight is dangerously low. You've said it yourself. She is not eating. It doesn't look like you'll be able to get her to eat. There are trained professionals who have experience in dealing with this exact situation. She's also been very violent toward others and has now been causing harm to herself."

"I can get her to eat. I can take care of her."

"By yourself, Mr. Edwards?" There was a pause. "I will not lie to you, Mr. Edwards. If your daughter's health does not improve, she will die soon. Placing your daughter in professional medical care is an act of compassion. Once her health is stabilized, she can return home to you."

"I can't do that." He shook his head. "I have to have my daughter with me. I can't lose her."

"Are you listening to yourself? This isn't about you. This is about what your daughter needs at this moment."

"In either case, I won't allow it. She's staying with me and that's final."

"I can't force you, since I'm only a visitor in your country, but I will pass on my recommendation to Dr. Schmidt. I hope you can understand."

"And you'll understand that I'll be taking my daughter right now. Where is she?"

"Of course," the doctor said. "She's in the other room, heavily sedated. You shouldn't have any problems taking her home."

Chapter XXXVII

"This is CTTV Live News. I'm David Hunter."

"And I'm Margaret Thomas."

"In today's news, Randy Chapman, the boy famous for appearing in a YouTube video where he underwent the rite of exorcism by the infamous Pastor Ed, was found dead in his garage in an apparent suicide by hanging. Police aren't releasing many details, but they did say they do not suspect any foul play."

"That's right, David. The disturbing news comes shortly after John Henry Edwards was deposed as pastor of his local church for what some members of his congregation call 'heretical' and others would say 'extremist' views. With us over Skype are long-time churchgoers Albert Muller and Lisa Phillips. Thank you for agreeing to talk to us."

"You're welcome," both Albert and Lisa said.

"What can the two of you tell us about Randy's death? Lisa, why don't you go first?"

"We're all like really sad that he's passed away at such a young age. My heart goes out to his parents, Mr. and Mrs. Chapman."

"Do you believe that his suicide had anything to do with Pastor Ed's exorcism?"

"I can answer that, Margaret," Albert said.

"Please, go right ahead."

"I without a doubt believe that Pastor Ed's exorcism directly resulted in the boy's suicide, and just to be clear, our church and the members of our congregation were never in favor of what Pastor Ed was doing."

"Hold on there, Albert," David said. "There have been videos on YouTube of Pastor Ed performing exorcisms at your church."

"He managed to convince some of the newer members to go along with his circus show, but the majority of us were strictly against it."

"Yeah, that's true," Lisa said. "And I want everyone to know that we in no way endorsed what he was doing. Our church should in no way be affiliated with what Pastor Ed was doing."

"It shows on your website that Pastor Ed was pastoring the church for several years now. Why did it take this long for your congregation to remove him from his post as pastor?"

"Pastor Ed was actually a good pastor," Albert responded. "In fact, we were good friends, and I always admired his preaching until he got it in his head to go into the exorcism business. After what occurred in Mexico, it was like he went crazy. Suddenly, he was talking all this nonsense and preaching stuff that wasn't Christian. Extreme occult-like stuff."

"Oh wow! The occult," David resounded. "Do you think he was trying to start his own cult?"

"More like he was joining the biggest cult in the world. The Ca—"

"And what's most sad about all this," Lisa interjected, "is that a young boy is now dead."

"Yes, sad indeed," Margaret said. "All for more views."

Chapter xxxviii

Pastor Ed laid his heavily sedated daughter in her bed. He closed the door behind him and made his way to the living room, where a bottle of Jack sat on the table. Pouring himself a shot, he lifted it mid-air for a brief second before gulping it down. After several shots, and the alcohol had taken effect, Father Ortiz called.

"Pastor Ed, how's your daughter?"

"They're going to take her away from me."

"What? Who?"

"They want to place her in a psychiatric ward."

"Dios mío."

Pastor Ed wiped his nose, staring at the now half empty bottle. "I don't know what to do."

There was a momentary pause. "I've been doing research on your daughter's claim that Sella is possessing her. All of my research shows that humans can't possess someone. It's completely unanimous."

"I don't see how this helps," Pastor Ed said in a cracked voice.

"Yes, but recently, I ran across a case that occurred in Germany in 1975. Her name was Anneliese Michel. The two priests conducting the exorcism took meticulous notes and even used what, at the time, were excellent audio recordings. I read the notes and listened to the audio, and what I found shocked me. During her exorcism, not only did a demon manifest itself, but also Judas Iscariot, Nero, and Hitler."

"I thought you said humans couldn't possess someone?"

"True, so it's believed that the demon was playing tricks. The two priests who conducted the exorcism, however, claimed that it was not possible since the demon was under their control."

"Under their control?"

"Yes, exorcists over the years have noticed that there are instances during an exorcism when God will force the demon to be under the complete control of the exorcist. Exorcists have used these rare instances to extract knowledge from demons. The exorcist redacts that information from their reports and conveys it directly to the chief exorcist at the Vatican."

"Wait, how does the exorcist know when the demon is under his control?"

"Exorcists have several ways of knowing. One example is that they'll have the demon kiss a crucifix or a relic of a saint."

"That makes sense, since a demon would never do that."

"Right. So I did a little digging to see what the expert opinions were on the matter, and that's when I came across one of Dr. Tayler Marshall's videos where he and a guest were discussing the matter of exorcism. The guest said that Adam Blai, a consultant to the Catholic Church on matters of demonic possession, explained that during a demonic possession demons will descend into hell and bring tormented spirits with them to a possession, much like a person will bring their luggage with them on a trip."

A jolt of adrenaline spiked throughout Pastor Ed's body. "Sella!"

"The demon must have dragged Sella's tormented spirit with it and is now hiding behind her."

Pastor Ed gazed at his daughter's bedroom door. "How do I go about getting an exorcism performed?"

"Okay, okay. First, you need to convince the local priest in your dioceses. I have to tell you, Pastor Ed, ever since Vatican II there have been some priests that unfortunately don't believe in demonic possession."

"I thought you guys agreed to not disagree."

"Well, yes, that's true. However, not all of us are well catechized. When the devil unleashed its most power weapon, the sexual revolution, against the Church in the 1960s, thousands of priests and nuns left, leaving a big void. Unfortunately, that void was filled by not-so-Catholic men and women."

"Spare me the history lesson, Father."

"All I'm saying is that you might meet with some resistance. I just want you to be ready."

"Okay, then what happens?"

"Well, it's like I told you before. They'll run an investigation and, based on that, they will send for approval from the Vatican."

"I don't have that kind of time. They're going to take my daughter away, and even if I'm able to fend them off, the doctors said that she could die soon."

The priest cleared his throat. "You're going to have to convince the bishop to expedite your case, but start off by convincing the priest. I'll be praying for you."

* * *

Pastor Ed made his way to Patricia's room. Standing by the door, and placing his hand on the doorknob apprehensively, he twisted the knob and slid the door open. Deeply sedated, Patricia slept. Gripping the rope he had retrieved from the garage, he made his way to her bedside. He tied one end to the bed's frame before grabbing Patricia's painfully thin right arm and tying it. He walked to the other side and tied her other arm. Closing the door behind him, he made his way outside, where an Uber driver pulled up shortly after.

"St. Michael's Catholic Church?" asked the driver.

"Yes, and please drive as fast as you can."

The church was a massive red brick building. Its most distinctive feature was a Gothic West font, much like Notre-Dame de Paris. Making his way past the fountain, Pastor Ed walked around the perimeter searching for the priest. Three columns of long bench seats faced the altar, iconography depicting the stations of the cross decorated the interior, and three Filipino ladies prayed before the statue of the Virgin Mary. *God forgive them, for they don't know what they do.*

"Are you looking for the priest?" an elderly lady with a black veil over her face asked.

"Yes, is he here?"

"He's in his office." She pointed at a door. "Go through there and turn left, then go straight. You can't miss it."

Pastor Ed made his way to the office. The priest's secretary looked up at him with a startled look on her face.

She must know who I am. "Hello, is the priest in today? It's an emergency."

The secretary turned her attention to behind him.

"How can I help you?" came a voice.

Pastor Ed turned around to find a man of average height, with dark wavy hair, brown eyes, and thick eyebrows, looking more Italian than Hispanic.

"Are you Father Garcia?" Pastor Ed asked.

"I am."

Pastor Ed cleared his throat. "My daughter is possessed by a demon." He shut his eyes, realizing how crazy that sounded.

"I'll make sure to tune in to the show, Pastor Ed."

Pastor Ed bowed his head. "I know how that came across." He slowly raised his head. "Is there a place we can talk in private?"

The priest's gaze pierced right through him. "Have you been drinking?"

Pastor Ed flicked a glance to the side, then shifted his weight. Standing up straight, muscles tightening across his chest and abdomen as if he were readying himself to receive a blow, he nodded. "Yes."

The priest shifted his gaze to his secretary for a moment before resting his eyes on Pastor Ed, extending his left arm toward an open door. "This way."

Pastor Ed walked into a bare office. There was a desktop, a Bible, and an icon of Jesus on the wall. He recognized it as the Pantocrator. Pastor Ed took a seat and watched as the priest leisurely made his way behind his desk.

"You were saying?" the priest said.

Pastor Ed took a deep breath and explained to the priest what had occurred. The priest listened attentively, not once interrupting, and waited patiently until Pastor Ed had said everything he had to say.

"So what do you say, Father, will you help my daughter?"

"I'm afraid I can't."

"Why not?"

"Because I'm not a doctor. I'm a priest. I understand you believe in demonic possession, but these things don't happen anymore."

"Since when?"

"Since we learned about mental illness."

"But the Catechism of the Catholic Church says that demonic possession is real."

"The Catholic Church can't change its mind on anything that it's declared infallible. Once something's declared to be true by the Church, it can never be reversed. Since it has declared demonic possession to be true, it can't reverse it, but we all know that what people believed to be possession was simply mental illness."

"No. I'm telling you, she's possessed. I've taken her to several doctors, and they don't know what's wrong with her. She knows things and can do things that are beyond what a normal person can do." He paused and looked around. "Your fellow priest in Mexico was a witness to what happened in Juarez, and he said that Sella's case was approved by the Vatican. So don't tell me demonic possessions are not true."

"Have you seen the approval for exorcism with your own eyes, Pastor Ed?"

"No."

"How do you know the priest in Mexico isn't lying to you?"

"What? No, he wouldn't lie."

"Priests can lie, you know? There's a reason we all go to confession. Even the pope goes to confession."

"He wouldn't lie to me."

"Everything you've told me can be explained by natural circumstances. People have been known to have superhuman strength. There are recorded instances of women lifting vehicles to save their children."

"Come see her for yourself."

"I'm afraid I can't do that either."

"Why not?"

"If I'm not mistaken, you've been very vocal about the Catholic Church—"

"You're refusing to help my daughter because of my views?"

"No, what I'm saying is that I don't know if you are going to record me and upload it to your YouTube channel."

Pastor Ed slammed his hand on the table. "I don't have a YouTube channel anymore!"

The priest looked at him silently.

Pastor Ed closed his eyes. "I'm sorry." He leaned back in his chair. "Look, I've made some mistakes. Call Father Ortiz in Mexico. He'll explain everything. Just, please, don't say no until you've spoken to him."

The priest took a good look at him. "Give me his information."

Chapter XXXIX

Booming profanities came blowing from Patricia's room. Pastor Ed sat in his living room, glancing at his phone from time to time. It was eight o'clock, and almost a week since he had spoken with the priest. Earlier that day, the priest's secretary had called to let him know that Father Garcia would visit him that evening.

At that moment, a notification flew by his screen. It was from Dr. Schmidt: *Mr. Edwards, I'm concerned about your daughter. She hasn't been to any of her scheduled appointments. We need to discuss viable options for bringing her back to health.*

Dismissing the notification, Pastor Ed put his phone back in his pocket.

"You stinking rat," Patricia howled, seconds before someone knocked on the door.

Pastor Ed opened the door. "Norma?"

"Hey, can I come in?"

Pastor Ed looked behind her to see if the priest was anywhere in sight.

"Should I come back at another time?"

"No, it's fine. Come in."

She walked past Pastor Ed, who was still looking outside. "I just wanted to say how sorry I am about what happened."

"Liar," Patricia shouted from behind her bedroom door.

Norma turned to Patricia's door with a bewildered look. "I was pretty stressed out," she said in a low voice. "I just needed someone to talk. So I told Katy and she must have told Lisa."

"Liar, she told Lisa."

Norma shook her head. "No, I didn't. I—"

"She told her over the phone right after she finished telling Katy," Patricia shouted.

Pastor Ed knew Norma wasn't telling the whole truth. "It doesn't matter anymore. What matters is that my daughter makes it through this alive."

Patricia broke out into a maniacal laugh.

"Please forgive me." She placed her hands on Pastor Ed's arms. "Let me help."

Patricia ceased laughing, and for a handful of seconds, a much-desired silence spread throughout the house. Then came a knock on the door.

"Are you waiting for someone?" Norma asked.

Pastor Ed nodded. Another knock, this one more rapidly than the previous. Pastor Ed answered the door.

"Norma," said the priest. "I haven't seen you at mass for some time now."

"I'm sorry about that, it's just that—"

"You don't have to give me any excuses. I've heard them all." Father Garcia made his way into the living room. "Now, where is your daughter, Pastor Ed?"

"Right this way." Pastor Ed led him to Patricia's room. He opened the door, and they walked in. The priest pulled out a napkin and placed it over his mouth. Patricia laid in her bed. She stared at the priest, following his every movement.

"Hello, Patricia," said the priest, making his way to the side of the bed. "Your father says you're sick."

"Yes, I am," she said in a sweet voice.

"How do you feel right now?"

"Fine."

"Your father says that you have the spirit of a woman in you. Is that true?"

Patricia let out an innocent laugh, and turned her head toward Pastor Ed. "Daddy, why would you say that?" She then turned to the priest and lowered her head. "Help me," she whispered, revealing the restraints on her arms.

The priest lifted his head in the direction of the restraints for a moment, before turning his head back toward her. "How did you get those scratches on your face?"

She turned her eyes on Pastor Ed. "I don't know."

Pastor Ed clenched his fists. "Reveal yourself, demon."

The priest lifted his hand to Pastor Ed. "If you don't mind, please don't interrupt."

Norma placed her hand on his shoulder. It had a calming effect.

"I spoke with the dean at your school," said the priest. "He told me you ripped off someone's crucifix and threw it. Is that true?"

"No. It was a simple misunderstanding."

"I see. So you wouldn't mind if I place my crucifix on your forehead, would you?" He pulled out his crucifix.

"You're not going to hurt me with it, are you?"

"No, child. I'm just going to place it near you." He drew it close.

She squeezed her eyes and turned her head away, opening her mouth and letting out a faint moan. Her breath was foul, and Pastor Ed could smell it from three feet away. Norma lifted her hand over her mouth, gasping, as Patricia's features contorted into a malevolent mask, her green eyes turning black, her lips pulling tight, and a wolfish tongue hanging from her mouth. The priest withdrew his crucifix, looking up at Pastor Ed, who was hopeful. *This has got to prove it.*

"Cur non tibi licet?" the priest said to Patricia.

"What?" replied Patricia, whose face had ceased contorting. "I don't speak Spanish. My mom never taught me."

"I think you're lying, Patricia. I think your father is telling the truth."

"No, he's not. He just wants to get more views for his channel. You should hear what he says about your church. What was that you called it, Daddy? 'Whore of Babylon'?"

"I'm not interested," said the priest. Making his way to the foot of the bed, he pulled out a slender flask from his pocket.

Patricia's eyes widened. "What's that in your hand?" she asked in a raspy voice, drawing back rigidly against her pillows.

"This?" he said, holding it up. "Why, it's holy water."

"Keep that shit away from me," she said, tugging at the straps.

The priest held the flask up high for a second. Patricia whimpered. The priest let his arm fall, shooting sprinkles of the flask's contents on her.

"Oh, it burns! It burns!"

The priest squinted his eyes and stared silently at her before sprinkling her again.

"Aaaaaah!" she screamed. "Stop it! It burns!"

Again the priest stood silently, gazing at her for about a minute or two before sprinkling her for the third time. Patricia thrashed around and let out a scream that was several decibels louder than before, writhing in terror and in pain.

"Damn you, sly priest. You fox. You'll pay for that."

The priest closed his flask. Patricia lay breathing hard, staring at the priest and grinding her teeth. The priest signaled to Pastor Ed and Norma and then stepped out of the room. Pastor Ed closed the door behind them.

"I've seen enough," the priest said. "I'll report my findings to the bishop."

The priest took several steps toward the front door. Pastor Ed caught up to him and grabbed him by the arm. The priest looked down at his arm, and Pastor Ed released him. "I have to know, Father. What are you going to tell the bishop?"

The priest looked back at Patricia's door, then looked at Pastor Ed. "I sprinkled tap water on your daughter. Her reaction was fake."

Pastor Ed shook his head. "The demon," he bit his hand. "It's trying to trick you."

"It was," the priest responded. "That's why I switched flasks after the second time."

"That's why her reaction was so strong the third time," Norma said.

"Correct," the priest responded. "Now, if you don't mind, I have to talk to the bishop right away."

Pastor Ed shook his head. "But I don't understand. I sprinkled her with holy water and she didn't so much as flinch."

The priest lowered his eyes in thought. "When you sprinkled her with holy water, did you put your faith in the water or in Christ?"

Pastor Ed was speechless, stunned at having made such a simple mistake. *Are you even a competent theologian?*

Father Garcia must have read Pastor Ed's reaction. He stepped out of the house. Halting his steps, he turned around and gave one long look at the house before leaving.

CHAPTER XL

Two days later, Pastor Ed was driving twenty miles per hour over the speed limit. He parked his car at St. Michael's Catholic Church. It was a dark night, giving the church an ominous look. He made his way to the office. The secretary looked up at him. "Go ahead," she said. "They are waiting for you."

Pastor Ed made his way into the priest's office.

"Have a seat, Pastor Ed," the bishop said. He was a frail old white man with gentle mannerisms. He sat in the priest's chair.

Pastor Ed took a seat. "Thank you."

"I rarely meet with the afflicted family members. However, Father Garcia let me in on the situation and I thought it best to discuss it with you."

"This is all highly unorthodox," Father Garcia chimed in, standing behind the bishop.

The bishop folded his hands together on the table. "The reason we asked you to come in tonight is because your daughter is too frail to withstand an exorcism. At her stage, the rite would require several sessions, which can drag on for months, even years."

"No." Pastor Ed clutched his arm to his chest. "She won't make it."

The bishop looked down. "Father Garcia says her doctors want to admit her into a psychiatric ward."

"Yes, that's right. They want to force feed her."

Raising his head, the bishop said, "Perhaps we should hold off until her weight stabilizes."

Pastor Ed shook his head. "The demon won't let her eat. It wants to kill her."

"I'm afraid he's right, Your Excellency," Father Garcia said. "The demon will torment her until she passes away."

The bishop placed his fingers to his chin. "The demon will not kill its host unless it's certain it can take its soul with him to hell. If your daughter is still alive, it's because she hasn't submitted to the parasite."

"She may not hold out much longer," the priest said.

"There has to be a way," Pastor Ed said.

"There is," said the bishop. "If we can get the demon to give up its name, then the exorcist can gain dominion over it and command it back to hell."

The priest shook his head. "That'll take several sessions."

"It's our only chance," said the bishop. "We need to have the Vatican send us its most experienced exorcist."

"But, Your Excellency, even our most experienced exorcist would need several sessions just to know which demon it's dealing with."

The bishop turned toward the priest. "Father Garcia, you must trust in God. Now, send a message to Cardinal Thomas in Rome. Tell him I need to speak with him. Tell him it's urgent."

"Yes, Your Excellency," the priest said, and walked out of the room.

"Pastor Ed, go home and pray. We will let you know when the exorcist arrives."

"Are you sure they'll send him?"

"The cardinal will not fail us."

Pastor Ed got up.

"Hold on one minute. I almost forgot." The bishop withdrew a document from the desk drawer. "You'll have to sign this."

Pastor Ed grabbed the document. "What's this?"

"It's a release of liability, just in case."

"Just in case of what?"

"Just in case your daughter dies during the exorcism."

CHAPTER XLI

The evening was eerily quiet throughout the house. Patricia spent the whole day sleeping. Neither Sella nor the demon manifested itself. Dr. Schmidt had ceased texting. Pastor Ed and Norma sat in the living room praying, holding hands, waiting for the exorcist to arrive. They'd been waiting for three long days.

There came a knock on the door. Pastor Ed stopped praying. Norma looked up at him and nodded. "They're here."

Pastor Ed got up and approached the door, Norma following lockstep behind him. He paused for a moment before opening the door, revealing two police officers.

"Mr. Edwards?" one officer said.

Pastor Ed and Norma looked at each other. "Yes."

"We're conducting a welfare check on a Ms. Patricia Edwards. Is she here?"

Pastor Ed gazed at the police officer, then shifted his gaze to his partner's green eyes. "Was it Dr. Schmidt?"

"We're not at liberty to say," said the officer.

"Is that even legal?"

"Requesting a welfare check?" the policeman asked, with a quizzical look.

"No, I mean, isn't that like breaking some kind of HIPAA law?"

The cops looked at each other. "Again, I'm not at liberty to tell you who requested the welfare check. If you believe that a HIPAA violation has occurred, then you'll have to take that up with the courts."

"Well, Patricia isn't feeling well, and she's sleeping. I'm afraid I can't wake her up. It's best that she rests." Pastor Ed held his breath. *If she wakes up now, they'll hear her shouting.*

"We just need to make sure she's okay. We won't wake her. In fact, we'll be very quiet. Do you mind if we come in?"

Pastor Ed pulled the door toward himself. "I'm afraid I can't let you in."

The police officer looked at Pastor Ed and then at Norma. "It'll be quick. I promise."

"Unless you have a warrant, I'm afraid I can't."

The police officer looked at his partner, then looked back at Pastor Ed. "Very well then. Have it your way," he said, before turning around and leaving.

Pastor Ed closed the door. "Damn it," he said, peeking through his window.

"Did they leave?" asked Norma.

"No, I don't think they're going to leave." He pulled away from the blinders. "Where is the exorcist?"

Norma pulled Pastor Ed's hand. "Come, let's pray."

Before they could finish their first prayer, someone knocked on the door. Pastor Ed and Norma stared at each other. Then came a second, more rapid knock. Pastor Ed got up and made his way to the door. Holding the doorknob for a brief second, Pastor Ed felt an icy chill as he opened the door.

"Father Ortiz?" said Pastor Ed.

Father Ortiz stood next to Father Garcia, his scar visible from the side of his head. Behind them was an African American woman and a tall muscular white man.

"Hello, Pastor Ed," said Father Ortiz.

"Come in," Pastor Ed said.

The group cautiously stepped inside the house.

"Father Ortiz, this is Norma."

"Thank you for coming, Father," said Norma.

Father Ortiz turned to the woman standing behind him. "Pastor Ed, this is Dr. Davis. She will monitor your daughter's health during the exorcism, and the man standing beside her is Chris."

Pastor Ed shook their hands. His good manners kicking in, he headed to the kitchen and asked them if they wanted any water. Glancing back at them, he saw them on one knee with their heads bowed down before Father Ortiz, who bestowed a blessing on them. Father Ortiz then blessed Father Garcia, followed by Father Garcia blessing Father Ortiz.

Father Ortiz turned to Pastor Ed and Norma. "You may want to put on a sweater. It can get ice cold during an exorcism."

"I'll get them," said Norma as she walked into the laundry room, emerging wearing a blue sweater with Pastor Ed's church logo. She handed one to him, and he grabbed it and gazed at the logo for a moment before putting it on.

"You're all familiar with the rules concerning exorcism?" Father Ortiz asked.

Everyone looked at each other. "It's our first time," said Father Garcia.

Father Ortiz addressed the group. "No matter what happens, it is especially important that you avoid having conversations with the demon. Father Garcia and I may ask what is relevant." Father Ortiz placed his purple stole on himself. "But anything beyond that is extremely dangerous." He placed the second stole on Father Garcia. "It is imperative that you don't listen to anything it says. The demon is a liar and a trickster. It will mix lies with the truth in order to confuse you. The demon will do everything in its power to stop the rite of exorcism. You must not listen to it. Remember that. *Do not listen.*"

Norma's eyebrows curved up. She looked at Pastor Ed, who placed his arm around her. "You don't have to be there if you don't want to."

Norma placed her hand on his chest. "I want to be there for you and for her," she said.

Father Ortiz scoured the room. "Is there anything you would like to ask me now?"

No one said a word.

Father Ortiz nodded toward the doctor. "Please go in and get a preliminary assessment of the girl's physical health." He turned toward Chris. "You go with her."

Father Ortiz bent down and picked up two copies of *The Roman Ritual* and gave one to Father Garcia. "Do you have the holy water, Father Garcia?"

"Yes," he said, handing him a slender, cork-tipped vial from his pocket.

The doctor emerged from the room with a stern look on her face. "She's in really bad condition. She needs to be hospitalized as soon as possible."

Chris stood behind her. "God have mercy on us," he said with a shocked look on his face.

Father Ortiz whispered a solemn prayer, then nodded at Father Garcia. "If you would lead the way, please."

Father Garcia led the way to Patricia's room, followed by the exorcist, Chris, and finally the doctor. They marched in procession to do battle with the most unholy. Father Garcia stood at the door. The air thickened.

"Alright," said the exorcist softly.

Father Garcia opened the door. He almost fell back from a blast of the stench of decay, rotting flesh. They walked into the room and took position. The exorcist stood at the foot of the bed. To his left stood Father Garcia. Behind them to their flanks stood the rest of the group. The doctor went to the side of the bed and strapped a blood pressure cuff on Patricia. She held a tablet device in her arms, monitoring Patricia's heartbeat. The exorcist then made the sign of the cross over Father Garcia and then to the rest of the group individually.

Patricia laid on a single layer of ripped white sheets stained in red, her belly and crotch sticking up in the air. Her hands and feet were individually buckled to the corners of the bed, and her wrists were heavily restrained, scratched and bleeding. She wore a nightgown, ripped and torn, revealing her pale and bruised flesh. Turning her skeletal face, she watched the priests open their red leather-bound books.

Father Ortiz said, "Lord have mercy," and Father Garcia repeated, "Lord have mercy."

Father Ortiz: "Christ have mercy."

Father Garcia: "Christ have mercy."

"What the hell is this?" Patricia asked, turning wide-eyed to her father. "What're you doing with all these people? You're scaring me."

The room suddenly filled with an icy cold that seemed to seep from the walls and penetrate to the bone, and along with it came slow, tapping sounds.

"Saint Michael the Archangel, defend us in battle," the exorcist prayed. "Be our protection against the wickedness and snares of the Devil. May God rebuke him, we humbly pray. And do thou, O Prince of the Heavenly Host, by God's power, thrust into hell Satan and all evil spirits who wander the world seeking the ruin of souls. Amen."

"Why are you doing this?" Patricia asked.

"Our Father, who art in heaven, hallowed be they name…"

"I need medical help. Please. Call my psychiatrist, Dr. Schmidt, she'll tell you."

"Give us this day our daily bread and deliver us from evil. Amen."

They repeated the prayer, Pastor Ed expecting for the demon to manifest itself, but Patricia kept talking.

"Are you mad at me? Is that why you're doing this?" Patricia asked her father. "I know I've been acting weird, but that's because I have a scar on my brain. I can't help it." She turned to the group. "Please, someone do something." She shivered. "I'm so cold."

The priests continued praying.

Patricia's lips turned blue. "Dad, please. I'm freezing."

Pastor Ed took a step forward, but Father Garcia put his hands on his shoulders and whispered in his ears, "It could be a trick."

"Yes, I faked my lips turning blue, and made goosebumps appear on my skin," Patricia said. "I'm faking it like all the witches your church drowned in ice cold lakes."

"I command you, unclean spirit," the exorcist boomed. "In the name of Jesus Christ and the powers invested in me by His Holy Church, reveal yourself to me."

"This is illegal," she said. "You can't keep me tied up like this." She yanked at her restraints. "You'll all go to prison. You're all accomplices now."

The doctor and Chris looked at each other.

"I command you, unclean spirit, by the mysteries of the incarnation, passion, resurrection, and ascension of our Lord Jesus Christ. Reveal yourself to me."

"Please." Patricia turned her attention to the doctor and Chris. "I don't know your names. I don't know who you are, but if you release me, I swear I won't tell anyone. I promise."

"I command you in the name of Jesus Christ," said the exorcist, "to reveal yourself to me. Give me your name and the hour of your departure."

"Patricia Edwards, Okay, that's my name and I'll depart right now. Just let me go."

The priests continued praying from their red books.

"I'm scared," Patricia said. "I'm really, really scared. My father is crazy, he'll do anything for views. I wouldn't be surprised if he's got hidden cameras in here. Please, I'm not possessed. He's just doing this to get famous. I swear. It's all he cares about."

Pastor Ed looked down at the floor.

"Come on, this is crazy." Patricia yanked at her straps. "You have to know this is illegal. This is how people get killed."

"Silence!" the exorcist said. He unscrewed the bottle and sprayed holy water on Patricia.

She jerked her head up, her mouth and neck muscles trembling with rage. She screamed, then turned to the doctor and Chris. "It's not holy water. I swear. It's like acid or some other kind of chemical. I swear. It burns so bad."

The priest sprinkled more holy water on her.

Patricia squirmed on the bed, shaking violently, yanking at her straps. "I've done nothing to you," she said. "Please, please, please, just check his bottle. It's not holy water. It's some chemical." Red burn marks appeared on her skin. "Look at my skin. It's burning me."

"In the name of Jesus, I send you to the cross," the priest said. He poured more holy water on her. Patricia cried in pain. Tears fell from her eyes. "Please, he's going to kill me. It's not water. Just check it."

Then the exorcist did it again. "Reveal yourself to me, unholy spirit. I command you by the most high." Again, he sprinkled more holy water.

Patricia's body convulsed. She looked as though she was going into shock. The doctor dashed forward and inspected Patricia's eyes. She had a baffled look.

The priests again prayed the Lord's Prayer, but this time, everyone in the room joined in one voice. "Our father who art in heaven…"

Something broke behind Patricia's face and she crumbled into tears, her body shaking. "Daaaadddy, why are you doing this to me?"

The exorcist moved forward and placed his stole on Patricia's forehead. "I command you in the name of Jesus Christ. Reveal yourself."

"No!" she shouted. "No, get off me. Get off me! Daddy, help! Help! Heeeelp!"

The exorcist stepped back and sprinkled more holy water. "Come forward, demon," he commanded.

Another blast of holy water. "Come forward, father of lies. Reveal yourself, evil one."

Patricia had given up the struggle. Her chest heaved. She closed her eyes.

"Tell me your name, demon."

"Kanenas."

Pastor Ed shot up, uncertain if he'd heard correctly. It was so faint that he wasn't sure if he'd imagined it.

She said it again. "Kanenas."

"It's Kanenas," Pastor Ed shouted. "The demon's name is Kanenas."

Father Garcia placed his hand on his shoulder. "Kanenas means 'no one' in Greek. Now please stay quiet."

His heart sank.

"In the name of our Lord Jesus Christ, I command you by the authority of His Most Holy Church to give me your name, demon."

Patricia opened her bloodshot eyes, fully dilated, with tears rolling down the side of her face. "No," a deep male voice said from within, in a voice coarse and guttural, bristling with venom, "No, this filthy pig is mine."

"Get it out of me. Please, get it out," Patricia pleaded.

Patricia's face contorted into pure hatred, her mouth agape, shrieking until the demonic personality possessed her, filling her. "Stay inside where you belong, pig." Then it turned its attention to Father Ortiz and changed its face to that of a woman in sheer terror. "*Ayuda me, Padre!*" Sella's voice said, and just as quickly, the demon's contorted face returned.

Chapter XLII

The Shroud of Turin, also known as the Holy Shroud, is a length of linen cloth believed to be the fabric that wrapped Jesus's body after his crucifixion. On studying the Shroud of Turin, scientists discovered that before Jesus's crucifixion, they whipped him with a lead-tipped whip called a flagrum. A flagrum is comprised of three separate thongs, each ending in a set of two lead balls. Scientists also discovered that during crucifixion, the weight of the body pulled down on the arms, making breathing extremely difficult. Therefore, in order for our Lord to speak, He had to lift himself up by the arms. Every time He lifted his body up, His wounded back would rub up against the wooden beam, making every word spoken excruciatingly painful.

The exorcist stood up by the side of the bed, where he looked down into hate, and stared at the horror, at the emaciated, skeletal thing on the bed that was watching with mocking eyes, filled with cunning, and anger, and, most unsettling of all, a posture of towering authority.

Patricia licked her purple lips with a wolfish tongue, her chapped lips cracking as the tongue left a filmy substance. "You didn't pray correctly before the sacrament, Ortiz," said Patricia. "Why, you even forgot to kiss the stole before putting it on. You incompetent fool." Patricia turned to her father. "Sella is dead because of you. Are you going to let your pig daughter die too?"

The exorcist lifted his hand and traced the sign of the cross above the bed. He plucked the cap from the vial of holy water.

"Ah, yes. The piss of saints," the demonic voice hissed, turning toward Pastor Ed. "You should know, Edwards." She pronounced his name with such emphasis it made him shiver. "Your precious daughter is mine, and I can do more harm to her than you can do to me."

The exorcist sprinkled holy water on Patricia. "Be silent!" His words echoed throughout the room. Patricia moaned, thrashing about, trembling, shaking in rapid motion. The exorcist capped the vial of holy water and slipped it into his pocket. He then knelt down by the bed and closed his eyes. "Our father who art in heaven…" he began.

Patricia spat, hitting the exorcist in the eye with deadly accuracy, the yellowish mucus sliding down the side of his face.

"… thy kingdom come…" The exorcist continued to pray without skipping a beat. He pulled out a handkerchief and wiped the side of his face. "… lead us not into temptation…"

"But deliver us from evil," Father Garcia responded.

The exorcist looked up at Patricia, whose eyes rolled down into their sockets until only the white of the sclera was visible. "Lord Jesus Christ, I humbly beg you. Give me the strength to vanquish this unclean spirit in your name."

"Amen," responded Father Garcia.

The exorcist stood up and continued the Roman Ritual. "O God, whose nature is always to forgive and show mercy, receive our prayer for this, your servant, Patricia Edwards, who is bound in chains by the power of the devil: may your faithful love and compassion mercifully grant her release. Through Christ our Lord."

"Amen," responded Father Garcia.

Patricia sat erect with the whites of her eyes exposed, hissing while her tongue flickered in and out in rapid succession like a snake, weaving her head slowly from side to side. The doctor's tablet began to beep: the heartbeat monitor rose steadily, and a heart-shaped alert icon flashed.

The exorcist continued his prayer. "O God, who sees that in your weakness we fail, we humbly entreat you for this our sister Patricia Edwards, that you will drive the evil spirit away from her and restore her to the full freedom of your children, so that with your saints and your elect she may praise you without end. Through Christ our Lord."

"Amen," replied Father Garcia.

The exorcist quoted a verse from the Bible. "Behold, I have given you the authority to tread upon serpents…" Norma gasped as she squeezed Paster Ed's arm. Patricia's bed elevated from the floor, one foot of the bed rising, then another and another, until it floated in mid-air. By this time, Patricia's heartbeat was racing at an unbelievable rate. A wave of apprehension washed over the doctor's face.

"Father Garcia?" said the exorcist.

"*Dios mío*," said Father Garcia.

"Father Garcia?" repeated the exorcist.

Pastor Ed shook the priest. He snapped out of his trance and turned to the exorcist.

"The response, please."

Father Garcia looked down at his book. "You, O Lord, are my refuge."

The exorcist prayed a lengthy prayer. It was only then that Pastor Ed noticed Norma's presence was missing. She had left the room in fear. The exorcist reached up his hand and gently traced the sign of the cross on Patricia's forehead repeatedly while reading the prayer. The bed floated down like a feather, landing gently on the floor.

Patricia's hissing stopped. In its place, she squealed like a pig for slaughter.

"O Lord, our defender and our refuge, free your servant Patricia Edwards from the snares of the demon stalking her and from the evil word of those pursuing her…"

Patricia squealed louder, the sounds bouncing off the walls.

"Protect her under the shadow of your wings, surround her with the shield of your strength, and in your mercy show her your salvation..." The exorcist reached up with his stole in hand and placed it on Patricia's neck. Holding it there, he continued his prayer. "Through our Lord..." Patricia fell silent for a moment, then gagged, and from her mouth flowed spiders, insects, and worms. The creatures ran down her chin, down her neck, and up the exorcist's arm. Spiders bit down on him, and his muscles tensed, but he did not move his hand. "The word became flesh and dwelt amongst us..."

Father Garcia flicked the insects off with his stole.

"I cast you out in the name of the Most High, demon. It is he who commands you..."

The creatures stopped pouring out of Patricia's mouth. She lifted her head, staring at the exorcist with the whites of her eyes.

"He who flung you from heaven! I command you to give me your name, demon."

Patricia's heart was still racing fast as ever. Beads of sweat appeared on Pastor Ed's forehead. The doctor ran over to Patricia's side and placed her fingertips on her wrist, staring down at her watch, shaking her head.

Patricia's ghostly white eyes turned until she fixed them on Pastor Ed. "Are you going to let him kill your daughter?"

The exorcist raised his crucifix. "Behold the cross of the Lord. Be gone, all hostile powers."

Patricia turned her head slowly toward the exorcist. The lights flickered on and off. A muffled pounding jolted the room. Then another. Then steadily it grew louder and more frequent. Through the floor, through the ceiling, shuddering through the walls. The pounding was locked step with Patricia's heart rate.

"...By the Judge of the living and the dead, by your Creator, by the Creator of all the universe, I command you, demon, to give me your name."

The pounding grew deafening and sped up to a deadly tempo. Patricia's heart hammered at a speed too fast to gauge. The doctor stumbled her way to her medical bag. She pulled a syringe and felt her way back to Patricia's side. The exorcist signaled to the doctor to stop with his hand, and while he continued his prayer he reached calmly on Patricia's breastplate and with his thumb traced the sign of the cross. His words of prayer were suppressed by the pounding. All senses became confused. Up was down. Down was up. The mouth could hear, the ears could taste, and the eyes could smell. The heart monitor slowed down. The exorcist continued tracing the cross on Patricia's chest. The doctor breathed a sigh of relief as Patricia's heart rate normalized.

"You incompetent bastard," the demon spat. "She will die. You will lose." The lights stopped flickering, and the demon unleashed a barrage of insults.

"May the holy cross be your light," the exorcist said. Then he leaned over Patricia and let out three breaths.

The demon spat on the exorcist's face.

"By the breath of your mouth, O Lord, drive out all the evil spirits…" He reached out for his handkerchief and wiped his face.

"Look at me, you scum," said the demon. "You hypocrite. You care nothing for the pig whore. You're no different from her father. You do this for yourself, for your reputation in a church that's looking more Protestant by the day. Oh, what's that? Contraception is bad? Not according to your Papa Francis. You're all crazy! Haven't you heard? I'm not real. The Jesuit superior general, Arturo Sosa, says I'm just a symbol. A fuckin' symbol!"

The exorcist sprinkled holy water on Patricia. "Give me your name, demon!"

Patricia's head fell back on her bed, stretching out her neck, and her breathing becoming raspy, rotted, putrid, here, yet far, and sinister. "I am he who dwelled within Nero," a demonic voice said. "I am he who dwelled within Muhammed, and I am he who dwelled within Luther." Patricia's body stiffened like a board, her hands claw-like. "I am he who dwelled within Calvin." She raised her head. "I am he who dwelled within Cardinal McCarrick. And I will not rest until the gates of hell prevail against the Church."

The exorcist continued praying. "O God of heaven and earth, God of the angels and archangels…"

The demon turned its white gaze onto Pastor Ed. "Why didn't

you save me?" it said in his wife's voice.

Pastor Ed's hands trembled.

"Don't send me back to hell. Let me stay here with our daughter. I'll keep her safe."

"Don't listen, Pastor Ed," said Father Garcia.

"...deliver this servant who is made in your image..." continued the exorcist.

"You don't know what it's like down there. The things they do to me. The things they make me do. Even the demons fear hell. It's your fault I'm here. The least you can do is let me stay here with our daughter."

Father Garcia placed his hand on Pastor Ed's shoulder. "Don't listen."

Pastor Ed closed his eyes, tears falling from his face. "You're not my wife!"

"Please don't send me back. Don't you love me anymore?"

"...it is Christ who compels you..."

Pastor Ed clenched his fists. "You're not my wife!"

The exorcist raised the vial of holy water. "I command you in the name of Jesus Christ with the authority vested in me by His One Holy Apostolic Catholic Church to give me your name!"

The exorcist let his arm drop and with it fell droplets of holy water, splashing across the demon's face. It let out a silent cry, the veins in her neck bulging. "I ... am ... Adramelech, grand chancellor of demons, president of the devil's general council, and governor of Satan's wardrobe."

The exorcist closed his red leather book. Making the sign of the cross, he commanded the demon, "Adramelech, I cast you out in the name of Jesus Christ."

Silence filled the room. Patricia's muscles relaxed. Her pupils rolled back into place. Seconds later, Patricia cried out for her father. "Daaaady!"

Pastor Ed took a deep breath and ran to his daughter's side. "You're safe. You're going to be okay." He clasped his daughter in his arms.

Patricia's face trembled, crying, large tears rolling down her face. "They're going to kill me."

"What?" Pastor Ed shook his head. "No, no. It's gone."

Patricia's eyes rolled up in their sockets. "Adramelech is gone. I get the pig whore," a demonic voice came from inside her. "No, I'm next in command. Her soul belongs to me." Three demonic voices fought inside Patricia for possession of her soul.

"No! No!" Pastor Ed fell to the ground. "Dear God, no!"

BOOM! BOOM! BOOM!

"This is the police! We have a search warrant!"

The exorcist opened his red leather book. "Our Father who art in heaven…"

"Open the door!"

BOOM BOOM BAAAAAM!

Marching boots pounded into the living room. Norma screamed.

"Get on the floor! Get on the floor!"

Pastor Ed became disoriented, crumbling to the floor in a daze of horror, the swirling of images and sounds in the bedroom. His head spun, blurring vision, unfocused, his ears ringing loud with chaotic distortions as he weakly tried to raise himself off the floor, pushing up with his hands, faltering, looking up at the bed as the demons laughed.

Something pulled at his chest. Falling through space, everything became muffled. He closed his eyes before being jolted awake. He now stood at the foot of the cross. The Lord was above him with His hands stretched out across the beam of the cross.

"My Lord. My God." Pastor Ed fell to his knees. "Save my daughter. Please, I beg of you."

The Lord turned His gaze on him, raising Himself up, His whipped back rubbing against the wooden beam, His face in agony. "Man," he said. "Behold your mother."

Pastor Ed turned to his side and gazed at the Blessed Virgin Mary's sorrowful face, looking up at her dying son. "Mary," he said. "I'm sorry. I'm so sorry."

Suddenly Pastor Ed was again in Patricia's room. He closed his eyes and clasped his hands in front of him. "Hail Mary, full of grace, the Lord is with thee. Blessed art thou among women, and blessed is the fruit of thy womb, Jesus. Holy Mary, Mother of God, pray for us sinners now, and at the hour of our death. Amen."

The scent of roses filled the room. "Do you smell that?" Father Garcia asked.

"The woman!" three demonic voices yelled within Patricia. "The woman! Noooooo!" The demonic voices dissipated into the background. The sweet scent of roses filled the room. A calm, loving, motherly sense enveloped the room.

"Dad," said Patricia.

Pastor Ed made his way to the side of the bed and squeezed his daughter tight.

"She's so beautiful," she said.

The police marched into the room. "On the ground! Everyone on the ground!"

Suddenly Pastor Ed was on the ground, face-down, his arms yanked back, the cold steel of handcuffs tightened around his wrists. He was yanked up and dragged away, followed by the two priests, the doctor, and Chris.

Chapter XLIII

The church was shrouded in darkness. Outside, a fire burned, and from it, a candle representing Jesus Christ, the light of the world, was lit. Under the moonlight, Father Garcia progressed into the dark church, stopping three times, proclaiming, "Christ, our light!" By the time he reached the sanctuary, the whole church was blazing with candles, lit by the Easter candle, becoming a wave of lights that spoke of Jesus Christ.

It was Easter Vigil, and Pastor Ed along with Patricia were being admitted into the Catholic Church, having spent several months in the RCIA program — Right of Christian Initiation for Adults. They were about to partake in holy communion. Amongst the attendants were Norma and Frank, the only ones from Pastor Ed's church to attend.

Inside the church, still in darkness, several readings from scripture were read, from Genesis through to the New Testament, interspersed with chanted hymns and passages. Afterward, during the baptismal liturgy, Patricia, having never been baptized, bowed her head before Father Garcia, who poured the waters of baptism, saying, "I baptize you in the name of the Father, and of the Son, and of the Holy Spirit." Pastor Ed, having been baptized in his Protestant denomination, professed his faith.

Afterward, the liturgy of the Eucharist was celebrated. Father Garcia, standing behind the altar, washed his hands and offered prayers of thanks to God for the gifts of bread and wine that were before him on the altar that would be changed into Christ's body and blood. He invited the people to pray that their sacrifice would be acceptable to God. The Eucharist prayer followed, in which the holiness of God was honored. Recalling the Last Supper, the bread and wine were consecrated. Father Garcia elevated the host and chalice. "Through him, with him, in him, in the unity of the Holy Spirit, all glory and honor is yours, almighty Father, forever and ever."

"Amen," the people responded. Then, all in unison, they prayed. "Lord, I am not worthy that you should enter under my roof, but only say the word and my soul shall be healed."

Father Garcia stepped forth with the bread, where Pastor Ed, followed by Patricia and the rest of the RCIA members, awaited to receive Jesus Christ. Father Garcia lifted the bread before Pastor Ed. *"Ecce Agnus Dei, ecce qui tollit peccata mundi,"* Latin for "behold, the lamb of God, who takes away the sins of the world."

Pastor Ed said, "Amen," and opened his mouth, truly receiving Jesus and establishing a most personal relationship with him. Patricia followed suit, as did the rest of the RCIA members.

* * *

The following day, Easter Sunday, Pastor Ed invited Frank, Norma, and his fellow RCIA members, whom he and Patricia befriended, over to his house to celebrate Easter. Surrounded by their friends, Pastor Ed gave thanks.

"Thank you, everyone, for showing up. I want to take the time to give thanks to our Lord Jesus Christ, and to his blessed mother, Mama Mary. Some of you may not know this, but Mama Mary saved my daughter's life and, in effect, my life too, because without my precious Patricia I would have surely died."

He turned and gave a warm smile to Patricia, who had by now recovered and was close to her normal weight.

"If you would have told me a year ago that today I'd be standing before a crowd preaching on Mary, I would have thought that you'd lost your marbles."

The attendants let out a short laugh.

"Because I had such misconceptions about what Catholics believed, I thought the Catholic Church was just crazy! I mean, the immaculate conception? What part of all have sin do you not understand? And don't even get me started on the assumption of the Virgin Mary. I used to say that the assumption was the greatest assumption ever made."

The members laughed.

"He'll be here all night!" Father Garcia said jokingly.

"However, my fundamentalist lens with which I read the Bible didn't allow me to see the fact that Mary is in heaven, body and soul. In Revelation, chapter twelve, John says he saw a woman in heaven, clothed with the sun, the moon beneath her feet, and a crown of twelve stars on her head. He talks about how the woman gave birth to the messiah. This passage is clearly speaking about Mary, and notice how he mentions her head and body. It's not just Mary's soul in heaven, it's Mary's soul and body in heaven. And let me ask you this: What type of woman wears a crown?"

He gave the crowd time to think.

"I used to ask Catholics, why do you call Mary queen of heaven? Don't you know that Jeremiah 7:17-18 says that the queen of heaven is a pagan goddess?"

Holding up Brant Pitre's book, *Jesus and the Jewish Roots of Mary*, he continued, "But thanks to this book, I now know that just because there were pagans who worshiped an idol as the queen of heaven doesn't mean that the term is now only meant to mean idolatry. If that were the case, then we couldn't call Jesus the Son of God, because Caesar was called the Son of God and worshiped by the Romans before Jesus' birth. So why do Catholics call Mary the Queen of Heaven? Well, because of Jesus, that's why. Jesus wasn't only the new Adam and the new Moses. The Bible tells us that He was also the new Davidic king and that His kingdom would have no end. So we have to ask ourselves, if Jesus is the new Davidic king, then who is the queen? Unlike in other monarchies, in the Davidic Kingdom, the mother was always the queen. That's why John, in Revelation, chapter twelve, says that the woman whom we identified as Mary had a crown of twelve stars. If Mary is the mother of Jesus, who is the Davidic king, then she is the queen mother. And let's talk about Mary being the mother of Jesus. If Jesus is God, then that means that Mary is the mother of God, but if you had told me that a year ago, I would have said that that's heresy. I would have said that Mary was only the mother of Jesus' body, because God is eternal. How can Mary be the mother of God if she was created by God? But, folks, when we Catholics say that Mary is the mother of God, we don't mean that she is the creator of God, but that she gave birth to Jesus, who is God. Much like how your mother, who only gave you your body and not your soul, is still your mother."

As Pastor Ed continued preaching on Mary, Patricia's phone vibrated. Pulling it out of her jeans pocket, she looked down at the screen. Noticing the international number, a wave of apprehension washed over her. Pressing the answer button, she slowly put the phone up to her ear.

"Hello," she said.

"Patricia Edwards?" a man asked.

"Yes, this is her."

"This is Mexican Federal Agent Francisco Mejia. I'm calling you from Juarez, Mexico."

Patricia didn't respond. Her heart hammered in her chest.

"I'm calling you because we are seeking your help in locating Doña Gloria. I believe you had an encounter with one of her clients, Sella Castañon."

"I don't know anyone by that name."

"I just texted you a picture. Look at it and tell us if you've seen her."

At that moment, the text notification buzzed. Lowering the phone, Patricia tapped on the notification, revealing a picture of Doña

Gloria.

Patricia gasped.

"You've seen her, haven't you?" the man's voice came across from the phone's speaker. "In your visions."

Patricia's hand trembled.

"Will you help us?"

The Author Recommends

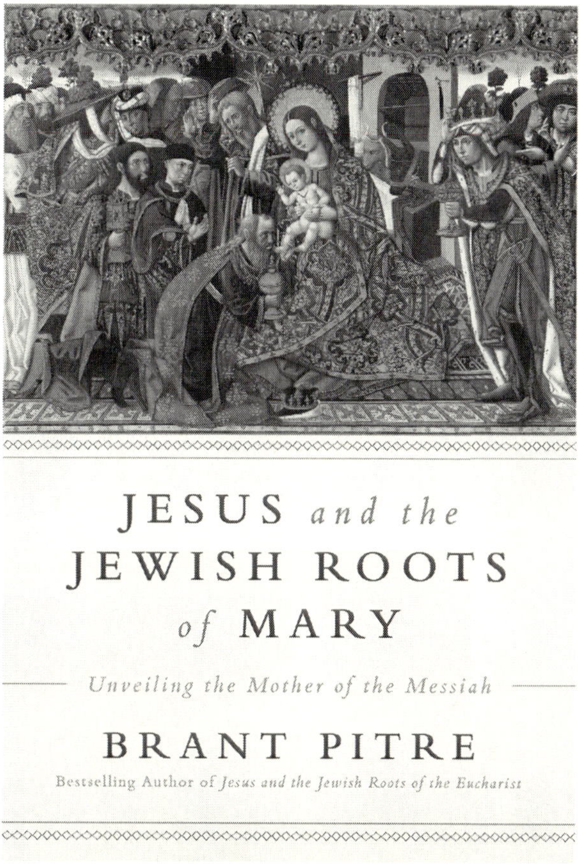

The Author Recommends

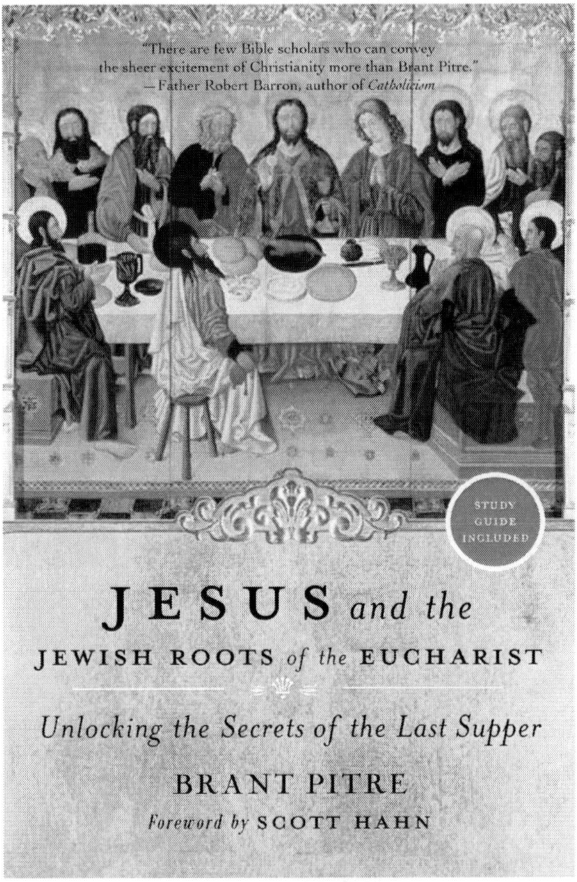

The Author Recommends

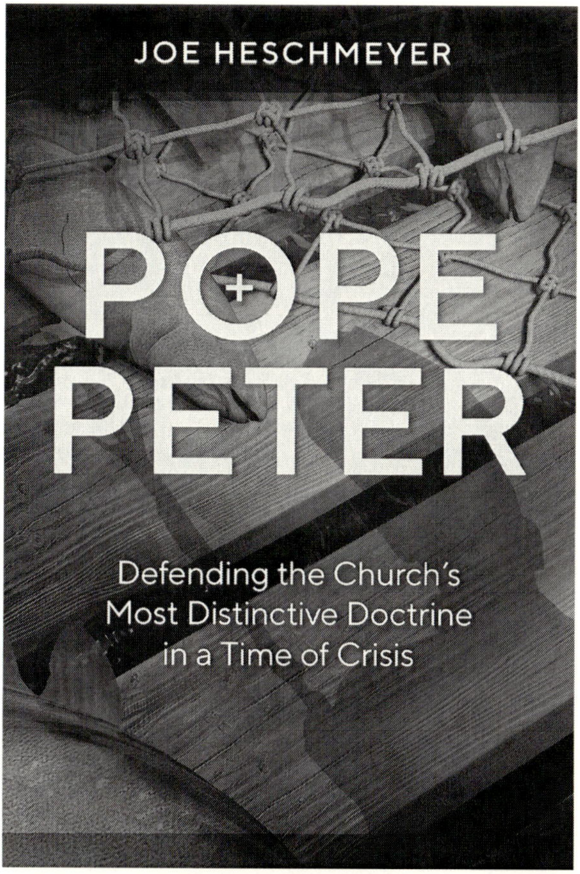

The Author Recommends

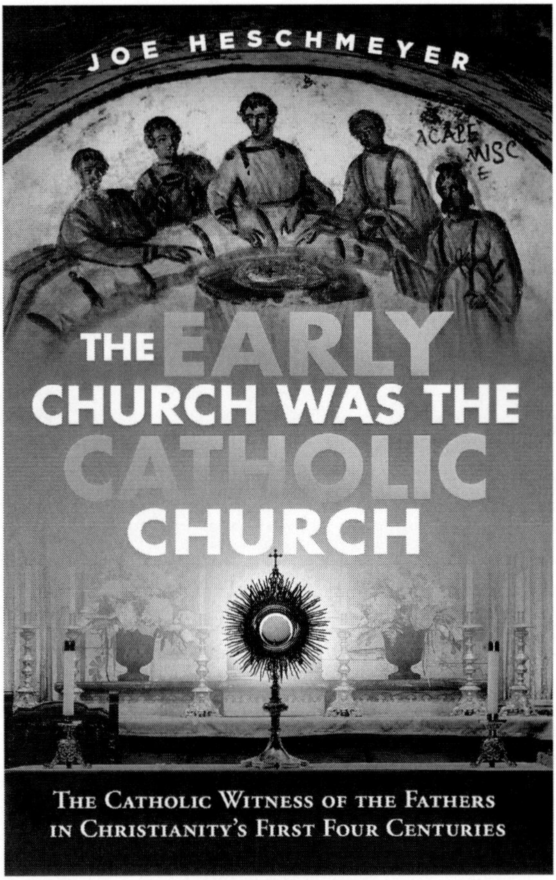

The Author Recommends

The Author Recommends

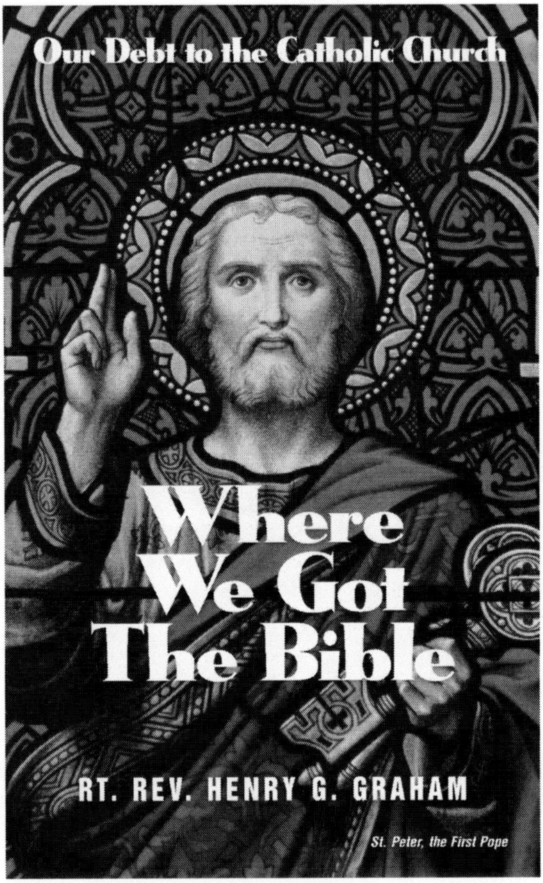

Recommended Content Creators

Apocrypha Apocalypse

Blue Collar Catholic

Brad Schepisi

Capturing Christianity

Catholic 4 Rednecks

Catholic Answers

Catholic Converts

Catholic Productions

Catholic Travel Nurse

Catholic Truth

Church Militant

Douglas Beaumont

Dr Taylor Marshall

Gospel Simplicity

How To Be Christian

Keith Nester

La Fe de la Iglesia

Lizzies Answers

Orthodox Jeremy

Patristic Pillars

Pints With Aquinas

Reason and Theology

Renewal Ministries

Rincón Apologético

Robert Haddad

That One Catholic Girl

The Coming Home Network International

The Counsel of Trent

The Jewish Catholic

The Religious Hippie

Made in United States
North Haven, CT
03 July 2023

38543843R00150